The DACHSHUND Whisperer

MILLNER PRESS

THE DACHSHUND WHISPERER
Copyright © 2024 by Caitlin McKenna
Colorado Christmas Magic Excerpt Copyright © 2021 by
Caitlin McKenna

MILLNER PRESS

Published by Millner Press
PAPERBACK: 979-8-9914198-0-2
EBOOK: 979-8-9914198-1-9
FIRST EDITION
All rights reserved.

Except for use in any review, the reproduction or utilization of this work in whole or in part in any form by any electronic, mechanical or other means, now known or hereinafter invented, including xerography, photocopying and recording, or in any information storage or retrieval system, is forbidden without the written permission of the publisher.

This is a work of fiction. Names, characters, places and incidents are either the product of the author's imagination or are used fictitiously, and any resemblance to actual persons, living or dead, business establishments, events or locales is entirely coincidental.

AI RESTRICTION: The author expressly prohibits any entity from using this publication for purposes of training artificial intelligence (AI) technologies to generate text, including without limitation technologies that are capable of generating works in the same style or genre as this publication. The author reserves all rights to license uses of this work for generative AI training and development of machine learning language models."

Cover Design & Interior Layout by The Killion Group, Inc.

MORE GREAT READS BY CAITLIN MCKENNA

A Movie Magic Christmas
Colorado Christmas Magic
No Such Luck
Super Natalie
Manifesting Mr. Right
My Big Fake Irish Life
Logging Off

The DACHSHUND Whisperer

CAITLIN McKENNA

MILLNER PRESS

For Sugar, Spice, Cocoa, Jammer, Sage, Chiot, and Barnaby—my beloved dachshunds.

*For Kahlua, Scruffy, Suzie, and Shadow—
who often pretended to be dachshunds.*

CHAPTER ONE

"Whoa, Pupperton, slow down." Sydney Elder transferred three dog leashes to one hand so she could get a tighter grip on the hyper Mountain Cur she'd only been walking for a few days. The name Pupperton didn't seem to fit the all-muscle, forty-five-pound ball of energy who still had another five months to go before he was fully grown.

"If you want to go on a hike, you need to walk calmly like everyone else." She made eye contact with Pupperton, then commanded him to heel. But the super excited puppy ignored her. After three more failed attempts, she realized it was time to put her intuitive animal communication skills into action.

She visualized Pupperton relaxed and walking by her side as she told him to heel one more time. She ran this image of him heeling, over and over in her head, while she telepathically projected it to him. A few minutes later, he stopped pulling on the leash, and a few minutes more, he was doing as she requested.

"Yes!" She rewarded him with a treat, and his whole body wagged, not just his tail. "Glad to know I can reach you telepathically." Sydney gave him a pat on his side before she continued walking with the rest of the pack toward her favorite hiking trail.

When she reached a park bench near the foot of the trail, she gave them a break. "Time to get hydrated," she said, pouring bottled water into a travel bowl as she spotted a woman approaching, dressed in dark-gray slacks and a pink silk blouse.

The woman also wore high heels, in a park no less, so she knew it had to be her sister.

Sydney chuckled to herself. No stranger would ever think they were sisters. They didn't look or act like they were remotely related. Interior designer Rachael, with her wavy, dark-brown hair and big blue eyes, was always nicely dressed—while dog walker and pet sitter Sydney, with her straight, auburn hair and hazel-green eyes, lived in leggings and a T-shirt.

In a way, they reflected the residents of their beloved hometown. Pinecrest, Minnesota, was a serene small town an hour north of St. Paul. Locals consisted of artists, nature lovers like Sydney, and hard-working families who had lived there all of their lives. But a growing number of the residents were corporate executives—potential clients of Rachael's—who worked in the city but had moved out to Pinecrest for some peace and quiet.

"Thought I'd find you here." Rachael handed over a mocha cookie crumble Frappuccino, collapsed on the bench next to her, and took a deep breath. Everyone loved Mulberry Park. It sat on fifty well-maintained acres and was a hiker's dream, with several trails extending into beautifully wooded rolling hills.

"Thanks." She took a sip of her favorite drink, then eyed her sister suspiciously. "Is this because you love me, or is it a bribe?"

Rachael smiled and flicked her a sideways glance. "Your telepathy training definitely sharpened your psychic skills."

"Hardly," she said with a laugh. "I've always been able to read you, and I'm sensing an important client of yours is in need of a good dog walker."

"Close. My boss thinks her boyfriend is proposing tonight, and her dog sitter just canceled."

Sydney shot her a surprised look. "Perfectionist Dana has a dog? The interior designer whose favorite color is white allows muddy paws in her house?"

"Not really. He's a very new addition, and truth be told, it doesn't sound like he's going to be a permanent one."

Sydney released a disgusted snort, which had all the dogs' heads turning in her direction. "Why don't people ever think about how their lives will be altered when a dog is added to their family? All they see is how cute the pup is, but when they're inconvenienced for the first time, they turn around and abandon the poor thing at an overcrowded shelter."

"I know." Rachael sighed. "I wholeheartedly agree, but in Dana's case, she found him next to her trash cans. He was visibly shaking, so she brought him inside to get warm, while she posted his photo in hopes of finding his owner. That was two weeks ago, and unfortunately, he's really destructive when left alone."

She pictured a beast of a dog snacking on the end of Dana's couch and realized she shouldn't have judged her so quickly. "Since Dana got him off the streets, how can I say no? What's his breed? Or is he a cute mutt?"

"Hmm." Rachael inspected the group of dogs who were politely sitting at their feet. "None of these. It's one of those wiener dogs with short legs and a long back."

"A dachshund?"

"That's it!"

Sydney exploded with a laugh. "A tiny little dachshund needs a sitter? You made it sound like Dana took in an unruly Saint Bernard with a taste for Louis Vuitton."

"Not exactly, but just as destructive. He goes ballistic if he's locked in a crate and chews everything in sight if he isn't." Rachael frowned. "He really needs your special kind of help."

Sydney's shoulders stiffened. "Did you tell her what I can do?"

"Of course not. I'd never want to put any pressure on you."

A few years back, Sydney began pursuing animal communication as a career. She had been lucky enough to study under one of the best psychic mediums and animal communicators in the business. Soon Sydney discovered she could telepathically connect to any animal, anywhere, so she began practicing on her friends' pets. At first, it was fun. She loved discovering the reasons for some of their pets' idiosyncrasies.

But when it came to more serious issues, like trying to find a lost dog or attempting to figure out a cat's medical condition, she'd found it incredibly stressful. Her friends' calls were always urgent, filled with panic or tears, forcing Sydney to drop everything in order to telepathically talk to their beloved animal. The stress was worth it when she received a lot of correct information. But sometimes her psychic "hits" weren't detailed enough to help the pet when it mattered most.

Heartbroken by the ones she felt she had failed, Sydney stopped pursuing intuitive animal communication as a professional career and turned toward pet care. Now she used her telepathic skills to correct behavioral issues with some of her clients' pets.

Sydney sipped her Frappuccino, thinking about the cute little dachshund. "Sounds like he might have separation anxiety." She let out a long exhale. "I suppose I could try to reach him telepathically tonight."

"Seriously? You'd be willing to do that?"

"For you, yes." Besides, it wasn't like she had a date or anything interesting going on in her life, so she could at least help a wayward pup. She suspected the poor thing had been confined in a cage for too long, and now feared being left alone. If she could connect with him, she'd assure him that he was in a safe place. Hopefully, he would stop his destructive behavior, which could change Dana's feelings about his temporary status.

"Thank you." Relief spread across Rachael's face. "Dana hasn't been herself since she rescued the little guy, and it's stressing everyone out." Rachael sent off a quick text to her boss and got a reply back immediately. "Dana said to tell you thank you with a bunch of smiley faces, and asked if you could come over at seven."

Sydney nodded. "Text me her address."

"Done." Her sister got up. "I better get back to work. I really appreciate this, Syd."

"No problem."

After Rachael left, Sydney enjoyed the rest of her Frappuccino while the dogs basked in the morning sun. Molly, a five-year-old beagle, put her paws on Sydney's legs, wanting some affection. She leaned toward Molly and ran a hand down the beagle's back. "You're such a sweet little girl." Molly wagged her tail and gazed at Sydney with big brown eyes.

Pupperton joined them, also wanting affection, which she was more than happy to give. "If only men were as loving and attentive as you two."

Her friends had been pressuring her to start dating again, but why should she when every guy she ever dated had disappointed her? And it wasn't as if she was completely alone. Her furry friends gave her unconditional love and were fearlessly loyal—traits she couldn't say she had ever found in the men she'd dated. Too many of them were self-absorbed or didn't like dogs—or both. But they'd all agreed on one thing: she spent too much time with dogs.

She happened to strongly disagree, and lately she'd been feeling like she was supposed to be doing more to help animals. She'd been considering working at a shelter, despite her reservations about seeing animals euthanized due to overcrowding. But caring for clients' dogs had kept her too busy to explore her options. She let out a long sigh. Already twenty-four, and she still hadn't figured out her career.

Pupperton whined, letting her know it was time to go.

"Okay, gang. Are you ready for a hike?"

All four swiftly sprang to their feet, making her smile. She led them up their favorite hiking trail with a sigh of contentment. It was a beautiful sunny day, and she was out in the fresh air with happy, loving dogs. Perhaps taking care of other people's animals was exactly where she was meant to be.

Carter Hansen sat in front of his computer, doing a final read on an article he'd written about another surprise tax hike for the residents of Pinecrest. The city had promised taxpayers that it would take no more than a year to bury all of the power lines underground, but to date, they had only finished a quarter of the work.

Now they had run out of money, *again*, and blamed the high cost of materials on inflation. It sounded like a legitimate excuse, but it wasn't. Very little of the taxpayers' hard-earned money had gone to fund the overwhelmingly approved measure in the first place. Instead, their taxes—*his* taxes—were being used for city officials' "team-building" getaways and lavish dinners during the holidays. Enough was enough, and he was certain the good folks of Pinecrest would agree.

"Carter, I need you to cover a story breaking right now," Russell said, striding over to his desk.

"On it." He quickly sent the finished article to his boss before closing his laptop and grabbing his jacket off the back of his chair. "Where am I going?"

Russell flipped through a pad of paper. "Oakwood and Ridge."

A bank was on the corner of Oakwood and Ridge, *his* bank. He pulled his phone from the charging station and threw it in his jacket. "A bank robbery?" His pulse quickened at the thought that he might finally see some real action. Would it turn into a hostage situation? Pinecrest had only made the national news once, and it had hardly been newsworthy. Two huge bull moose had been entangled in a heated battle on the main road into town, stopping traffic in both directions for ten whole minutes.

"Not a robbery," Russell said, "but a life and death situation. Several ducklings are trapped inside a storm drain."

Carter's shoulders dropped as he felt his excitement seep out of him like a leaky balloon. "Another animal assignment?"

Russell always gave superstar Shep the good stories, and it was irritating as hell. Sure, Shep had seniority; he'd been with the newspaper for five years, whereas Carter had only been there for two. But it was more than that. Shep didn't need a break. The guy always seemed to be in the right place at the right time—like the morning he went to the gym an hour early and a four-alarm fire broke out in a business next door. Or the time Shep had been filling up his car with gas when the cashier had a heart attack and a doctor saved his life right in front of him.

Carter glanced toward Shep's desk. He wasn't there, which meant Russell had already sent him to cover whatever else was more important.

"Where's Dario?" Carter searched for the young intern. "Send him. He's the new kid on the block."

"Dario's out sick, and you're the only one who can turn this into a heart-stopping story." *Heart-stopping from boredom is what he really meant.*

"I thought you were going to let me cover hard-hitting news."

"I will. As soon as we have some."

Carter couldn't believe he had to cover another story on

Pinecrest's wayward wildlife, especially when they were always so cliché, like a bear in a resident's backyard or a deer stuck in a fence. Would he ever move away from stories starring animals?

"Fine. But I just sent you something on corruption by city officials. Will you give it the spotlight it deserves?"

"I'll give it serious consideration."

"You should, Russell. You're paying for something you're not getting, either."

"Oh?" Russell raised a brow. "What's this about?"

"Read my article," Carter said. "And after this, I'm not covering any more animal stories."

He grabbed his key fob off his desk and stormed out the door, wondering why he was still living in Pinecrest. He peeled out of the parking lot, shaking his head. Frankly, he didn't know what he was waiting for. He'd grown up in Pinecrest, and even though he had wanted to move to a bigger city for his career, his family and lifelong friends were here. So instead of saving his money to eventually live in Chicago or New York, he'd ended up buying a house. A few months later he had proposed to Jade, his then-girlfriend, and it felt like his life was falling right into place—until their engagement abruptly ended.

Now another year had gone by. He was twenty-six, still single, and his house felt too big and lonely. He'd pack up and leave tomorrow, but his parents had come to depend on him, and his older sister was expecting her first child. He couldn't leave, and in truth, he didn't want to. He just wanted some excitement in his life—*real* excitement, not ducks trapped in a storm drain.

Carter saw police cars ahead, blocking off traffic at the intersection of Oakwood and Ridge. He arrived on scene just as a fire truck rolled up, which was no surprise since Russell listened to the police scanner for any breaking news. Pinecrest was so laid back that if it weren't for *The Pinecrest News*, none of the residents would ever know what was going on around them.

He grabbed his camera and headed over to where a growing number of concerned onlookers were gathering. The ducklings' frantic mama seemed like she was quacking at them to help her as she paced in front of the storm drain.

Three firefighters climbed out of their truck with crowbars

and got to work. Two raised the heavy iron grate and held it back for the smallest of the three men to climb inside.

The mama duck paced faster, quacking louder, while the firefighter bent down, scooped up the first duckling, and set it on the pavement. The mama duck checked over her baby quickly, then went back to pacing and quacking.

The firefighter brought up five more before he reached for his flashlight. "I think there's still one farther in the drain."

He crouched down, ready to crawl inside, when the mama duck suddenly flew in next to him. She kept quacking, and soon her baby responded. As the duckling came closer to the opening, the firefighter caught him in his gloved hands and released him onto the pavement.

With a couple of quacks, no doubt a thank-you to the firefighter, mama and her brood waddled away to a nearby pond. The onlookers clapped, and a few children squealed with delight, as everyone watched the duck family make it safely to the water.

Carter had taken video and several pictures throughout the ordeal, and got the names of the three hero firefighters before he headed back to work with a small smile he couldn't quite shake. As much as he wanted to hate his human-interest assignments, he couldn't. They always managed to conclude with a happy ending—something he wouldn't mind having one day for himself.

CHAPTER TWO

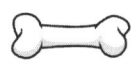

Shortly after Sydney had finished up her dog walking responsibilities, she received a text from Molly's human mom. The family was moving and no longer required her services. Sydney teared up, knowing that she'd never see the sweet girl again. She'd been taking care of Molly since she was a six-month-old puppy, and her owner hadn't even had the decency to let her know earlier, so she could say goodbye. She stared at the cold text in her hand and didn't know how to respond.

She scrolled through all the pictures she'd taken of Molly over the years and knew the next few days were going to be rough. She had loved their routine of tummy rubs and lounging on the couch whenever she was lucky enough to pet sit her. Sydney wiped away the tears flowing freely down her cheeks. She had wanted a dog of her own for so long, but she lived in an apartment complex that didn't allow pets. Irony at its very best. She went back to the cold text and sent a one-sentence reply: **I will really miss Molly.**

And only Molly, she thought, before she stuffed her phone in her pocket and headed home. She wasn't the least bit hungry, but she reheated some soup for dinner anyway, and hoped that Dana's dog would be able to cheer her up.

Right at seven, she pulled up in front of Dana's home, ready to pet sit the ferocious wiener dog. As soon as she rang the bell, she heard excited barking, followed by Dana instructing him to be quiet. But Dana's wishes were falling on deaf dachshund ears.

The door finally whipped open. Dana appeared a little frazzled, even though she was wearing an elegant black dress and had her hair up in a simple French twist. "Hi, Sydney. Thank you for coming on such short notice."

"I'm happy to help." Sydney stepped into the two-story English Tudor with dark-stained hardwood floors, impressive matching beams, and mostly white fabrics in between.

Dana led her into the living room where a dog enclosure, three-feet in height, took up half of the room. Inside the gated area was a plush dog bed, a ceramic water bowl, three chew toys, a squeaky toy, and a fluffy dog blanket. Sitting next to the bed was an adorable short-haired, chocolate and tan miniature dachshund. He looked to be five, maybe six years old, and had a pattern on his chest in the shape of a large heart.

"Oh my gosh. He's the cutest thing I've ever seen." She set down her handbag and stepped over to the enclosure. "What's his name?"

"Dudley."

"Dudley! What a perfect name. It suits him." Sydney knelt down so she could reach out and let him sniff her hand. "Hi, Dudley," she said in a gentle, soft voice.

Dudley only slightly wagged his tail. He seemed to be in a bit of a mood as he turned his back on Sydney and lay down. She was surprised by his behavior. She had never met a dog who hadn't loved her instantly.

"I'm not sure how long he's been a stray, so he might take a while to warm up to you," Dana said. "He's already been fed, but he can have a treat or two, which I've left out on the kitchen counter. He can come out of his enclosure as long as you're watching him. He's not allowed on the furniture at any time. If he needs to go out, he'll let you know. My backyard is not fenced in, so he'll need to be on a leash when he goes outside."

She was about to ask if Dudley had anything he particularly enjoyed doing, but Dana seemed distracted and a little anxious.

The doorbell rang and Dana sharply inhaled. "That must be Mark." She grabbed her evening bag. "You have my cell. Call me if you need anything."

"Have a good time," Sydney replied, but Dana had already hurried out the door.

"Well, Dudley, it looks like it's just you and me." She opened the gate on his enclosure and made herself comfortable on the floor, hoping to win him over with her expert tummy rubs. But Dudley bolted past her, raced to the couch, and leaped on top of it.

She groaned, getting up. "You had to go straight to the forbidden zone, didn't you? Listen, Mr. Dudley, you shouldn't be jumping on the furniture. Your new mom might not know about your breed, but dachshunds aren't supposed to jump—not with that long back of yours. Come here, so I can help you get down." She reached for him, and he raced to the opposite side of the couch.

"Is that any way to treat a new friend? You might really need me one day, so let's not make this difficult." She picked up a charcoal-gray throw draped across the end of the couch and spread it over the cushions. "Why don't you sit on this blanket instead of Dana's white couch?"

Dudley didn't move a muscle.

"You heard your mom. No dogs named Dudley on the couch."

Then that excludes me.

She laughed, thinking she'd heard what he'd say if he could talk. She telepathically sent him a picture of her picking him up and setting him on the floor. "If you get off the couch, I'll give you a treat." She reached for him, and he rolled over on his back to avoid capture. She tried again, and he raced to the other side of the couch, only now he was sitting on the throw.

Sydney let out a sigh. "You're not directly on the couch, so I guess you can stay—as long as you remain on the blanket. Got it?"

He eyed her, then stretched himself out, as if he understood everything she'd said.

She definitely wanted to connect with him psychically, but she needed to let him feel comfortable with her first. She reached for the remote control, which looked similar to hers, and scrolled through the channels, landing on Canine TV.

"Look at this. Dana has a channel dedicated to you." She set the remote down and studied Dudley. "Do you like listening to relaxing music?"

Dudley rolled on his side and closed his eyes.

"I'll take that as a yes." She was about to get settled in next to him when her cell phone rang. "Hey, Jacqui."

"Sydney, I'm at the animal hospital." Jacqui's voice was shaky, and she sounded like she was holding back tears. "Taffy is really sick, and they don't know what's wrong with her. Are you still doing pet psychic sessions?"

"Not really. I'm a little out of practice, but I can try," she answered honestly, fearing that her friend needed an instant miracle. "Hold on, Jacqui. I'm putting you on speakerphone so I can pull up Taffy's photo to read her energy." Sydney searched through her pictures. "What's wrong with her?"

"She's got a fever, is lethargic, and hasn't eaten in a few days. The vet thought it was Lyme disease, but the lab test came back negative. Are you seeing anything?"

"Give me a couple of minutes, and I'll call you back."

She hung up, briefly closed her eyes to center herself, then stared at Taffy's picture, trying to connect with the canine telepathically. *Hi, Taffy, I'm one of your mom's friends, and she's very worried about you. Can you tell me how you're feeling?*

Taffy psychically sent her one word: *Tired.*

Sydney released a nervous breath. She had a connection. *Tired. I hear you. I'm so sorry. Let's figure it out.*

Dudley suddenly got up and came over to her. He nudged her arm with his nose, so he could see what held her attention.

"Dudley, I've got to concentrate on Taffy right now." *Taffy, do you know what's wrong with you?*

A creature is feeding on me.

I think it's a tick, Taffy. Did you feel sick before you felt the creature?

No.

Her cell rang again. She was going to ignore it until she saw that it was her friend calling again.

"Anything?" Jacqui asked anxiously.

"I've only had time to ask a couple of questions, but Taffy has a tick on her. I know you said it wasn't Lyme disease, but she told me that she felt fine before the tick started feeding on her."

"Taffy *had* a tick when I brought her in, but the vet already removed it and checked her thoroughly for any more."

"Let me ask for clarification." Sydney stared at Taffy's picture. *Is the creature still on you?*

Yes. Below ear.

"Jacqui, Taffy is telling me that the creature is still on her."

"Creature?" Jacqui asked. "What are you talking about?"

"Taffy's referring to the tick as a creature. Have your vet feel her lymph nodes."

Dudley barked and wagged his tail.

"That's the first thing she did when we came in," Jacqui said, "but hold on." She relayed the information to the vet.

Sydney stared at Taffy's picture. "What's making you sick?" she quietly said out loud.

Dudley put a paw on Sydney's arm, and she instantly saw an image of a tick moving between lemons and limes in a fruit bowl. *What the heck?*

"Sydney, you're right," Jacqui said as she got back on the phone. "The vet just found another tick on one of her lymph nodes, and she's doing a smear test on it right now."

"That's good," Sydney said. "I'm not sure what this means, but I'm seeing a bowl of lemons and limes. I'm guessing limes represent Lyme disease. Is there a disease that acts like Lyme disease and is carried by ticks?"

Dudley barked again, and Sydney finally looked at him. "What is it? Do you have to go out?"

Dudley barked twice before he sat next to her. He pawed at Taffy's photo, and sneezed.

"Sydney, the vet is saying she's seeing something strange in the tick's blood and is going to send it out for testing. She says Taffy could definitely have another tick-borne disease."

Dudley barked, and Sydney suddenly heard a word in her head. "Anaplasmosis?"

Jacqui relayed what Sydney said to the vet, then came back on the phone. "Anaplasmosis can be transmitted to dogs by ticks. Sydney, you're a lifesaver. The vet is going to test for it, but she'll start Taffy on antibiotics for it now, since it sometimes doesn't show up as a positive case for weeks."

"I'm glad I was able to help. Give Taffy a kiss for me, and tell her I hope she feels better soon."

"Apparently, you can tell her yourself," Jacqui said, sounding relieved. "Thank you, Sydney. You really should be doing this for a living."

"I'll think about it. Keep me posted." She hung up and flung herself back on the couch. "Well, that was stressful."

But rewarding. She clearly heard a male voice in her head.

"Rewarding, if Taffy gets well again," she replied automatically, as if she were having a normal conversation with a friend. And then it hit her. Sydney slowly turned toward Dudley and froze. "Was that you?" She studied Dudley. He appeared to be a perfectly normal, average-looking dog. "Did I just hear your snooty, upper-crust, and possibly fake British accent in my head?"

Dudley looked offended. *I do not have a snooty voice, and I most certainly do not have an accent—fake or otherwise. I am a well-educated species—a visionary, really, with a consciousness well ahead of my time.*

Sydney's head jerked back. "You can understand me?"

Of course I can understand you. I'm not an imbecile. He looked insulted.

Sydney sprang off the couch, her gaze glued to the dachshund. What was happening? When she used to do animal communication sessions, she'd receive impressions or simple images from the animals she connected with. She'd also hear short phrases or a couple of words, like she had with Taffy. But this? No. She'd never heard an animal's *own* voice in her head—especially one so well-spoken.

"I can telepathically hear you loud and clear," she said to Dudley. "How are you able to speak to me so easily?"

The dog let out a long sigh. *Did I not just explain how exceptional I am? Aside from being a visionary, I understand over a thousand languages across countless species, and English happens to be one of them. As much as I'd like to take all the credit for this conversation, you seem to have quite a gift of your own. Well done on that diagnosis for your friend.*

"Were you the one putting that information in my head?"

Not at first. That was Taffy. She informed you about the tick on her lymph node. I, on the other hand, gave you the image of the fruit bowl and the name anaplasmosis, as many who are not veterinarians are unaware that those vile, blood-sucking entities you refer to as ticks *can spread other nasty diseases besides Lyme disease.*

Sydney slowly sat back down, shaking her head. "I can't believe we're talking so easily. Why haven't I been able to hear others like I'm hearing you?"

Once again, I am a well-educated species—a visionary with a consciousness well ahead of my time. Although I must inform you that I shall not be able to telepathically hear you as well as you are currently hearing me.

"Why not?" She squinted at him in confusion. "That's how telepathy works."

True, but your species has an extremely short attention span and is constantly distracted, so your telepathic connections aren't clear and precise like mine. Why should I struggle to understand your muddled telepathic voice when I can hear you perfectly well speaking out loud?

"Makes sense." She eyed the little guy. "Okay. I'll communicate with you verbally, and you'll answer me telepathically."

Brilliant.

"I assume this means you haven't been able to reach any other person telepathically."

Not in the least, which has been incredibly frustrating.

"I can certainly understand that. I've had more than my share of frustrating conversations." And they were usually with men. She studied him. "So tell me about yourself, Dudley."

Let's begin with that wretched name. Does my appearance resemble anything close to a Dudley?

"I think it's a great name. Did Dana come up with it?"

She did.

"I'm assuming you didn't have a collar on when she found you."

I'm not a piece of merchandise, therefore, I would never wear a tag around my neck. But, I suppose, I shouldn't be so hard on my new human servant. At first, I was monumentally impressed by her. She actually sat with me, seeming to truly want to know my real name, so I intently stared at her and telepathically said, "My name is Durlindemore, King of the Dachshunds."

Sydney laughed. "The dachshund breed has a king?"

Naturally, and one should never interrupt a king.

"My apologies." She cleared her throat. "Please continue."

As I was saying, my human servant you refer to as Dana kept staring at me. "Is your name Rover? Tex? Buster?"

She clearly hadn't heard me in the least. I was about to bring forth the slop out of my stomach she had mistaken for breakfast—to show her my displeasure—when I chose to ignore her instead. I turned away and curled up on the floor.

This did not deter her in the least. My human servant remained focused on me. "Don't any of those names appeal to you?"

"Absolutely not," I replied, but she hadn't heard me. I tried one more time. "Durlindemore. It's not that difficult. Durlindemore, Durlindemore, Durlindemore!"

"Wait, I think I'm getting something," she said excitedly.

I immediately ran over to her, feeling like I was at last getting through to her. "Durlindemore, Durlindemore, Durlindemore!"

She cocked her head. "Dudley?"

"No!" I barked. "No!"

But she was smiling at me, so proud of herself, thinking she had heard me correctly. "It's Dudley, isn't it?"

I gave her two very distinct barks.

"Which means no," Sydney said.

Precisely. One bark for yes. Two barks for no. Everyone knows that—except of course for my newest human servant. Well, she started making baby noises, ruffling my coat with her cold, poky fingers, telling me that I was such a good boy, and for that, we were going to the pet store to pick up a torture collar that would proudly display the name Dudley.

Sydney squelched a smile. "I'll be happy to tell Dana that Durlindemore is your real name, though she might take offense. As you mentioned, she sat with you and tried really hard to learn your name."

He scanned his enclosure, seeming to take note of everything Dana had bought him. *I see your point. The poor woman will be crushed.* He released a dramatic sigh.

She bit her lip to keep from laughing. His theatrical expressions were hysterical. "She *will* be crushed, but I can certainly call you Durlindemore."

I'd appreciate that.

Now that she'd agreed to it, she realized his name would end up being a five-minute conversation every time someone asked about him. Not only did he look like a Dudley, but the name was much easier to pronounce. Could she convince him of that?

"Why do you dislike the name so much?"

Dudley sounds like a commoner's name.

She grabbed her phone to research its origin and was surprised by what she found. "Did you know that the name Dudley is of British origin and has aristocratic roots?"

He gave her the side-eye, full of veiled curiosity. *Go on.*

"Back in the sixteenth century, there was a nobleman by the name of Robert Dudley who was very close to Queen Elizabeth the first. He was the first Earl of Leicester."

An Earl. His snout raised an inch or two in the air. *But I'm a king.*

She laughed. "Indeed, you are." She decided to drop it and let him have time to think about it. "I understand you haven't been with Dana very long. Do you have any family I can contact?"

I'm a world traveler. I have no time for foolish family stuff.

She had always suspected that a dog's feelings could be hurt, and now she knew it was true. She sensed that he had become attached to a family with children, and for some horrible reason, he'd been separated from them, or worse, dumped.

"I heard Dana found you near her trash cans. Have you been on the streets all your life?"

Hardly. I stay with someone for as long as it suits me, then when it becomes too confining, I move on.

"That must be difficult—not knowing where your next meal is coming from."

Does it look like I've missed a meal?

She had to admit, he did not. In fact, he was a tad chubby, though she chose to keep that to herself. "You look like a perfectly healthy dachshund."

Thank you. When I choose a new place to stay, I use the rubbish bin test.

"And what is that, exactly?"

I watch someone for a day or two, and then when I know they'll see me, I stand by their bins, which implies that I'm starving. A Good

Samaritan will always take me in, whereas a heartless git will throw something at me and tell me to get lost.*

"Very smart of you, though you must know that Dana isn't going to want to have you around if you keep being so destructive."

I'm aware. I realized after a few days here that we're not the right fit. She's not one to fawn over me. I actually thought she'd forget I was here and leave the door open one day while retrieving a package off the porch, but she did not. I had to take matters into my own paws. I went on a chewing spree, thinking she'd give me the boot when she discovered the carnage. However, she didn't do that, either. Instead, she refused to let me out of her sight. Sometimes I'm too adorable for my own good. He sighed. *I've been attempting to make an escape for a week now and have failed every time.*

"Which is why you continually act out."

Precisely. Perhaps you can break the news to her that we must part ways.

"I've never had a dog ask me to help them break up with someone." She smirked. "Are you sure you don't want to stay? Dana wouldn't have bought you all of this stuff if she didn't care about you."

I'm afraid she can't have me as I am meant for another.

"Oh?" She gave him a surprised look. "And who is that?"

Why, you, of course. I shall go home with you.

Her eyes widened. "Me?"

Is there anyone else here that I'm speaking to?

"Dudley, I mean, Durlindemore, I'd love to have you stay with me, I really would, but I live in an apartment and they don't allow dogs."

I'm clearly more than a mere canine.

"Clearly, though I'm not sure how I'd explain a telepathic dog to my landlady."

Perhaps we can think of something together. We'd make an extraordinary team. He put a paw on her arm and gazed into her eyes. *Do have a serious think on it, dear Sydney. With me by your side, the possibilities are endless.*

An animal communicator and a dog who was fluent in a thousand languages including her own. They *would* make an extraordinary team because their line of communication was clear and concise. She would no longer have to grapple with insufficient information and guesswork. They could step in where other trainers and behaviorists had failed. They could help so many animals in need. But how would it work? Dudley was currently Dana's dog.

"We might be getting ahead of ourselves. As you said, you're quite adorable. Dana might not want to let you go. What if she's speaking to her boyfriend about you this very minute and plans on making you a permanent addition to their relationship?"

I highly doubt it. I've only met the chap once, and he was very standoffish. Needless to say, we did not bond.

"I'm sorry to hear that."

I'm not. I don't belong here, Sydney.

She stared into his eyes and knew he was right. He didn't belong with Dana. He belonged with her.

CHAPTER THREE

Carter finished up the story on the ducklings, and sent it to the copy editor right as Russell's cat jumped up on his lap. "Hey, Chester, how's your day been going?" The cat purred, arching his back as Carter pet him.

"Good job covering the tax hike," Russell said, hovering above him. "It will be tomorrow's headline."

"Are you serious?" Carter set Chester aside. "My story will be on the front page?"

"You suspected corruption, and I should have listened. Hopefully, we can get enough residents fired up to demand transparency, and to shame at least some of the city council members into doing their job." He leaned against his desk. "I've lived here all my life. I didn't want to believe that our quaint town could ever elect corrupt officials. But the truth of the matter is Pinecrest isn't so little anymore. Thirty years ago, our population was just two thousand. Now it's over fifty thousand. If we don't want to lose our safe, small-town feel, we need the right people in charge. Your article might serve as a wake-up call to voters to elect a new mayor next fall."

"Thank you, sir, I really appreciate it." Carter sat taller, unable to stop smiling.

"Great work. Now go on and get out of here. Say hello to your folks for me."

"Will do." He grabbed his jacket off the back of his chair and headed out the door with a spring in his step. He felt like celebrating and wanted to pick up dessert from the local bakery, but he was already late for his family's Tuesday night dinner. More than likely, his mom had already made dessert anyway.

Ten minutes later, he pulled up in front of his parents' house and saw his sister, Lorelai, through the living room window with her husband, Jeff. Carter hoped that the dinner conversation would remain focused on all of the preparations for their baby's arrival—instead of why he wasn't dating.

After Jade left, he was done. No more dates, no more hurt feelings, end of discussion. But it never *was* the end of the discussion. He continually had to explain that not everyone found love. Not everyone got married and settled down. There was nothing wrong with being single.

Carter walked in the front door. "Hello, hello."

He was met with ear-piercing barks mixed with aggressive growling from his parents' new dog. He eyed Penelope warily. The fifteen-pound Cavalier King Charles spaniel might have everyone fooled with her doe-like eyes, but Carter knew better. She was a savage beast who'd bite your hand off if you got too close to her toy or the people she'd claimed as her own.

"Penelope, be nice," his mother said as she greeted him with a kiss on the cheek.

"I see Penelope still despises me."

"Oh, she does not," his mom said with a laugh. "It's only been a few weeks. Give her time. She just gets fussy when someone takes my attention away from her."

Penelope sneezed, as if she had understood her human mom and was punctuating her sentence.

The dog was already spoiled rotten. He couldn't imagine what she was going to be like by the end of the year.

"You're never this late." A very pregnant Lorelai slowly made her way over. "Did something dramatic happen today?"

"Depends on who you talk to. Ducklings fell into a storm drain."

"Oh no." His mother put both hands to her cheeks. "Were they rescued?"

"Of course. Our fire department saved the day once again."

"You seem to be continually surrounded by animals in distress," Jeff said, handing him a bottle of beer.

"Yeah, something I've been trying to outgrow." Carter took a much-needed sip. "Good to see you, man. How are things going with the remodel?"

"Done. Finally."

"Just in time." Lorelai swirled a hand over her baby bump. "We're decorating the nursery now."

"We haven't moved past the paint color," Jeff said through a tight jaw. "I've repainted it three times."

"That's because the color wasn't quite right," Lorelai said. "But now it's perfect. He or she is going to love the silvery, light-blue color. It will make any baby fall asleep."

"I have to agree since it already worked on me." Jeff yawned.

"Sleep is very important for babies and new parents," Carter's mom said. "You were a good sleeper, Lorelai, but your brother was a night owl. He had me up every hour."

"I was helping you get a lot more accomplished."

"Hardly," she groused. "You'll see one day when you have kids of your own."

"He's got to get a girlfriend first," Lorelai said. "How's the search going?"

And there it was. He'd been in the door less than five minutes before his dating life was front and center. "No search in progress, and not interested in being set up again, so don't even go there."

"You don't have to worry about that. Lorelai is completely over her matchmaking." Jeff gestured like a baseball umpire, signaling that Carter was safe.

"It's true." She put her hands up in surrender. "I'll be the first to admit that my choice of the perfect girlfriend for you was an utter failure. I've never seen two people act so awkward around each other in my entire life."

"The woman was a beekeeper and owned a pet snake," he said. "How could you have ever thought we'd be a good match?"

"I assumed you'd find that cool." She shrugged.

"Why?"

"Well, you love honey, and one of your friends in high school owned a snake."

"A snake that wrapped itself around my leg and tried to kill me."

"I kind of forgot about that part." She chuckled. "Don't worry. I have no desire to set you up with anyone ever again—though maybe I should get you a dog."

"That's a wonderful idea!" His mom's face lit with excitement.

"I don't need a dog or a cat, and I'll never *ever* need a snake. I'm good on my own."

"Are you?" Lorelai gave him an intense look that only his sister could get away with, and he immediately broke eye contact before he gave away too much.

His sister seemed to constantly worry he'd never get over Jade, which was ridiculous because it had only been a year. But his whole family, especially Lorelai, had been so shocked when they'd called it off. Jade's acceptance into a prestigious art school in Paris had been such a long shot that no one thought it would happen. Then it did, and he couldn't ask her to turn it down— not when it was the opportunity of a lifetime for her.

But should he have gone to Paris with her? Even though he'd thought about moving to a big city for his own career, he'd never been good at learning languages, and he didn't want to be so far from his family.

At least that's what he'd told himself. He'd never seriously considered following her to France because she'd never asked him to come. That had said a lot about their relationship— something he hadn't been willing to see at the time.

"I'm good, Lorelai, really, and you have more important things to be worrying about."

"I will always worry about you, little brother." She put her arm around him as the service door to the garage opened.

"You made it," his dad said, coming in with greasy hands.

"Working on the car, I see."

"That's all I ever seem to do. They don't make 'em like they used to."

"Hon, get cleaned up. Dinner's ready," his mom said.

"Good. I'm starving." His dad went into the laundry room and washed up in the utility sink.

Carter was relieved the attention was finally off him—except for Penelope, who was still growling. He took a step toward the dining room, and she went ballistic. Penelope's hair stood on end, and she bared her teeth like he was an intruder. "This is why I'll never own a dog."

"Penelope, go lie down." His mom snapped her fingers, pointing to the dog bed on the floor, and Penelope reluctantly obeyed. "That's just her way of saying she likes you."

"If that's true, then I feel sorry for anyone she hates." He followed his mom into the dining room, keeping a close eye on Cujo for any surprise attacks. *No wonder I have trouble reading women.*

Sydney and Dudley had barely moved, talking endlessly, like good friends catching up. "I took classes from one of the best in the business," she said. "My mentor, Isabelle Scott, is a much better pet psychic than me. She's been speaking telepathically to animals since she was a child, so it comes naturally to her, whereas I had to learn it."

Doesn't matter. A gift is a gift, and this is one that appears to be quite rare. You're the first to hear me, although I do hope you're not the last. How lovely would it be to have more like us?

"It would make things a lot easier," she said as she heard the front door open. "Quick. Get down." She reached for Dudley, and this time he jumped into her arms. She got him off the couch and onto the floor right as Dana came into the living room. "Hi, Dana."

Dana's gaze anxiously darted around the room, then relaxed when she saw that everything looked in order. "How did it go with Dudley?"

"Insanely good." Sydney got off the floor where he was suddenly playing with one of his toys.

"I can see that." Dana nodded in approval. "He only played with that toy the first day I bought it for him."

I had to put on a good show. Dudley's words filled Sydney's head.

"Well, he seems to love it tonight," she said. "We've been playing all night."

And telepathically talking. He rolled on his back and gave it a good scratch on Dana's rug.

Sydney turned away from him, trying to concentrate on the

verbal conversation she was having instead of the telepathic thoughts flying into her head. "How was your evening?"

"Amazing." Dana flashed Sydney her new engagement ring.

"Oh, Dana, it's beautiful. Congratulations!"

Dudley sat up to take a look at the ring for himself. *Well done snagging Mark,* he interjected, even though Sydney was the only one who could hear him. *Perhaps we may celebrate by sharing that pint of ice cream you've been hoarding.*

"Thank you." She admired the rock on her hand. "I wish you could have met Mark tonight, but he's extremely allergic to dogs, even with an antihistamine, which is why he didn't come inside."

"He's allergic?" Sydney set her gaze on Dudley.

Come to think of it, the poor fellow had *been sneezing is head off.*

"Very allergic," Dana replied. "Mark loves dogs, but he was only around Dudley for fifteen minutes before he broke out in hives."

"Hives?" She stared at Dudley, shocked.

Oh dear. I might have forgotten that bit. He pulled up his snout and bared his teeth in an attempted grin.

She suppressed a laugh and kept her attention on Dana. "How horrible for Mark. I don't know what I would do if I were allergic. I love dogs too much to be without them."

Dana sat on the ottoman to pet Dudley. "You know, Sydney, I'd love to keep Dudley, but with Mark's allergy, I don't think I can. Would it be possible for you to take him?"

"Yes, yes, yes!" She threw her hands in the air. "Wait. What am I thinking?" She slowly sank to the floor next to Dudley. "My landlady doesn't allow dogs."

I won't be staying with your landlady.

"Not even a small one?" Dana looked as disappointed as she felt.

"Not even a tiny teacup dog. She has a very strict, no-pet policy. If there was any way around it, I would have already found it."

Dana tapped a finger on the side of the ottoman. "Have you considered moving? My mother's a real estate agent and can find you an apartment that allows pets, or even a house rental that isn't much more expensive. I know she'd be happy to help."

Could she move? Aside from Dudley being totally worth the trouble, a move would get her away from noisy neighbors and a nosy landlady. But could she afford it?

Dudley made himself at home in Sydney's lap before he gazed at her with real puppy eyes.

"He seems so enamored with you."

And she was with him. She'd only spent a few hours with him, and she was already attached. "Do you really think your mom could find me a dog-friendly place within my budget?"

Dana nodded. "She's done it for others."

Should the woman fail, fear not. I'm irresistible and will charm your landlady into allowing me to stay.

Sydney already knew there was no charming her landlady, but she couldn't risk losing Dudley to someone else. "I've wanted a dog for a long time now."

And here I am. Dudley wagged his tail, staring up at her.

"How can you say no to that face?" Dana asked.

She laughed. "I can't. Would you like to come live with me, Dudley?"

Dudley barked excitedly. *Excellent decision, Sydney. You are the smartest human I've ever known.*

"He really does understand you," Dana said. "I'll give my mom a call and get this going. In the meantime, can I pay you to take care of Dudley tomorrow?"

"I'm already committed to dog walking all day, but he can go with me if you're okay with that. I'll be taking the dogs to the park for exercise and fresh air."

At last. Something worth getting out of bed for.

"I think that's a great idea. He's getting a little tubby and could use the exercise," Dana whispered.

Look who's talking. You were stress-eating all week, thinking Mark would get cold feet.

Sydney chuckled at both of their comments. "What time should I pick him up?"

"How's eight?"

"Eight is great."

Dana handed her money for the evening. "Here's a little extra for your move."

"Much appreciated." Sydney tucked it away in her pocket. "You know, Dana, I admire you for taking him in when dogs really don't fit into your lifestyle. Most people would have chased him away."

"When I discovered the damage he'd done by chewing everything in sight, I was going to take him to the shelter. But then I couldn't. It was like he had read my mind and immediately poured on the charm."

She's smarter than I gave her credit for.

"He's definitely a charmer." Sydney gathered her belongings, then gave him a pat. "You behave for Dana. All right, Durlindemore?"

I suppose I can keep my antics down to a minimum.

"Dur what?" Dana's brows pushed together. "Are you already renaming him?"

You were quite right, Sydney. I can see the hurt look on her face. Soon she'll be losing me, her shining star, so no need to explain about my real name. Let us leave her thinking she came up with a brilliant name.

No need to explain? But that's exactly what she now had to do. "No, I'd never rename him." Sydney ran a hand through her hair, trying to come up with something plausible. "We were watching an old movie, and there was a character by that name. Dudley cocked his head every time he heard it. It was so cute."

Dana fixed her gaze on Dudley. "Oh, I've got to see this. What was the name?"

No, Sydney. Don't say it.

"Durlindemore."

Dudley had no choice but to cock his head to one side.

Dana laughed. "That's so funny! Durlindemore."

He cocked his head to the other side.

"Durlindemore, Durlindemore, Durlindemore!"

Now she was laughing with Dana, watching Dudley cock his head every time he heard his name.

You humans are so childish.

Sydney let Dana say his name a few more times before she cleared her throat. "I think he'd prefer to hear the name you gave him instead."

"Would you?" Dana bent down next to him. "It's a great name, if I say so myself. You look exactly like a Dudley, don't you?" She raked her fingers through his coat. "Don't you?"

Dudley had a look of disgust on his face. *Grumpy Cat made quite a name for herself, but I'm about to surpass her grumpiness if Pokey Fingers here continues.*

Sydney squelched a grin. "Well, I better get going."

Dana stood up and went to the door with her. "Thanks again, Sydney."

"My pleasure." She stepped out onto the porch. "See you both tomorrow."

I'll be right here by the door, waiting for you at eight sharp.

She chuckled under her breath, wondering if the dog could tell time as she walked to her car. Never did she think pet sitting would turn into the most unreal night of her life.

As soon as she got inside her car, she called Rachael. "You're not going to believe this. Dana's dachshund talks, and I mean *a lot*."

"Really?" Her sister sounded surprised. "I met him yesterday, and he didn't seem that energetic."

"No, I'm not saying that he *barks* a lot, I'm saying that I could hear him telepathically."

"That's awesome, Syd. I've always said you were a great animal communicator."

"But it's not me. It's the dachshund. We talked the entire time Dana was gone."

"You mean he's a talking dog?"

"No. What I'm saying is that I telepathically had a three-and-a-half-hour conversation with him."

"That's really long," Rachael said. "But isn't that the way it normally works when you're communicating with animals?"

She was clearly having difficulty explaining. How could a dog understand her better than her own sister?

She tried again. "I usually get impressions, or pictures in my head, and sometimes a few short sentences. But then I have to piece it together. With Dudley, I didn't have to guess what he was trying to tell me because I psychically heard every word loud and clear."

"Sounds like your communication skills are sharpening."

Rachael didn't sound as excited about it as Sydney thought she would, which meant she still wasn't explaining it correctly. She decided to drop it. "You were right about Dana. She got engaged tonight and asked me to take Dudley permanently."

Rachael gasped. "Can you? I didn't think your apartment building allowed dogs."

"It doesn't. Dana volunteered her mom to help me find a new place."

"Oh, Syd, I feel horrible that I've sent you down this path. You pet sit for a few hours, and now you feel the need to move?"

"I can't let Dudley go to someone else, now that I know he's so special. Besides, I think the apartment above me has been turned into a bowling alley, and I'm sick of the constant noise. Can you stop by the park tomorrow?"

"I don't know yet. We've got a new client in the morning, but I'll text you. Thanks again for taking care of Dudley tonight."

"It was nothing," Sydney said before disconnecting the call. But it was so much more than nothing. Durlindemore, King of the Dachshunds, had just changed her life forever.

CHAPTER FOUR

Carter came home with the usual doggy bag of goodies from his mom, which he always loved. He now had dinner for tomorrow night, and one less thing to worry about. He turned on some lights and got the mail, which was all junk, except for a postcard from his real estate agent. Grace had been bugging him to rent out his guesthouse. She told him he could make decent money doing it, so maybe he should consider it. Summertime was when most people looked for a new place to live, and it was already May.

He stepped out the back door and walked along the flagstones he'd laid for Jade. The daffodils he'd planted for her were bowing their heads, closed up for the night, but come the morning sun, they'd be back in full bloom, brightening up his yard—though he could do without the reminder.

He unlocked the front door to the guesthouse, turned on the light, and instantly recalled how happy she'd been when he'd finally shown her what he'd been working on late at night. He'd placed easels by one of the well-lit windows and sketchpads on a long table, along with jars filled with paintbrushes, charcoal, and pencils.

"Oh, Carter, it's beautiful." She'd thrown her arms around him and told him how much she loved him, and he'd foolishly believed that day was the first among many to come.

He picked up one of the sketches that she'd left behind—a drawing of their wedding she had envisioned—a ceremony in a meadow of wildflowers. It seemed too perfect, too easy, and it was.

When she'd received her acceptance letter from the art school in Paris, her priorities changed overnight—as did her love for him. She'd said she didn't want to tie him down, waiting for her to finish school, when in reality she had wanted to keep her future open to wherever her career would take her.

He couldn't blame her for the choice she'd made. Living in Paris had been her dream, but it hadn't been his.

He tossed Jade's sketch back on the table, turned off the light, and locked up. He definitely needed to rent the place. If anything, having someone else in that space, *her* space, might help bury the memories that continued to plague him.

Sydney barely slept, unable to stop thinking about Dudley and how their telepathic conversation had been so effortless. Dudley said he'd never been able to get through to anyone before her, and she'd never been able to telepathically hear any other animal like she had with him. What was allowing their exceptional communication to occur?

She shoveled down a bowl of cereal and headed over to Dana's, anxious to see him again. What if they'd only been able to communicate last night because of some random, unknown reason, and now they couldn't?

"Good morning," Dana said as she opened the front door.

"Morning." Sydney immediately noticed Dudley sitting just inside the door.

It's bloody well about time. You're two minutes late. Is this going to be a thing with you? Just how much longer must I endure it here? Really, Sydney, I do hope you've made arrangements for me to accompany you home today. I suppose I shouldn't refer to you as my new human servant. What is your preference? My soon-to-be flatmate?

A big grin took over her face. Their connection hadn't dwindled one bit. He was just as articulate as the night before. "Good morning to you, Sir Dudley, my soon-to-be new roommate."

Dudley wagged his tail and barked. *Good on you for hearing me. I have to say, I once spent an entire hour attempting to tell a previous human servant that I was in dire need of stepping outside. But he never heard me, so I had no choice but to relieve myself right there, in front of him, on his brand-new oriental rug.*

Sydney laughed, picturing it.

"What's so funny?" Dana asked, slipping on an earring.

"Uh...Dudley. He's just too cute for words."

"I've got good news." Dana motioned her inside. "My mother knows of three rentals that allow pets, and she just sent over the listings. I'll forward them to you right now, along with her contact info, and you can give her a call when it's convenient."

Sydney's phone buzzed. "Got it. Thanks, Dana."

"Here's Dudley's leash, and a key for you to get back inside. Call me if you need anything else."

As soon as Dana was out the door, Sydney sat with Dudley and opened Dana's text. "Let's take a look at these possible new places." She didn't care for the first one—too old and too much wood. The second apartment was on a busy street, which she didn't love, either. Then there was a house rental. It was a two-bedroom, one-bath, with a small backyard, but it was a hundred dollars a month over her budget. "It looks nice, but it's too expensive." She sighed and put her phone away.

No need to move. I'll come home with you and be quiet as a mouse. Actually, quieter than a mouse. They make a racket at night—particularly when they're scurrying about in your walls.

"I don't have mice in my apartment."

Are you sure?

No, she wasn't. "C'mon. I've got clients to pick up."

Sydney loaded Dudley into the passenger seat and rolled down the window so he could get some good sniffs on their very short ride.

I do like your definition of walking. His eyes were closed, his ears were flapping in the wind, and he looked like he was in heaven.

"Yes, you lucked out. All of my other clients live near one another, so we'll be on foot after this."

Perhaps the others would also prefer to ride rather than walk.

"I'm sure they would, but we won't be burning calories or keeping our hearts in good condition by riding around town." She pulled up in front of her client's house and parked. "We're here."

She helped Dudley down to the ground, then wrapped his leash around her hand and walked him up to the front door. "This is where Pupperton lives. He's a very enthusiastic puppy who doesn't know he's a big dog. Any help would be greatly appreciated."

Someone named a big dog Pupperton? It appears I have a better understanding of the English language than your own species. Pupperton for a big dog, and Dudley for me, when I should have been named Einstein.

She chuckled, opened the door, and located Pupperton in his crate, who was very happy to see her. "Morning, Pupperton. I have someone I'd like you to meet."

Pupperton locked on to Dudley and wagged his tail even more. "This is Durlindemore."

Pupperton cocked his head at the sound of the name, and Sydney had to laugh.

If anyone is confused about an odd name choice, it should be Pupperton.

The big dog wagged his tail as Dudley stood in front of him.

Hello, Pupperton. I'm Durlindemore, King of the Dachshunds. Dudley talked to him with a lot of rolling barks, a few sneezes, and some body language clearly stating that he was in charge.

Pupperton stuck his butt in the air. For a second, she thought Dudley had told him to bow, but then she realized he was just stretching.

She hooked Pupperton's leash onto his collar first before she allowed him to come out of his kennel. Dudley said something to him and he sat, cocking his head again.

It appears Pupperton is having difficulty with my name, most likely due to his lower-class education. At least I was able to get him to sit.

"Thank you, Durlindemore." She worked hard to keep a straight face.

Dudley let out a long sigh. *I suppose I can be known as Dudley from now on, if you wish.*

"It might be easier on the masses," she said, playing along. "Let's go get Finn."

Carter yawned as he poured himself a cup of coffee. After he took a much-needed sip, he opened the front door to retrieve the paper and smiled. Russell had kept his word. Plastered on the front page was his headline: *What are Taxpayers Really Funding?*

A few pages in, he also saw his story on the duckling rescue. As much as he wanted to believe the citizens of Pinecrest would be incensed once they read his front-page article, he knew most would find the duckling rescue more appealing. Not that he could blame them. Misappropriated taxes would continue to happen, and there was little anyone could do about it.

But there was something dangerous about the mayor. He was charming, slick, and the type of guy who could smile while lying to your face, without feeling the least bit guilty about it. Kessler had campaigned on keeping Pinecrest quaint, but his actions in office had proven otherwise. He had encouraged new construction by eliminating environmental restrictions with breakneck speed.

At the same time, he continued to push for more renovations, convincing residents that another incremental tax increase would do wonders for the town's overdue improvements. But he never explained *what* those improvements were. If Carter's article could enlighten more residents, maybe they could finally see some accountability.

He set his dirty dishes in the sink and glanced out the window into the backyard. He could clean out the guesthouse this weekend and get Grace to list it by Monday. Having a steady stream of income coming in would help if he decided to venture out of Pinecrest in search of a position at a bigger paper.

He poured coffee in his travel mug and hit the road, wondering what exciting story he'd be covering today. A neighbor dispute over a fallen tree? A fender-bender due to an old man running a stop sign? A family of raccoons taking up residence in someone's garage? Oh, the possibilities were endless.

Carter pulled into the parking lot and got out just as Dario, the new intern, parked beside him. Dario dragged himself out of his car, then blew his red, blotchy nose.

"Shouldn't you be home drinking chicken noodle soup or something?"

"Can't," Dario said, a little hoarse. "The boss called me in." He grabbed his laptop out of the back seat and walked with Carter. "Besides, it's just a head cold. I always get them in the spring."

"Maybe you're allergic to something blooming."

"Yeah, you might be right."

Carter opened the door and noticed that the place was abuzz. Dario was immediately called over to help one of the editors while Carter found Russell. "What's going on?"

"An eight-year-old kid and his dog have gone missing at Mulberry Park."

"When?"

"An hour ago. Shep is already on scene, but it's a big park, so I want you to get down there too."

"On it." Carter dashed out, his pulse racing a little faster, thinking that this might turn out to be very intense. Kids wandered off, especially at a park, but something told him there would be a lot more to the story. He just hoped it would have a happy ending.

CHAPTER FIVE

Sydney was walking at a good clip with Pupperton, Dudley, a sweet border collie named Cocoa Puff, and a retired greyhound named Finn. Cocoa Puff had been too excited about the walk to pay any attention to Dudley, but Finn warmed right up to him. She could see Dudley and Finn bonding quickly since they were both serious couch potatoes.

She slowed the dogs down as Mulberry Park came into view. Several cop cars were in the parking lot, along with a large crowd of people. A guy around her age pulled up right in front of her. When he got out of his car, she couldn't help but notice him. He was tall and lean, but muscular, with dusty brown hair, a pointed, turned-up nose, and a determined chin. He made eye contact for a split second and gave her a quick smile before he popped his trunk and pulled out a camera. He then began loading up his vest pockets with additional equipment. She assumed he was a reporter or a freelance photographer, at the ready to capture something newsworthy.

"Morning," she said with a warm smile. "Do you know what's going on here?"

The guy glanced up, then did a quick assessment of her and the four dogs. He turned toward her, meeting her gaze, and his eyes softened as the hurried air about him slowed. "A boy and his dog went missing."

"Oh no!" She immediately thought of a frantic mom searching for her son.

I suppose I shall have to find him. Dudley put his nose in the air.

She bent down next to Dudley and looked him directly in the eye. "You think you can do that?"

Of course. It's not rocket science.

"Do what?" the guy asked her.

"Oh, sorry." She let out an embarrassed laugh as she stood. "I was talking to my dog."

The guy closed the trunk and studied Dudley, who was scratching his ear. "Did he answer you?" He raised a brow to her, suppressing a smile.

She automatically stiffened, feeling like he was making fun of her. But when she stared into his deep blue-green eyes, she saw a flirty playfulness about him.

She threw him a half smile as she raised her chin a notch. "As a matter of fact, he did."

He nodded as if he accepted her answer as truth, then skimmed over the rest of her pack. "It sounds like you're the person I should be talking to. I'm a journalist with *The Pinecrest News*." He held up his camera. "Do you walk your dogs here often?"

"Every day. I'm a professional dog walker."

He had a surprised look on his face, and she could only assume he'd thought they were all hers. "Have you seen anyone suspicious around here in the past few days?"

Could this be a kidnapping? She hadn't thought of that. Pinecrest registered so low on the crime scale that she rarely thought about worst-case scenarios. "No. Not that I recall."

"That's good." He breathed out a relieved sigh, then noticed a lot of people gathering on the other side of the parking lot. "Hopefully the kid is just lost."

"Yeah, I hope so too."

"Thanks for your help," he said, seeming torn between staying to talk and going to do his job. Police officers arrived with bloodhounds, so his job won out. "I better go. Stay safe out there."

He didn't even know her and he was worried about her safety? Who *was* this guy? She watched him hurry toward the growing crowd, then released a loud sigh.

Oh dear. Dudley invaded her thoughts.

She cleared her throat and focused on him. "What's wrong?"

You've been bitten by the bug.

She inspected her exposed skin and didn't see any red welts. "What bug?"

The love bug.

"Oh, please." She rolled her eyes. "Come on." She gathered the leashes tighter in her hand, knowing that cute guys were bad news, including the one she'd just met.

Are we going to find your dashing young journalist?

"He's not my—" She couldn't believe how perceptive he was, but she certainly wasn't going to discuss it with him. "No, we're going to see if we can help find the missing boy."

Oh, I think we'll find more than the boy.

She ignored his comment and headed straight to what appeared to be a makeshift command center under a large tent. Volunteers were setting supplies on long tables while others were milling around, waiting for someone in charge to tell them where to start searching. A few minutes later, a police officer made his way to the front of an ever-growing group of volunteers.

"Thank you all for coming," he said, and held up an oversized photo of the eight-year-old missing boy with his golden retriever. "This is Zachary and his dog, Scout. Mrs. Phillips, Zach's mom, said he was throwing a squeaky toy for Scout when her phone rang. She answered it and was on the phone for less than a minute. When she looked up, they were both gone. Zachary is wearing a light-blue shirt and dark-brown pants. Scout's squeaky toy is a big yellow ball. Since the park includes several hiking trails, they might have started up one of those and got lost, or they could be with another adult."

A concerned murmur rippled through the group before the officer continued.

"If there are any volunteers who haven't checked in, please do so, and we'll assign you to a search team. Any questions?" The officer scanned the group, all seeming anxious to get on with it. "All right, let's go find Zachary and Scout."

As everyone got ready to leave, the police officer spoke to three handlers with bloodhounds. One by one, the bloodhounds smelled Zachary's sweatshirt, then each team took off across the park. The rest of the volunteers formed smaller groups before they left to join the search.

"What's the plan?" Sydney said to Dudley.

Get me next to the lad's sweatshirt, so I can pick up his scent.

"Are you here to volunteer?" a young woman asked, sitting behind a table with walkie-talkies, bottled water, and first-aid kits.

"I can try, but I'll have to go at my own pace since I have four dogs with me."

"Any help is greatly appreciated. I'm Valerie, and I'm the on-scene coordinator. I can have you search nearby, instead of the trails. Will that work?"

She eyed Dudley. *Anything nearby that won't force me to exert myself is jolly good with me.*

"Nearby is fine," she said.

"Great. I'll need you to fill this out." Valerie gave her a form on a clipboard, which asked for her name, cell number, emergency contact, and how much experience she'd had with search and rescue. "Just your name and cell number are all I need since you won't need to search through rough terrain today."

Sydney nodded and jotted down the requested information. "Can my dachshund sniff the boy's sweatshirt?"

Valerie held back a smile. "Sure."

Tell her I'm far superior to any of those pathetic bloodhounds. I will crush them in the skill department and win the day.

"He's got a nose for this," Sydney said. "He is a hound, after all."

"He is indeed." She brought the sweatshirt over to Dudley, who sniffed it all over, and then started licking part of the sweatshirt.

He had pancakes for breakfast with real maple syrup. Delicious!

"What's he doing?" Valerie gave Dudley an odd look.

"Oh, he uses all of his senses."

The lad smells like animal cookies, which happen to be another one of my favorites.

"Whatever works." Valerie shrugged, then grabbed a few things for Sydney. "Here's a map of the park and a walkie-talkie. The channel is preset so don't change it, and here's the base camp number if you need to use your cell phone instead. If you see or find anything you feel might be relevant, let me know, and I can get someone over to you right away."

"Thank you."

"Help yourself to some bottled water for you and your pups. Good luck and stay in touch."

"I will." She turned toward the park. "C'mon, everyone. Let's go!"

Valerie stood up to stretch as Carter watched the woman with the four dogs. "Who was that?" he asked, trying not to sound too interested.

"A concerned resident who thinks her wiener dog can find the missing boy." Valerie caught his eye and they shared a smile, both knowing there was zero chance of that ever happening.

Carter watched the odd pair. The woman was getting jerked around by the dachshund who went from having his nose to the ground, to stopping at a tree and barking at a squirrel—which got the other dogs riled up and barking too. They looked comical, and he would have laughed out loud if the situation hadn't been so serious.

He leaned back and took a peek at the list of volunteers. Her name was Sydney Elder. Her handwriting was so neat that he could clearly read her phone number, and he quickly memorized it. Even though she had four dogs with her, they all looked so docile that he found himself worrying about her. She was a tiny thing, searching alone for Zachary. What if some lowlife was the reason for the kid's disappearance and the concerned dog walker was literally walking into a bad situation?

"Hey, Valerie." Shep approached the table. "What do you have for me?" Shep looked more like he was going on a safari than covering a story for the paper. He had on a khaki hat and binoculars around his neck. His cell phone was clipped to his belt, and two cameras hung from his shoulder. He did a double take when he saw Carter. "What are you doing here?"

"Russell sent me."

"Why? I don't need any help."

"I'm not here to help you, Shep. I'm here to cover the story. It's a large park with miles of hiking trails, and you might not be in the right place at the right time." *For once.*

Shep burst with a laugh. "That will never happen." He moved closer to Valerie and turned on the charm. "Now what were you saying?"

Irritated, Carter stepped closer to the volunteers working the phones, keeping an ear out for any important information coming in over the walkies. His gaze drifted to Sydney, the dog walker. The dachshund was barking at a bird, and she was saying something to him, but he appeared to be ignoring her. The doxie then flipped on his back and started scratching it in the grass.

A chuckle escaped his lips, which had Shep and Valerie looking at him. He turned away, hoping to speak with Zachary's mother, but she was crying and someone was comforting her. He needed information on the professional search and rescue teams from Valerie, but Shep was still taking up her time, so he spoke with another volunteer to see if any witnesses had come forward. Unfortunately, none had. He'd already checked for any CCTV cameras when he pulled into the parking lot. There weren't any of those, either, so if Zachary had left with someone, it hadn't been recorded.

Valerie laughed at something Shep said, and Carter knew that waiting for his annoying colleague to go away was a waste of time. Carter would have to speak to Valerie and Zach's mom later since he had to figure out the best place to cover any breaking news. He could attempt to join one of the groups already searching, or he could wait to hear something over the walkie. Either way, Carter knew that Shep would somehow be exactly where he needed to be to capture the story first.

Sydney kept her eyes closed as she telepathically connected to Zach's dog. "I'm getting very little from Scout on his whereabouts," she said to Dudley. "I'm seeing pictures of trees. But are those trees in this park?" She shrugged. "He just sent me a picture of Zachary, which I can only assume means they're together, but where exactly? Wait. I just heard, 'up and down.' What does that mean?"

She opened her eyes and stared at Dudley who was still on his back, taking a sunbath. "Are you sensing any of this? Honestly, Dudley, I thought you were serious about helping."

I am. Can't you see I'm hard at work?

"Quit messing around."

I'm not. I'm very busy gathering intel.

"Do you think I'm that stupid?"

Do you speak bird?

"What?"

Bird! My newest acquaintance, Twilley Anna, is on the case.

She let out a sigh. "What are you talking about?"

I suppose you thought I spent a mere two seconds attempting to pick up Zachary's scent before I was distracted by a squirrel, then a bird, and then the grass.

"It had crossed my mind. You already told me you've been trapped inside Dana's house for the past week, and now you're getting a long walk at a park—so it does stand to reason."

I loathe long walks. A long walk to me is from the couch to the refrigerator.

"You seemed to have been enjoying it while we were picking up the other dogs."

Did I have a choice? I wasn't going to complain and have you change your mind about my living arrangements. But we're getting off topic. I had a chat with Gudorineezop and—

"Who?"

Mr. Squirrel to you. Anyway, Gudorineezop was horrified because he saw Scout bolt after Gudorineezop's girlfriend. Luckily, the boy chased after Scout, which allowed Gudorineezop's girlfriend to run to a nearby tree.

"What happened to Zach and Scout?"

They went in that direction. Dudley gazed off toward one of the hiking trails.

"Then what are we doing hanging out here? Lead the way."

Dudley refused to budge. *Not until I get a bird's eye view of the little bugger's precise location.*

Sydney squinted at him in confusion, then finally got it. "You gave Twilley bird his description and she's searching for him?"

Her name is Twilley Anna, and yes. She's searching, and I'm warming up for the thousand-yard dash—although I do hope it's not a thousand yards. I'm ready for a nap.

Carter was in the middle of interviewing one of the volunteers, who happened to be Zachary's babysitter, when he heard a loud yelp. Sydney was being dragged across the park by the four dogs. He took off, racing to help her, as the dogs ran toward one of the hiking trails.

"Let me help," he said, slightly winded, as he finally caught up to her. He reached for the leashes to pull them back, but she yanked them away.

"What are you doing?" Sydney scowled at him, still in a full-out run.

"Helping you to get control of these dogs."

"They're not out of control. They're leading me to the boy!"

The dachshund pulled on the leash, and they ran faster.

Carter kept up, even though he knew there was no way the dogs were leading her to Zachary. More likely one of them saw a squirrel, and she was too embarrassed to admit the truth. He was breathing hard now, and ready to stop, but he couldn't let a petite dog walker outrun him.

"Zachary?" she called, out of breath, as they ran up the trail.

The dachshund was leading the pack, which seemed odd when the long-legged greyhound could easily overtake a short-legged, slightly overweight dachshund.

"What was that?" Sydney said, as if she were talking to the dachshund. "Are you sure?" she asked, then came to dead stop. "Zachary?"

Breathing hard, she peered over the edge of the trail, as did Carter. He'd never noticed the steep incline on the small hill before, and he'd been up this particular trail several times.

Sydney looked directly at the dachshund. "I don't see anything, Dudley. Are you sure?"

The vibrant color of red columbine below caught Carter's eye. "I think I see something yellow in that patch of columbine."

She scanned the area he was pointing to and found it. "Dudley, tell Pupperton to go down there and see what it is."

The dachshund began barking his head off, as if he understood everything she'd said—which was impossible. Sydney unleashed the dog she called Pupperton, and he ran down the hill, then immediately leaped into the columbine. Dudley barked at Pupperton, as if he was giving the bigger dog instructions. Pupperton started sniffing the ground. A moment later, he had a yellow ball in his mouth and was making it squeak incessantly. The dog was a total goofball, playing with his newfound toy.

"Good boy, Pupperton!" Sydney called out.

Carter gave her a sideways glance. "Pupperton seems like an odd name for such a big puppy."

"That's exactly what Dudley and I said." She caught his gaze and beamed him a broad smile.

Pupperton raced up the hill, but Dudley barked at him, so he bounced back down the hill and ran around in that area, playing with the squeaky toy.

A moment later, a golden retriever emerged from behind a bunch of big trees and ran toward the squeaking sound.

Dudley barked at the golden retriever, who spotted him and barked back.

"Scout, wait!" A young boy appeared, limping heavily toward his dog, looking a little worse for wear. His chin was scraped up and his clothes were dirty, indicating he'd most likely fallen down the embankment.

"Zachary?" Sydney shouted. "Are you Zachary Phillips?"

He stopped and glanced up at her, squinting from the sun. "Yeah."

"Your mom is worried sick. We're with a group of people out here looking for you."

"I fell." The boy rubbed the back of his head.

"I'll go down," Carter said to Sydney. "Wait here." He started sidestepping down the steep terrain. "My name is Carter," he called out to Zachary. "I'm coming down to help you."

"I can't leave my dog," the boy said.

"You won't." Carter heard Sydney on the walkie-talkie behind him as he continued making his way down to Zachary.

"Help is on the way," she called out, holding up the walkie-talkie.

Carter reached the bottom, and Pupperton greeted him with a lick on the back of his hand, which made Zachary smile.

"Let's get you off that ankle." He picked up Zachary and set him on top of a boulder, then pulled out a bottled water from his vest. "You must be thirsty." He twisted off the cap and handed it to him.

The boy took a small drink before he gave the rest to Scout. Pupperton came over to get in on the action and licked Zachary in the face, which made him giggle.

"He's so cute." Zachary patted his big head. "What's his name?"

"Pupperton."

The boy giggled. "That's a funny name. Hi, Pupperton."

Pupperton grabbed the ball again and dropped it in his lap.

"Zachary!" His mom arrived, out of breath, with a rescue team. "Are you okay?"

Zachary nodded, more interested in Pupperton and Scout playing with the ball.

"He's twisted his ankle," Carter called up to the team.

A few minutes later, two paramedics were on the way down. But as Carter glanced up from below, it was only the dog walker in the gathering crowd who held his attention.

CHAPTER SIX

Sydney watched the rescue from above with Dudley, Cocoa Puff, and Finn by her side. Several volunteers poured into the area, along with a pushy photographer who was taking pictures at every angle—including some of her. She was glad they'd been able to help the boy, but now she wanted to escape. That wasn't going to happen anytime soon.

Pupperton was taking his new rescue duty very seriously and didn't want to leave the little boy's side. Once the paramedics wrapped Zachary's ankle and put him on a stretcher, Sydney called for him, but the big puppy ignored her. As everyone headed up the embankment, it was Dudley who finally got him to obey.

"You did it!" She picked up Dudley and hugged him as Pupperton joined them with his tail wagging. "Good boy, Pupperton." She gave him a rub on his side.

I do believe it was quite a team effort.

Twilley Anna did a flyby, then circled back.

"You're right, Dudley." She watched the bird glide over to them. "Thank you, Twilley Anna."

The bird chirped and flew off. Sydney gathered the dogs and got them out of the way as the paramedics set the stretcher down on the trail. Zachary's mom threw her arms around him with happy tears running down her cheeks.

The aggressive photographer pushed Carter back so he'd be the one to capture the reunion. Sydney frowned. She could feel the competitive tension between the two men.

"Mom, I can't breathe," Zachary said, and she finally let go as everyone laughed.

"Looks like I was in the right place at the right time again," the photographer smugly said to Carter. "I captured everything I needed for an exciting article."

"I got a lot of coverage myself, Shep." Carter's voice was laced with irritation.

"Russell will be the judge, but I'm sure he'll agree with me. You can't objectively cover a story when you're part of it." Shep held up his camera with a big grin, then took off down the trail, before he turned and crouched down to get more pictures of everyone descending out of the woods.

"Friend of yours?" Sydney couldn't help but ask.

"We both work at *The Pinecrest News*, but Shep always manages to cover any major story."

She hated to see disappointment in those blue-green eyes of his. "You helped save that boy. I'd say your take on what happened here is far more valuable."

"Thanks." He offered her a warm smile. "I'm hoping my boss will agree."

When she and Carter reached the command post, Shep was talking to Zach and his mom before leaving the scene. No doubt he was wanting to get back to the paper first.

Carter didn't seem to care. He'd had plenty of time to talk to the boy while they waited for help. "Zach, can I get a quick picture of you and the dogs before you go? You'll be on the front page tomorrow."

"Cool!"

"Mind if I borrow Dudley and Pupperton?" he asked Sydney.

"No problem." She handed over their leashes, knowing Pupperton's pet parents wouldn't mind him being in the paper after doing something so praiseworthy.

Zachary sat on the back of the ambulance with the dogs around him while Carter quickly snapped several photos. "That should do it." He stepped back. "Take care, Zach."

"Thank you for finding my son," Zach's mom said to both her and Carter, then squeezed Sydney's hand.

She had to clear her throat from emotion in order to speak. "It was our pleasure."

After the ambulance headed out, Sydney exhaled a sigh of

relief. "Well, that was one exciting morning." She gave each dog a treat, and a few extras for Dudley and Pupperton. Dudley snarfed them down and looked for another, so she sneaked him one more. "Incredible work, good sir."

It was nothing, really. Dudley thumped his tail, looking pleased with himself.

"Can I get a photo of you and your dogs?" Carter asked.

"Oh, I don't know." She ran a hand over her hair.

She suddenly felt very self-conscious, standing so close to Carter and having all of his attention on her. He had a studious, sexy vibe about him—book smart on a geek level. Yet, she imagined he'd be very romantic because he paid attention to detail. She felt a strong pull toward him, and her pulse quickened.

I can't believe you're attracted to this chap. Dudley sounded like he couldn't fathom such a thing.

She blinked, and refocused on Dudley. "Why not?"

"Great," Carter said, stepping back and aiming his camera in her direction.

"No, wait, I…" She couldn't exactly say her answer had been for Dudley.

"How about I take a picture of the first search team on scene?" Valerie said behind them.

"I'm not one for being in front of the camera." Carter took a step back, lowering his head in a shy manner.

"But you were part of the rescue. Do you represent accurate news or whatever fits your narrative?" She raised a challenging brow.

"Okay, I see where this is going." Carter took a deep breath and finger-combed his hair.

Sydney laughed as she got the dogs to sit at their feet.

"You two need to get a little closer together." Valerie directed with a wave of her hand as she studied the shot through the viewfinder.

Sydney and Carter shared an uncomfortable look.

Dudley stared at them. *The two of you are acting like children. It's a stunner how your species has managed to procreate at all.*

"Right." Carter moved closer, and their shoulders touched.

Heat flew down her arm, making her glance at him. He must

have felt it, too, because his gaze locked with hers and wouldn't let go.

"Those are great. Now I need a few of you two looking into the camera." Valerie snapped off four or five more photos, then shifted into another position, ready to take more when Carter walked toward her.

"Thanks, Valerie." He took back his camera. "That should be plenty." He snapped on the lens cap. "You sound like a professional photographer."

"I am. I do weddings, engagement parties, anniversaries, any special occasion." She handed him her card. "For the future." Her gaze darted between him and Sydney. "Hopefully, you two will be less self-conscious by then," she said, then walked away.

Sydney laughed uncomfortably. "That was..."

"Yeah." Carter shook his head before he focused on her. "I don't think we were properly introduced."

"I'm Sydney. Or Syd. Short for Sydney. Obviously. My sister calls me Syd, so I answer to both," she said, turning red with embarrassment. "Elder," she added. "That's my last name."

Awwwkward. Dudley had to chime in.

"Great to officially meet you, Sydney or Syd. I'm Carter."

"Carter...?"

Wow. It's like watching a train wreck.

"Hansen." His voice hitched. He sounded nervous. She felt equally jumpy, and they simultaneously glanced at Dudley, getting the attention off themselves. "How did your dog know where to find Zachary and Scout?"

"He has a good nose." She spit out a generic reply, assuming he'd never believe the truth even if she was willing to tell him.

"More than the bloodhounds who sniffed out that trail before he did?"

Go ahead. Tell him I'm a genius.

"All hounds are great at scent work."

"Uh-huh." Carter made a few notes on his phone. "So, this little dachshund initiated the search. I believe you said his name is Dudley?"

"Yes."

If my name is going to be in the paper, I want my proper title.

Sydney closed her eyes and scratched the side of her nose, reluctant to say what she was about to. "His, uh, real name is Durlindemore, King of the Dachshunds."

Carter laughed and looked up from his phone. "Who came up with that?"

"He did."

"And pigs can fly," he said under his breath. "Were you the one who nicknamed him Dudley?"

"No, the woman who found him sniffing around her trash cans did."

"She chose a great name. I think it fits him perfectly."

I don't care for this fellow. Dudley turned his back on Carter.

"So do I, but apparently Durlindemore, King of the Dachshunds, doesn't care for the name Dudley."

Carter bent down, eye level with Dudley, and gave him a gentle rub down his back. "You know, Durlindemore, King of the Dachshunds, your title is a mouthful to say. How about, for the newspaper, I let the world know your title, but I'll explain to the reader how everyone calls you Dudley for short?"

Oh, he's good. Dudley melted to his touch.

"I think that's a nice compromise," she said to both Dudley and Carter.

"Great." Carter stood, and noted it on his phone.

How is Dudley short for Durlindemore? It should be Durley or Durlind.

"Is that what you want, instead?" she asked Dudley. "Durley or Durlind?"

Carter glanced at her, and then at Dudley, no doubt thinking she was playing along.

I'm not fond of Durley or Durlind, either.

"He's thinking about it," Sydney said, a little embarrassed.

"Durley, Durlind, or Dudley. A tough decision," Carter said to him. "But if I'm to report the news accurately, I heard Sydney call you Dudley earlier."

"He's got you there." She lifted a brow to the dog.

Cheeky bugger. Dudley released a big breath. *I suppose it will have to do.*

"He's fine with that."

"Good." Carter eyed the other dogs. "Are you all okay with your names?"

She laughed. "Yes, they're perfectly fine with them."

Says the woman who doesn't speak dog.

"Would you mind texting me the proper spelling of Dudley's official name when you have a chance?" He handed her his card.

"No problem."

"Thanks." He held her gaze a little longer than normal before he reluctantly broke eye contact. "I have to get back to work," he said, though he wasn't making any move in that direction. "I'd love to hear more about Dudley's extraordinary scent work, if you want to grab a coffee sometime."

Rather forward of him, don't you think? Put him in his place, Sydney.

"Sure. I've got a pretty flexible schedule these days." Her eyes lingered on him. "And I'll text you Dudley's info."

"Great." He couldn't seem to stop smiling. "Thanks again. Bye, Durlindemore, King of the Dachshunds." He ruffled his fur.

Don't try to get on my good side.

"He said he enjoyed working with you and is looking forward to seeing you again soon."

Carter chuckled. "He's one talkative dog."

"Oh, you have no idea."

Carter glanced back at Sydney before he got in his car and saw her chattering away to the little doxie. Ordinarily he would have thought she was a crazy dog lady, but she was too young and way too pretty to fit the stereotype. There was something about her—something very captivating. If his phone hadn't been blowing up with calls and messages, he would have asked her out for coffee right then. Not that he was interested. Okay, he *was* interested, but that didn't matter. He wasn't going to put himself out there again. He was the worst at reading women, and he always paid the price for that inability. And yet…

He started his car and headed back to the office, unable to stop thinking about Sydney. Where had that physical attraction suddenly come from? He'd felt drawn to her the second their shoulders touched. He couldn't stop gazing at her. But who could blame him?

For a town where nothing happened, a hell of a lot had just happened. Now, he was damn curious about her and that dog. They seemed to have such a strong connection to each other. Of course, she appeared to have command over the other three as well. He'd have to do some research on her. Maybe she was a dog trainer in addition to being a dog walker. The Tasmanian devil his mom had mistaken for a dog could definitely use some serious training.

He stopped for a light as his cell buzzed. Sydney had texted him Dudley's preferred title. He smiled and was already composing a pithy reply when he abruptly quit typing. What was he doing? He said no more animal stories and no more dating, which meant women with animals were automatically off his list. If he had a list. Which he didn't.

An image of Dudley rolling around in the grass with Sydney looking exasperated, popped into his head and made him laugh. Maybe he shouldn't make promises he couldn't keep—even if they were only to himself.

CHAPTER SEVEN

"I can't believe we found Zach and Scout," Sydney said to Dudley as she took her morning clients home. "Our unique set of skills did that."

Did I not tell you we'd be a remarkable team?

"You did, and now I wholeheartedly agree." She opened the door to Pupperton's house and got him settled in his crate. "Okay, Pupperton. You be a good boy, and we'll see you tomorrow."

Dudley barked at him, which made the big dog's tail wag.

She locked the front door and was about to ask Dudley what he'd said when a text came in from Carter. She opened it and smiled. "Can you read English?"

Can you read dog?

"I'll take that as a no." She bent down and showed him one of the photos Carter had taken. "The caption reads, 'Sydney and her lifesavers.'"

Not completely accurate. While Pupperton and I were engaged, Cocoa Puff was more interested in a butterfly and Finn was licking his butt.

She chuckled. "I wish he had sent me the photo of the whole team."

Tell him one lifesaver is missing.

"I like that."

A moment later, a text and a photo came in. She looked stiff and awkward, and Carter looked a little uncomfortable too.

Let me see. Dudley studied the photo. *At least I look good.*

"So does Carter. He's very handsome."

And tall. Women seem to like tall men. He's much taller than you.

"Well, I am short."

Are you? He looked up at her.

"Okay, not as short as you."

Dudley studied the photo. *You both have strained smiles.*

Carter sent another text. "He says I look good and that you look majestic."

He got it half right.

"Ha-ha." She typed a reply to Carter. **You look like a hero.** She immediately regretted it, as he might take it as flirting.

Luckily, he quickly texted back: **If heroes look awkward, then yes.**

She smiled as her phone rang with a number she didn't recognize. "This is Sydney."

"Hello, Sydney. This is Grace Fielding. My daughter, Dana, gave me your number."

"Oh, yes, hi. Thank you for sending the photos, but I'm just not sure about any of them."

"That's the reason I'm calling. The house for rent was just reduced by fifty dollars a month, which means it will be snapped up quickly. I don't mean to pressure you, but if that makes a difference, you should see it today."

"It does." She looked at the time. "I could meet you at two."

"Two is great. I'll text you the address. See you then."

"Well, Dudley. It looks like you'll be going home with me so I can get a quick bite to eat before we see a rental. Then we'll pick up my afternoon crew at three. Sound good?"

Dudley barked once and ran to her car.

Carter entered *The Pinecrest News*, and the paper's small group of employees started clapping—even Shep.

"Well done," Jamie, the copy editor, clapped even louder.

"What's going on?" Carter glanced around, confused.

"Take a look." Shep led him to their news design table where he had taken it upon himself to help Russell figure out the layout of the paper. Two of Shep's photos told the story. The first photo showed Sydney with her dogs anxiously watching Zachary, Carter, and the paramedics climb up the embankment.

The second captured Zachary's mom hugging her son tightly. Below these two photos read, *A Rescue in Action*.

He was surprised that Shep had selected a photo with him in it, then realized what he was doing. "Russell might want to revise the front page when he takes a look at my photos."

"Go ahead and ask him." Shep shrugged. "But you know as well as I do that you can't be reporting on yourself."

"We'll see about that." Carter marched over to Russell's office and saw him on the phone.

Russell waved him in and finished the call. "Just the guy I was looking for."

"Tell me you haven't approved of Shep's photos because I—"

"Shut the door behind you." Carter did as requested, wondering what was up. Russell looked troubled. "You did a great job in the park today and with that boy."

"Thank you."

"You also did a great job with your investigative reporting on the town's power lines project, but it struck a nerve." Russell met his gaze. "The mayor is furious."

"Why, because I'm exposing the truth?"

"An inconvenient truth. While you were at the park, Mayor Kessler asked for your resignation, stating your reporting is an outrageous lie and that your article reflects poorly on our city. He then went on to remind me that our little independent newspaper relies heavily on ad revenue, and our biggest advertiser happens to be his brother-in-law. The mayor thought I should give his suggestion very serious consideration should I want to keep the lights on."

"A threat?" Carter clenched his jaw. "The mayor wants to take away free speech? Talk about outrageous. Our newspaper has integrity, it's unbiased, it's—"

"Failing. I appreciate how much you love this paper, but it doesn't take any investigative reporting to discover that *The Pinecrest News* is dying a slow death. As it is, I'm going to have to lay off two more employees by Christmas."

"What?" Carter sat back, stunned. "I know we've had a drop in subscriptions and ad revenue, but I didn't realize we were in such dire straits."

"We are, like every other paper in this country."

"So that's it? I'm done?"

"No. Kessler doesn't run this paper, I do. But I also know when not to poke a sleeping bear. You're young, Carter, and you're a very good investigative reporter. However, if you choose to stay, you can't pursue what you've uncovered or any other story about the mayor."

He let out a long, resigned breath. "You know the guy's a scumbag."

"And hopefully our residents will vote him out of office in November. But I've still got to pay the bills, and so does everyone here."

"Okay, I'll back off. Will you at least run my story on today's rescue, or are you going with Shep's?"

His boss leaned forward. "Did you notice something different when you entered the office?"

"Yeah, everyone clapping for me, which I'm sure Shep put them up to so I wouldn't complain about him taking full credit for the story."

"Not that. Do you hear the phones ringing off the hook?"

Carter turned his head, listening.

"Residents are inquiring about the woman with the dogs," Russell said. "What's her name?"

"Sydney Elder, but why are they calling us?"

"Because of Shep." Russell jotted down her name. "A lot of people recognized him out there. Look, we both know you're a better reporter than he is, but our town loves him, and I can't afford to lose him. So, this is what I'm going to do. The paper will run a two-part story starting tomorrow. Shep will take part one, which will be about the rescue, but it will also highlight Ms. Elder with her dogs. Then you'll do an in-depth interview with her that will run on Friday."

"You're giving me another human-interest story—starring dogs?" Carter shook his head at the irony.

"I know that's not what you wanted to hear, and I can send Shep to interview her if you—"

"I'll do it."

"Are you sure?"

Of course he was sure. There was no way he'd allow Shep near Sydney when the guy had practically dated every available woman in town. "I was there with her. It makes sense for me to do the interview."

"And that's how I'm selling it. One of our own reporters, part of the rescue, sitting down for an intimate one-on-one interview with the woman who reunited the boy with his mom. I love it," Russell said. "Your writing style engages readers, and I think your interview will bring back some of our readership. Once we get back on our feet again, you can go after Mayor Kessler as much as you want."

That alone would get him out of bed in the morning. "It will be my pleasure."

Sydney pulled up in front of her apartment building and groaned. The very woman she hoped to avoid was sitting on her balcony, scrutinizing anyone and everyone coming and going from the apartment complex. She didn't understand it. Her landlady was in her sixties and could be having lunch with friends, or visiting her kids, or getting an updated hairstyle so that birds would stop trying to nest in it. But no, Mrs. Seidleman chose to give everyone a hard time instead—especially her.

After Mrs. Seidleman had discovered another tenant with cats, she put Sydney on her watch list. The woman constantly accused her of sneaking dogs into her apartment, which was absurd. She'd never do that. Okay, maybe she was about to do that very thing, but this was different. It was temporary, and as Dudley continued to point out, he was no ordinary dog.

"Dudley, my nosy landlady is hanging out on her balcony. Can you fit inside my handbag?" Sydney dumped out the contents, then held it open for Dudley.

He gave her a look of disgust. *Surely members of my species are allowed to visit.*

"They are, but my landlady knows what I do for a living. She expressly forbade me to bring any four-legged clients here, and I don't need to get evicted at the moment."

Seems I've come along just in time to rescue you from this unfriendly prison. Dudley hopped in her handbag but didn't quite fit. *I do hope the house rental meets your expectations.*

"It's still a little pricey, but we'll see." Sydney covered up the rest of Dudley with a sweater she kept in the back seat, then got out and staggered to her feet. "You're like carrying a cinder block."

I'm all muscle.

"That's what all dachshunds think." She could feel Mrs. Seidleman's eyes on her as she hurried up the entrance to her building. "Stop squirming," she said under her breath.

"What do you have there, Sydney?"

Crap. She turned and faced her. "What do you mean?"

Mrs. Seidleman shooed away a bird that was trying to land on her head. "In your bag?"

Sydney wanted to say it was none of her business, but she didn't want to get on her bad side if she had to break her lease. "A bowling ball, Mrs. Seidleman."

"Why would you carry a bowling ball in your purse?"

"I'd love to talk, but I've got to run." Sydney hurried into the apartment complex and up the stairs to the second floor. "I swear that woman has a sixth sense better than me." Out of breath, she unlocked her front door and went inside.

Dudley hopped out of her handbag and took himself on a tour of her one-bedroom apartment while she set down a bowl of water for him. She wasn't hearing him say anything, so she suspected he wasn't impressed.

"You didn't know how good you really had it at Dana's, did you?"

Her place is magnificent, but I would have been tossed out when the allergic fiancé moved in.

Sydney grilled up some chicken tenders, then threw them in a cheese quesadilla.

Dudley stared at her with big eyes. *Don't I get lunch?*

"Dogs don't eat lunch, though I suppose I can make an exception since you worked hard today." She cut up a small portion of a chicken tender and served it on a teacup saucer.

Dudley inhaled it.

"Slow down."

Too late.

She quickly ate her quesadilla and glanced at the time. "We've gotta go."

So soon? How about a nap instead?

Her cell rang, and she hit speakerphone. "Hi, Carter."

"Am I interrupting?"

Just conversing with a genius. Dudley pretended to answer for her.

She rolled her eyes. "Not at all," she said as she tidied up the kitchen.

"Would you like to meet for coffee today?"

He doesn't waste any time.

"Wish I could, but I have afternoon clients, and I'll be working until five."

"What about after that?"

He seems a bit too pushy. Have him meet you in the park with me and the others, so I can keep an eye on him.

"Sure. I can meet after five. How about I'll call you when I'm done?"

"Sounds great. Talk soon."

You should rethink that. You need a chaperone.

"Since when?" She threw her cell in her handbag.

You just met this bloke. No doubt he has ulterior motives.

"Are you always this suspicious?"

I'm never wrong, Sydney. It comes with the territory of being a genius.

It was bad enough to have her sister constantly giving her dating advice. But a dog? Absolutely not. Sydney pulled out her gym bag from the hall closet and inspected the inside. It had a hard bottom to it, which would make it easier on her and Dudley.

"All right, genius, time to skate by my nosy landlady." She set a soft towel inside, then placed him on top of it.

Ah, this is the life.

Sydney locked up, then raced down the steps and ran right into her landlady, who tried to see inside Sydney's bag.

"That better not be a dog in there."

"Why would I carry a dog in my gym bag? Bye, Mrs. Seidleman."

Dudley made a soft sound of disgust. *I see a move in your future, and it's quite imminent.*

CHAPTER EIGHT

Carter sat at his desk with the cat on his lap, surrounded by colleagues listening to his first-hand account of the rescue.

"You're an actual hero," Jamie said, seeming to have stars in her eyes. "If you hadn't seen Scout's ball, poor Zachary would still be lost. His mother must be so grateful that you were there."

"Nothing but luck." Shep barged in on the conversation. "He was in the right place at the right time. How does it feel to be me?" He laughed, sitting down on the edge of his desk.

Chester jumped off Carter's lap as Jamie and the others went back to work.

"What do you want?" Carter eyed him warily.

Shep expelled an irritated breath. "I don't want anything, but Russell thought you should fact-check my article about today's drama since you were directly involved."

Carter could see how much it pained Shep to say that. "No problem. Just shoot it over to me, and I'll take a look."

Shep got up, then turned back around. "I don't mind doing the interview with Sydney. I know you're tired of animal assignments, and she might open up to me more than you—seeing as how I'm practically a celebrity in this town."

Carter held back a laugh. "She had no idea who you were in the park. Besides, I've already set it up."

Shep gave him a surprised look. "That was fast."

"I'm on a deadline."

"Or maybe you have your eye on Sydney too. But we both

know that no lady can resist me." Shep walked away with a smirk on his face.

Someone as caring and selfless as Sydney would never see anything in someone as shallow as Shep. Not that Carter knew her, but that's what he sensed, and his hunches were usually accurate.

Carter pulled up the video he'd recorded at the beginning of the search. He'd done a slow sweep of the park, which included the command post, the volunteers in the group, and Sydney. He hadn't realized he'd caught her on camera. She was talking on and on to Dudley, as if he were one of her friends, while the other dogs looked bored.

Sydney could easily be mistaken for one of those kooky women who talked to their pets and actually believed they talked back. However, in this case, Dudley looked like he was actively listening to her. At one point, he even shook his head. A few seconds later Carter could swear the dog nodded in reply. What was it about those two? Was there a story *behind* the story?

Shep's article came in through his email and Carter had to laugh at how Shep had mostly made it about himself—how he'd rushed to the scene the second he'd learned that a boy and his dog were in danger. How he'd suggested to Sydney and one of his colleagues (Carter wasn't mentioned by name) that they follow him up the trail because his reporter sense told him they'd find Zachary there. According to Shep, he'd instructed Carter to scan the area below the embankment, while he took a look farther up the trail.

Carter couldn't take reading any further and went to see Russell. He knocked on the doorframe but didn't wait for a response before he barged in.

"I know what you're going to say." His boss tossed a copy of Shep's article on his desk.

"The guy is a legend in his own mind," Carter said. "Did you read what I sent? Because that's how it happened. And if we're going to do another piece on Sydney, then he needs to stick to the facts, or you need to run mine."

"Agreed. I'll have him make the corrections." Russell sighed. "Have you been able to set up an interview with Ms. Elder?"

"Yes. I'm meeting her after work today."

"Good, though you might want to clean up a little." Russell motioned to the grass stains on Carter's jeans and muddy paw prints on his shirt.

"Right. Mind if I take lunch now so I can go home and change?"

"Go ahead. I'll have Shep straightened out before you get back."

"Thanks." Carter grabbed his phone from his desk and headed out.

When he arrived home, he took a quick shower and changed, then cooked up a hot dog. As he steamed the bun over the boiling water, his attention drifted toward his backyard, and more specifically to the guesthouse. He wished he hadn't renovated it specifically for Jade, because now it would most likely appeal more to a woman than a man. Carter wasn't so sure he wanted a woman as a tenant. She might be more inclined to involve him in her life than a guy who'd just see it as a place to keep his stuff. But now that he knew his job was tenuous, he was in no position to turn away any interested renters. Hopefully, his future tenant would be nice and dependable, and one who wouldn't complicate his life.

Sydney pulled up to the address Grace had given her and noticed the "For Rent" sign in the front yard. The grass was half dead, and the bushes were overgrown with weeds growing up around them. She really hoped it was nicer inside because she didn't want to settle for a run-down place in order to keep Dudley.

She glanced at him. He'd fallen asleep in the passenger seat the second she pulled into traffic. "Hey, genius. Wake up. We're here."

Dudley made a funny sound as he yawned, then glanced out the window. *Are we at the wrong address? This looks dreadful and not worth getting out of the car for.*

"Would you rather live in my gym bag, hiding from a nosy landlady?

Dudley grumbled something in an incomprehensible language, which must have been dog.

She and Dudley headed up the walkway when the front door was opened by a middle-aged woman dressed in business attire. She had short, highlighted hair and a broad, cheery smile. "Grace?"

"Yes, hi, Sydney. It's so nice to finally meet. Dana's told me all about you." She stared at the moving gym bag. "Is that little Dudley?"

"It sure is." Sydney swung him around in front of her so Grace could see him better.

"My goodness." She did a double take. "Dana said he had a heart-shaped pattern on his chest and he does! How adorable is that?"

Thank you.

"He says thank you."

"Oh!" She let out a big laugh.

"Come on in." Grace led the way into a two-bedroom, one bath home. "This was built in 1982, and as you can see, it's well-lived-in, but everything works."

Sydney could just imagine her sister's negative comments on the home's interior design as she noticed the living room's vertical blinds and worn, mauve-colored carpet. The kitchen had honey-colored oak cabinets, ceramic tiled countertops and wallpaper with a fruit design. The main bedroom was a decent size, as was the bathroom, which had two sinks and a glass-block wall surrounding the toilet. There was a small laundry room, a two-car garage, and a surprisingly large backyard.

"Not exactly built in the same century as my current apartment," Sydney said, which made Grace laugh.

"At least you'll get your own laundry room, garage, and backyard."

"A good trade off," Sydney had to admit, wondering if she could overlook the home's ancient design.

This could work quite well, don't you think? I shall survey my kingdom by the sliding glass door. Quite a few squirrels out there. Do you see them? Are you looking?

"Yes, I'm looking," Sydney said to Dudley, a little irritated.

"Beg pardon?" Grace asked.

"Sorry?"

"Sounds like you're looking at something you don't care for?"

"Oh, no, sorry. I was having a conversation in my head." Sydney gave her an embarrassed look.

"You should see me at breakfast, talking back to the TV." Grace laughed, but then her brows furrowed with concern. "Do you live alone, Sydney?"

"Yes. Maybe that's why I'm having conversations with myself."

"But surely you have a boyfriend…or a significant other?"

"Not at the moment."

"What? A pretty girl like you? You must not be putting yourself out there."

"I'm so busy these days that it's difficult. However, I'm a firm believer in perfect timing. When it's meant to happen, it will."

"What a wonderful, positive attitude. And you're absolutely right. Whoever is meant for you will show up at the perfect time, no doubt."

Who needs a human companion when you have me?

"You mentioned the rent had been reduced by fifty dollars a month. Does that include utilities?"

"I'm afraid not."

She nodded, glancing around one last time. "And it's a six-month lease?"

"Yes." Grace double-checked her listing. "Oh, I'm sorry. The owner changed that when the price was dropped. The lease is now for a full year with the first two months' rent up front and three recommendations. Dana, of course, will be happy to give you one."

Sydney inhaled sharply. "I don't know, Grace. I'm not sure if I want to make a year's commitment. Right now, my rent is month-to-month. I was willing to do six months, but I hadn't really thought about the utilities until now, which is another added expense."

"I understand," Grace said as they walked back outside. "There is one other—" Her phone rang. "I'm sorry, Sydney. I have to take this, but I'll make it quick."

"Well hello, stranger." She laughed, keeping her eye on Sydney, who just wanted to leave. "Is that so? When can it be ready? How much were you thinking? You know, I'm not far from you, and I have someone with me right now who might be interested. Do you mind if we stop by and take a quick peek?"

Sydney glanced at Grace, a little worried she'd be showing her something just as bad.

"That shouldn't be a problem," Grace said into the phone. "My client needs to get back to work too."

"All right. I'll tell her." She hung up. "Sydney, you're never going to believe this. Another client of mine, who happens to live about a mile away, has the most charming guesthouse rental in his backyard. He hasn't had a chance to clean it out, so it's not quite ready, but if you're willing to overlook that, you can see it before anyone else."

She didn't exactly want to live in someone's backyard—especially a man's backyard. Then again, it had to be better than having a bowling alley above her, and a nosy landlord watching her every move. "How big is it?"

"It's a studio, so it's smaller than your one-bedroom, but it has a full kitchen, a full bath, and its own private entrance. It really is quite charming, Sydney. The best part is it's two hundred dollars less than what you're currently paying, and it includes utilities."

"That's quite a bit of savings. Having lower rent would be welcome, especially since I haven't figured out how much this little guy is going to cost me." She looked at Dudley. "What do you think? Shall we go check it out?"

Sounds considerably smaller, but smaller often turns out to be far superior. I'm a perfect example of that.

She held back a laugh. "Yes, Grace, I believe we both would like to see it."

"Fantastic." Grace's eyes danced with excitement. "I'll text the owner and let him know we're on our way. Just follow me in your car."

Sydney set Dudley in the passenger seat and slid behind the wheel. "I hope small doesn't mean it's a closet."

Aren't you glad I'm compact?

"I'll remember you said that when I have to cut back on your food."

She followed Grace, and in no time, they were pulling up to a much nicer home than the one she just left. The main house was a well-maintained, one-story ranch that looked newly built. Hopefully the guesthouse would be in the same condition. She got out of the car and walked with Grace to the front door.

"The owner is a very considerate young man who happens to be quite handsome and *single*." Grace emphasized his marital status, as if it was a high-end feature that came with the rental.

"Will he be okay with Dudley?"

"Oh, shoot." She rang the doorbell. "I forgot to ask him that, but I'm sure he'll love Dudley as soon as he meets him."

The door opened and Sydney gasped when she saw the owner.

"Sydney?" Carter's gaze locked on her.

She blushed as a big grin took over her face. "Hi."

With Carter's blue-green eyes fixed on her, she realized just how gorgeous he was and immediately felt self-conscious. Her hair was a mess, and she smelled like dogs. He'd obviously had a chance to clean up from this morning's rescue. He had on a nicely pressed button-down shirt, crisp navy-blue pants, and his slightly curly hair was damp from the shower.

Grace threw glances between them. "Do you two know each other?"

"Just met this morning." Sydney couldn't take her eyes off him.

Well, this is unexpected. Dudley gave a tiny woof to remind everyone that he was there.

"Dudley! I didn't think I'd see you again so soon." Carter reached over and gave him a scratch behind the ear.

Why not? Sydney and I come as a combo pack.

Grace laughed. "It's like a family reunion."

"Isn't Dudley one of your client's dogs?" Carter asked Sydney.

"Actually, Grace's daughter is the woman I told you about who found him a couple of weeks ago. She had planned on keeping him, but her boyfriend just proposed, and he's highly allergic to dogs."

"So now you're his new mom?"

She nodded. "My apartment complex doesn't allow dogs, which is why I'm looking for another place to live. Do you allow pets?"

I am so not a pet.

"Ordinarily no," he said. "But for a hero who found a missing kid, I'll make an exception."

"I heard about Zachary from my son who works at the hospital," Grace said. "You three were involved in the rescue?"

We were the rescue.

"Dudley led us right to him." Sydney gave him a hug.

Grace leaned toward the dachshund. "You are so smart. People don't give you enough credit, do they?"

Not in the least.

"Come on in." Carter held open the door for them.

I smell hot dogs! The food of champions.

"You shouldn't be eating hot dogs."

Carter gave her an embarrassed look. "I only had one."

"Sorry, Carter. I was talking to Dudley. I, uh, saw him sniffing the air, and he got all excited, thinking *he* was getting a hot dog."

"Oh." He chuckled. "Sorry, little man, but your mom is right."

Is she? I've eaten more hot dogs than you could possibly dream of.

"Right this way." Carter led them through the kitchen, where he picked up the keys to the guesthouse, then out the back door into his backyard. "There's a separate entrance from the side of the house through a secured gate, which I'll show you on your way out."

Sydney wanted to squeal. The guesthouse was adorable—a quaint cottage with stepping stones leading up to the front, a gas lamp for a porch light, and flower boxes in the windows. There weren't any flowers, but she could envision just how perfect and inviting the place would look once she planted some.

"It's gorgeous," she said. "What's the square footage?"

"It's a little over six hundred."

Her one-bedroom was eight.

He put the key in the door, then glanced at Sydney. "I told Grace that I haven't had a chance to clean this out, but it will be spotless before anyone moves in."

He threw open the door, and she stepped inside. The guesthouse was flooded with natural light. Set in the corner between two big windows was an easel, a blank canvas, and paintbrushes in a glass jar on a small table off to the side. On the other side of the room was a long table cluttered with art supplies on one end, and several finished charcoal sketches displayed on the other. Sydney took note of the only sketch with color—a stunning wedding ceremony in a meadow.

"These are really good." She gazed at Carter. "Yours?"

He seemed to have a distant look on his face and sorrow behind his eyes. "No, my fia—my last tenant. She was an artist."

It seemed strange that an artist would leave all of her supplies behind. Maybe something unexpected had happened to her. Sydney wanted to ask but didn't want to pry.

The galley kitchen was small, with the appliances set along one wall, but it seemed to have everything she needed.

"You even have a dishwasher," Grace pointed out.

"I added it during the remodel," Carter said. "And the appliances have barely been used."

To the right of the kitchen was a pretty bathroom with two cabinets and plenty of storage. Next to it, and just off the living area would be her bedroom. She could easily bring in one or two privacy partitions to close off her bedroom entirely.

She looked around again and couldn't get over how much light was in the studio. She glanced out the window onto Carter's beautifully manicured lawn with colorful flower beds and a gorgeous willow tree. She stood there for a long moment, basking in a shaft of light, realizing that her apartment only received the morning sun, which she was never able to enjoy on work days. A feeling of complete serenity came over her and she had to fight the urge to close her eyes.

She let out a long breath and turned toward Carter. "I'm really impressed. Is your backyard fully enclosed?"

"Yes. I've also created a small, private sitting area behind the guesthouse."

He led the way out and around to the secluded area, which had a lot more shade from several mature trees lining the fence. There was a running water fountain, and a small outdoor table with two chairs. The place was a private little haven.

"I love it. Dudley, what do you think?"

There are three squirrels staring at me. I must speak with them immediately! He barked, squirming to get down, but she wouldn't let him, wanting him to be on his best behavior. "I believe it's a big yes for him too."

"That's great." Carter seemed happy with her answer.

"Wonderful!" Grace clapped her hands together. "I'll need to do the standard credit check, which I'm sure will be just fine, and then I can have a contract ready for both of you to sign sometime tomorrow. Are we doing a six-month lease, Carter?"

"If that works for you, Sydney?"

"Yes, I can do that. I'm supposed to give a thirty-day notice at my apartment complex, but I'll see if I can get it shortened."

"I'm flexible on when you want to move in," Carter said.

"This is amazing." She couldn't stop smiling. "Thank you."

"Well, I'd say this is perfect timing for both of you." Grace winked at Sydney as Dudley barked. "Excuse me, Mr. Dudley. I meant to say it's perfect timing for all three of you."

Dudley wagged his tail.

"I'm beginning to think he completely understands everything we're saying," Carter said, giving him another ear rub.

"You'd be right," Sydney said.

Dudley closed his eyes and leaned into the ear rub. *Okay. He can stay.*

Sydney checked the time on her phone. "I'd best get going. I've got to pick up my afternoon clients."

"And I better get back to work." Carter showed them out through the separate entrance on the side of his house. "Are we still on for coffee?"

"Absolutely, though it might be closer to six, if that still works." She definitely needed to take a shower and wear something nicer than leggings, sneakers, and a shirt covered in dog slobber.

"Anytime is good with me." He had a big grin on his face. "Let's touch base later this afternoon."

"That sounds great." She smiled, unable to break eye contact with him.

Dudley gave a small bark. *Look at you two with your googly eyes. Why don't you just make it dinner?*

CHAPTER NINE

Carter watched Sydney drive away, then went to close up the guesthouse. He couldn't believe what had just happened. He hadn't planned on calling Grace until after he'd had time to clean everything up. Now he was so glad he'd made that call. He never dreamed Sydney would be the one to see his place first.

As he shut the windows he had opened for the showing, he noticed how dirty they were and added them to his cleaning list. So much for not renting to a woman—or a woman with a dog. But these two weren't ordinary, by any means, and worth the risk. He definitely wanted to get the scoop on Dudley, but he wanted to get to know Sydney more.

Of course, that type of thinking could lead him down the road to another broken heart. If he were smart, he'd keep it professional and only help her move in if she asked. Most likely, he'd discover that there was nothing special about her communication with Dudley and that they had found Zachary due to sheer luck. No doubt, he'd regret renting to her and a dog who would inevitably mark his territory all over his very green lawn.

At least Sydney seemed competent and responsible, which was something he'd want in a tenant. She'd be the perfect type of person to have around should he need to go out of town. Having a watchdog around wasn't such a bad idea, either. There had been an uptick in mischievous teens vandalizing homes in the area lately—not that a little wiener dog could be considered a watchdog. What damage could he possibly do, except for nipping an ankle or two?

Carter turned to leave when his gaze fell on Jade's art supplies. He grabbed an empty box from under the kitchen sink and began packing them up. He'd put them in his car and donate them to the middle school the next time he was in the area. He picked up Jade's wedding sketch, thinking back to when she'd shown it to him, but that memory was suddenly replaced by Sydney studying it.

And he had studied her as she'd walked through the guesthouse in an almost reverent manner. Her hair had been pulled up in a ponytail, and when she stood in a shaft of light, the shine was intense. Some of the strands were the color of copper, and he suddenly wanted to know what her hair would look like falling over her shoulders and framing her beautiful face. The spell had been broken when she'd asked a question, and he'd been catapulted back to the present.

Carter took a deep breath, rolled up Jade's sketches, and put a rubber band around them. He'd stop by her parents' place and give them to her mom, or leave them on the front porch with a note. He'd clear out the rest of Jade's things this weekend, check the appliances to make sure everything was in working order, and then he would give it a thorough cleaning. He wasn't entirely sure why Jade had left her sketches and supplies behind—unless she had wanted to torture him. But it didn't matter now. It was time for him to move on.

He locked up and noticed the flower boxes under the windows needed filling. It wouldn't cost him much to plant something colorful. He'd stop by the nursery, maybe even snag a few dog treats to make his new tenants feel welcome.

He went inside and set the box on the kitchen table, reached for his keys, and realized he'd managed to get a big black smudge on his sleeve—no doubt from Jade's charcoal pencils. Annoyed, he went into his bedroom to change but didn't have much to choose from—a ratty T-shirt or an even dressier shirt than the one he had on. He took off his smudged shirt and dropped it in the hamper.

Sydney, with her beautiful hazel-green eyes, had definitely checked him over when he'd answered the door. Did her reaction mean she was attracted to him? He should have mentioned that his initial informal invite to coffee had evolved into an in-depth interview for the paper—one that would be recorded. He'd be springing it on her and hoped she wouldn't be upset by it. He didn't want her to think he invited her just to get an interview.

He slid his dressier shirt off the hanger and put it on. What was he doing? He kept telling himself he didn't want to get involved in another relationship, so why was he moving in that direction? She could have a boyfriend, for all he knew. And why wouldn't she? Sydney was a pretty girl with a dazzling smile and an infectious, friendly personality. He should just get the interview, help her move in, and then distance himself from her and that funny little dog of hers.

He buttoned up his dark-blue silk shirt and checked himself in the mirror. Maybe he should suggest dinner tonight instead of just coffee.

It took Sydney a little longer to drop off Dudley at Dana's than she thought, because he wouldn't stop talking—or rather he wouldn't stop jabbering about where he wanted his things set up in the guesthouse. He also gave her a list of foods he enjoyed and the type of blanket he preferred to snuggle into when they were watching TV.

She barely remembered any of it because she was too anxious about meeting Carter. She spent more time on her hair and makeup than she had in months, which was ridiculous, because the guy had asked her out for coffee, nothing more. And didn't he originally tell her it was because he wanted to know more about Dudley? Maybe that's all it was. Or maybe now he wanted to know what type of tenant she'd be before he signed the contract.

Did she really want to tell Carter the truth about her and Dudley, now that she was moving into his backyard? She was all for enlightening the world about animal communication, but Dudley put a whole different spin on it. She couldn't see Carter taking her seriously if she told him that her new doxie spoke a thousand languages, and that she could telepathically hear him speak. Would she be putting Dudley in harm's way by talking about how special he was to a journalist? It was possible. She'd need to downplay Dudley's abilities until she got to know Carter better.

She slipped on a shimmery, pale-gold blouse and straight black pants, then studied herself in the mirror. *What am I doing? It's just coffee.* Realizing she was way overdressed, she took off her blouse right as Carter texted her to ask if she wanted to grab dinner instead.

Dinner? What did this mean, exactly? Had his intentions changed, or was he just hungry? They *were* meeting at dinnertime, after all. She put back on her blouse, wishing she could read the guy's mind. She hadn't been out on a date in months because she was terrible at dating, often misreading intentions and body language, and first dates were the worst. They always felt like a job interview. She could never relax enough to be herself, which was why she felt more comfortable with dogs than men.

Of course, if this *was* a date, she and Carter wouldn't have to deal with the typical, awkward, strained conversations that seemed to accompany first dates because they already knew each other. Hell, they'd rescued a boy and his dog together.

She texted back and agreed to meet him at a popular bistro in town. She was nervous, but why? He was just a guy who was about to be her new landlord. A nice, very good-looking guy, who Grace said was single and who would be living a stone's throw away from her.

She took a breath, grabbed her purse, and walked out the door, wishing she still had Dudley with her for an easy distraction.

Carter had arrived first, secured them a quiet table on the bistro's outdoor patio, then texted Sydney to tell her where he was seated. It wasn't too crowded, the weather seemed perfect, and jazz was softly playing throughout the restaurant. The ambiance was ideal for a first date, which he absolutely was *not* about to have with Sydney. He was there to interview her for the paper. The only reason he had suggested dinner was so they wouldn't feel rushed.

Besides, it would be good to get to know her on a personal

level since she was about to be his tenant. She obviously loved animals and seemed very responsible. She was bright, funny, and surprisingly strong to be able to handle all those dogs at once. He could easily see them becoming friends—maybe even good friends.

Sydney walked out onto the patio, searching for him, and when they made eye contact, his jaw dropped. She smiled, making her way to the table. Her long hair fell past her shoulders in soft curls. She had on a beautiful silk blouse and sexy black pants that accentuated her every curve. He never paid much attention to a woman's makeup, but whatever she did, it made her gorgeous eyes grab hold of him and not let go.

Where were his manners? He shot out of his chair, jolting the table enough to knock over a glass of water. Sydney jumped back, avoiding the spill.

"Shit. Sorry." He righted the glass, thankful it didn't break, and threw down his cloth napkin to mop up the mess. He flicked her a glance. "Did I get it on you?"

"Not a drop."

"You have fast reflexes," he said as their waiter came over to finish the cleanup.

"Comes with dog territory." She pulled out a chair, and they finally sat.

He blew out a quick breath, attempting to appear relaxed. "I'm not normally a klutz. It's just you took me off guard because you look so amazing. Not that you didn't earlier." He slammed his mouth shut, forcing himself to stop talking.

"Thank you." She hung her purse on the side of her chair.

"Would you care for something to drink?" The waiter threw the wet towel onto his tray.

She eyed Carter. "What are you having?"

"I'm thinking a beer." He looked to the waiter. "Whatever IPA you have on tap."

He nodded. "And for you, miss?"

"I'll take a blonde ale."

Carter ran his hands over his thighs. He couldn't understand why he was so nervous. After the waiter left, he took a breath and refocused. "It's hard to believe we just met this morning."

"I know." She shook her head. "It's crazy, right?"

"This whole day has been unexpected, but in a good way."

"Obviously the rescue was completely unexpected, but so was this afternoon," she said. "I just started looking for a new place today, and I was already depressed about my options—that is, until Grace brought me to see your beautiful guesthouse."

"I was on my way back to work when I decided to give Grace a heads-up about wanting to rent out my guesthouse. When she asked to come over right away, I said no, but Grace can be very persuasive. I was cursing her under my breath until I opened the door and saw you standing there."

Sydney let out a short laugh. "When I was driving over to your house, I thought, what am I doing? I can't live in a complete stranger's backyard. And then when you opened the door, I can't tell you how relieved I was to see you."

The waiter dropped off their drinks, and Sydney raised her beer for a toast. "To opening doors."

He shared her smile. "To opening doors." They clinked glasses and took a sip. "You know, when I got back to the paper, the phone wouldn't stop ringing, and most of the calls were about you."

"Me?" She gave him a puzzled look. "Why me?"

"Because you found Zachary."

"Actually, it was Dudley, and also you. In fact, you were the one who saw Scout's ball."

"But I wouldn't have known to look for it if you hadn't stopped right there on the trail." He took another sip. "How did you know to stop?"

"Dudley's nose was in the air. I figured he must have picked up his scent."

"I still can't get over how fast you two found them, especially since Dudley was rubbing his back in the grass one minute, then taking off toward the trail the next."

Her eyes widened. "You saw that?"

"Why do you think I came over to help?"

"To be honest, I hadn't expected him to take off so quickly either, but it all worked out." She grabbed the menu and buried her face in it.

Was he making her feel uncomfortable? "How about we order an appetizer first? Do you like burrata?" he asked.

"Love it." She set the menu aside as he flagged down the waiter to put in their order. "Do you enjoy working at *The Pinecrest News*?"

"Yeah, I do, but we need a larger circulation to stay in business, and though living in a safe, small town has its advantages, there's not a whole lot to report on."

"What attracted you to the news industry?" she asked, sitting back.

"I'm not sure. Probably my need to know what's going on around me. That, and my cynical side. I'm forever looking for the truth, which isn't always given to the general public."

"Like what's happening with the tax hikes?"

"You saw my article?"

She nodded. "I'm sorry to tell you that I don't get the paper, but I saw the front page at a client's home. I hope your article got a lot of attention."

"Oh, it did." He scratched the back of his head. "But the wrong kind. Seems the mayor is no longer a fan of mine."

She let out a disgusted huff. "That guy's a jerk. He doesn't pick up after his dog."

Carter chuckled. "He seems the type."

"I hope he gets voted out in November," she said. "Which is a real possibility now that the whole town knows what's going on, thanks to you."

"Less than a quarter of our residents get the paper, so I don't think I'll be swaying many votes."

Shock registered on her face. "That's it? What about your online subscriptions?"

"They've helped, but they aren't as lucrative as one would think." He swirled his beer around in his glass before taking a drink. "Russell, my boss, is hoping to increase our readership from the sudden interest in the rescue. He's asked me to write an in-depth article about you and Dudley and how you two work so well together."

"Oh." She inhaled sharply. "I don't think people care about that."

"They do. With most of the news being so negative these days, readers need an escape. They want light, feel-good, human-interest stories, and let's be honest, who wouldn't love a story about a heroic dog walker and her sassy dachshund?"

She blushed. "I'm not seeing the fascination, but if it helps you, sure."

"Great." He set his phone in the center of the table. "Do I have your permission to record this for accuracy?"

"Oh, we're doing this now?" She stiffened.

"If that's okay." He froze, kicking himself for not mentioning it earlier. He hoped he hadn't just derailed the entire evening. "Russell would like to have you featured in two consecutive issues. Shep's article on the rescue will be published tomorrow, so my article about this interview will appear in Friday's paper."

"Shep? That pushy reporter in the park? Why didn't your boss ask you to write it? You were part of the rescue, not Shep."

"In fairness to my colleague, he was sent to the park before me. But now, because *I* was part of the rescue, I'm the one interviewing you, instead of Shep."

She nodded, but she still seemed to be thinking it through. "And what I say tonight will be known to all of Pinecrest in less than forty-eight hours?"

"Yes."

She blew out a breath. "That's fast."

"Has to be if we want to run the articles back-to-back, but I can tell my boss you'd prefer to wait." He reached for his phone.

She released a breath. "No, go ahead. It's fine."

"Are you sure?" He watched hesitation filter through her eyes. "I don't want you to feel pressured into doing something you don't want to do."

Her shoulders dropped, and she seemed to relax a little. "I'm sure."

"Thank you." He gave her a soft smile. "This will not only help the paper, but you'll be getting free advertising. I've no doubt you'll be picking up a lot of new clients."

"I wouldn't mind that." She ran a hand over her arm, looking like she still had reservations. "Just don't print anything embarrassing I might say."

"Like what?"

"I don't know, but I've heard about you reporter types—misquoting interviewees for a better story."

He chuckled. "You found a missing boy and his dog. I don't think I could make up anything better than that."

Her mouth softly curved up. "Right. Well, fire away."

"I'll be asking you the same question I asked earlier, so go ahead and expand on it if you can." Carter hit record and leaned toward the mic. "This is my interview with local hero, Sydney Elder." He winked. "Sydney, how did your dachshund know where to find Zachary and Scout in such a large park?"

"He picked up on the boy's scent."

Carter waited for her to expand on her answer, but she didn't. "You know, I initially assumed that. I did an article last year on scent work training, but Dudley wasn't acting like he'd done any scent work before. The bloodhounds immediately got Zachary's scent and took off running. But Dudley appeared a little confused. He only sniffed the ground a couple of times."

"Dudley's exceptionally good at what he does."

"Which is what, exactly?"

She took a healthy swallow of her beer. "He sees the whole picture and excels at communicating with other animals."

"I noticed that. I found it odd that you told him to tell Pupperton to go down the embankment when you could have told Pupperton to do it yourself."

"Right. Well, like I said. He's a very good communicator."

"How did Dudley know what you wanted him to do?"

"I told him." She shrugged.

"But he doesn't speak English."

She looked away, stifling a smile. "That dog understands more than you think."

"But how, exactly?"

She sat back, thinking about the question before she finally spoke. "I once planned on being a dog trainer, so I'm good at reading their behaviors and actions, almost before they do them. I can usually predict what Dudley's going to do, so if I want him to do something else, I give him a different signal."

"Interesting." It made perfect sense—except for one thing.

"I'm not sure I caught any of those training signals. I saw you put your hands on your hips, looking exasperated, when Dudley was taking a sunbath. Was that a signal?"

"Ha-ha. There are unspoken signals, Mr. Reporter. I am his mom, after all."

"A very new and extremely recent mom," he reminded her.

"What can I say? Some people bond instantly with animals—like Dudley and me." She took another big gulp of her beer. She looked uncomfortable, and he hadn't realized he'd been grilling her in his usual aggressive reporter fashion. He could see how she and Dudley had bonded so quickly. Nothing unusual there. Still, he felt like there was a missing piece to the story.

"You definitely have a way with dogs." He sat back, and she said nothing.

Luckily, their appetizer came to the table. While they helped themselves to burrata, he debated whether or not to abandon the interview. He didn't want her to think he was a callous journalist just intent on doing his job. He had already been fascinated by her and Dudley before she'd become his assignment.

He stole a glance at her. He wasn't sure what to talk about—other than dogs. "I'd love for you to meet my mom's new dog sometime. She hates me."

Sydney let out a big laugh. "Dogs don't hate people."

"Oh yes, they do, or at least Penelope hates one person—that being me."

"She probably feels threatened by you. You're a pushy reporter, and she's overprotective of her mom."

He *had* crossed the line. "Sorry, I didn't mean to be pushy," he said. "It's my inquisitive nature. In my line of work, we often get shut down quickly, so we tend to fire off questions and demand answers. It's a bad habit that I'm trying to break—though, if you ever buy a new car, I'm the guy to have with you."

She laughed. "I'll keep that in mind. And I'll be happy to meet Penelope anytime."

"Thanks."

"Do you have any more questions for me?"

"I do, but I don't want to—"

"I'm fine with it. Seriously. If I wasn't, I would have stopped the recording." She motioned to his phone recording their conversation.

He'd actually forgotten it was still on. Sydney was already affecting him to the point that he was forgetting what he was doing.

He took a sip of his beer. "You said you planned on being a dog trainer, but decided against it?"

She nodded. "I had a bad experience. I was actually in training when I was given an out-of-control American Staffordshire terrier to handle. Scraped-up skin, a faceplant on the pavement, and a big fear of it happening again had me rethinking my career plans."

He winced. She was no taller than five-three, and probably weighed less than a hundred pounds. He pictured how easy it would be for any large breed to drag her down the street. "I would have quit on the spot."

"I did, actually. Right after I went to the hospital to get stitches in my chin." She pointed to the scar.

He leaned toward her. "You can't even see it, and at least yours was earned." He ran his finger over a tiny scar barely visible above his right eyebrow.

"What happened?"

"I was being an idiot on a dirt bike, showing off with a few of my friends in high school."

"Yours sounds like it was a lot more fun to get."

"Maybe, but my dad grounded me for eternity."

She laughed, then took a small bite of burrata crostini. "I hate to admit this, but I'm still trying to figure out my career."

"Have you ever thought about becoming a veterinarian?"

"That's all I ever wanted to be when I was a kid. My mom had a habit of taking in any hurt animal wandering aimlessly around our neighborhood. Dogs, cats, birds, squirrels, even a mama opossum who'd been hit by a car."

"What happened to the opossum?"

"We rushed her to the vet and discovered that six babies were in her pouch. My mom paid for emergency surgery on the opossum's broken jaw, and then we, along with my sister, nursed her babies until she was well enough to do it herself."

"Did they survive?"

"Everyone one of them. Three months later, we released them back into the wild."

He couldn't help but admire her and felt guilty for complaining about covering animal stories. "So being a hero comes easy to you."

"Hardly. Anyone would have done the same."

"I'm not so sure," he said. "Sounds like you were a veterinarian-in-training at a very young age."

"I thought I was, but then I watched a minor surgery and fainted when our family vet made his first cut." She shook her head, looking embarrassed. "Vet school was not an option for me—then or now. But I've never stopped caring for animals. I've been thinking about becoming a canine behaviorist. I'd love to work with shelters and rescues to help get their adoptees into the right home."

"I imagine that's something that would be of great benefit right now."

"It is, but I need to do more research on it to see if there are enough opportunities in the field. I've still got to pay the bills, especially since I just leased a very cool guesthouse." Her eyes twinkled as a big smile took over her face.

"I'll remember you said that the first time something breaks," he said. "Can I ask you one more thing for the article?"

"Sure."

"How would you describe your communication with Dudley? Because it's unique."

"In what way?"

"He seemed to completely understand you, while the other dogs didn't."

"Uh…well…I haven't trained the others yet. Dudley's a very smart dog and learns fast."

"You really get into talking to him, too, as if he's somehow answering you."

She laughed. "I'd like to think he does, but who knows? He's just a dog, right?"

"Right." He quickly entered a few things on his phone.

"You're also taking notes?"

"Is that okay? It's for the article, and I promise this will help you gain clients."

She raised a brow. "You better be right." She then took her phone out and mimicked what he was doing.

"Are you taking notes about me?"

"Absolutely."

He set his phone aside. "Like what?"

"Like how you invited me to dinner under false pretenses, and how you tried to spill water on me the second I arrived."

"Full disclosure, I needed to ask you about Dudley for the article, but the water mishap was your fault entirely."

"How did you come to that conclusion?"

"You showed up looking so incredible that I temporarily lost control of my motor functions."

She broke into laugher. "I'm flattered to have received such a strong reaction."

"Just getting you ready for stardom."

"I thought you said your paper had a small readership?"

"It does, but a picture is worth a thousand words, and your face will be on the front page tomorrow morning."

She cringed. "You're in the photo, too, aren't you?"

"Unknown. Russell will be choosing the layout. But since we're running two stories about you, I guarantee you'll be front and center."

"Oh." She took a deep breath. "I'm not one for the spotlight."

"You did a good thing, and I believe only good will come from it," he said. "Just look what happened afterward. You found a new place to live, and you'll soon have a great landlord. I know him personally."

She lifted a brow. "How well do you know him?"

"Very well. Ask me anything about him."

"How much does he like dogs?"

"He loves them, except for his mom's new dog."

"Penelope is misunderstood, I promise you that, which Dudley and I will address. But back to my new landlord. Will he throw us out if, say, Dudley were to start barking when I happened to be away?"

"No, he'd never do that. He likes the little guy. Dudley's already growing on him. Though when you say away, do you mean away for the weekend, say…with your boyfriend?"

"Away, as in, to the gym or grocery store. I don't have a boyfriend."

Carter's grin widened. "I know he'll be very happy to hear that."

"Good. Then can I ask, are the rumors true? Is my new landlord single as Grace mentioned?"

"Grace has her intel correct."

She laughed. "I guess you're right. Good things *have* come from the rescue."

"And I have a hunch, as journalists do, that good things will continue to keep coming."

Three hours later, Sydney was finally on the way home, feeling good about her dinner with Carter. It had started out rocky, with him asking the one question she had trouble answering. But somewhere in the middle of their meal, they'd relaxed, learned a bit more about one another, and really enjoyed themselves. He was smart, honest, caring, and a little self-deprecating in a funny way, and she'd connected with him better than she'd ever connected with another guy.

She and Carter were well on their way to being good friends, and he had serious potential to become something more. The only hiccup was her unusual relationship with Dudley. Their special communication was the one question she wasn't sure how to answer. She'd tried to downplay everything, which left Carter unsatisfied.

At least she got to know him better, and from what she'd learned, she believed she would be able to tell him about Dudley's exceptional intelligence one day. But for right now, it was best to keep things vague.

Of course, once Dudley was living with her permanently, she'd need to figure out how she was going to handle their communication in Carter's presence. She didn't want to lie to him. She already felt bad about giving him half-truths on how they'd found Zachary so easily.

Maybe the answer was to never tell him. She and Dudley would continue working as they had in the park, and she would keep explaining that they simply understood each other exceptionally well. That was the truth, after all.

But how long could she keep that up? Carter was a smart guy *and* a reporter. He was already picking apart her answers. He knew she wasn't being completely transparent with him. She could see it in his eyes. He had a hunch that she was leaving something out, and he would keep digging until he found out what it was.

Even if she could continue the ruse, how was it not going to make her crazy—to hear Dudley jabbering on while she was trying to have a conversation? If Dudley could hear her thoughts clearly, they could communicate telepathically and their secret would remain safe. But he couldn't hear her very well, which meant she'd be talking to him way more than any normal dog owner would. At what point would Carter think she was a little nuts?

Sydney pulled into her apartment's parking lot and turned off the car. This was going to be a lot more complicated than she realized.

Carter thought about his dinner with Sydney all the way home. He should have stopped recording the conversation when they were no longer talking about the rescue or Dudley, but he'd kept it on. He wanted to listen to their conversation again—to hear her voice and how she'd responded to him. Hopefully, he hadn't sounded like an idiot—especially when he'd been trying to make her laugh. He couldn't believe they'd spent three hours together. It had felt like only one.

As he sat down to work on his article, he debated on how to present the interview. The objective was to go into further detail on the rescue, and how Sydney and Dudley had managed to find the boy and his dog when others had walked right past them.

But when he finished his first draft, he realized that she'd been very vague on her answers with respect to Dudley. He attempted to fill in the holes, but then the interview seemed too similar to Shep's article coming out tomorrow. His second draft was worse. It lacked excitement. It was a dry, mediocre read at best. Sydney wasn't mediocre—far from it, and she deserved a lot better.

Carter made a cup of coffee, then began again, wanting to present the interview more intimately, so he decided to tell it from his perspective. After all, he was part of the rescue team. Now, the interview felt much more personal, because it was.

As Sydney and Dudley had piqued his curiosity, he, in turn, piqued the reader's. Writing in first person gave him the flexibility he needed. He didn't have to explain exactly how the two had managed to locate Zachary and Scout since Sydney never quite answered the one question he'd asked several times throughout the evening. But one thing was clear: Sydney and Dudley had a very special way of communicating—something no one else could do. Their skills alone brought that boy home to his mom.

Carter sat back after reading it one last time and hoped she'd be pleased. Without a doubt, she'd be picking up new clients. The in-depth interview would leave readers wanting to work with her, and hopefully, it would also bring the paper more subscriptions.

He now needed the perfect title. *Meet The Heroes Who Found the Missing Boy?* No. He needed something catchy that would grab a reader's attention and not let go, something that would describe Sydney and Dudley's unusual communication skills.

He leaned back, running titles through his head, but nothing felt right. He pulled up a picture of the two on his phone and gazed at it for inspiration. In an instant, he had it. *The Dachshund Whisperer*.

CHAPTER TEN

From a dead sleep, Sydney slowly surfaced as she heard a barrage of texts come in on her cell. She glanced at the time. Not quite seven. She turned off her alarm and reached for her phone when it rang in her hand.

"Did you just send me a bunch of texts?" she asked her sister, barely awake.

"Only one, but can you blame me? Why didn't you tell me you rescued a boy and his dog yesterday?"

She sat up, now fully awake. "Oh. Right."

"Oh, right? Syd, that's incredible. I just read about it in the paper. I can't believe I'm the last to know."

"You're not. I haven't spoken to Mom or Dad either. Yesterday was a whirlwind, with the rescue in the morning, and finding a new place to live in the afternoon, and then I had dinner with Carter."

"Carter? You mean the guy who was with you during the rescue?"

"Yes." She hurried out of bed, now anxious to get a copy of the paper to read for herself.

"Are you dating him and neglected to tell me? And you're moving?" Her sister sounded exasperated. They'd always filled each other in about everything, but life generally moved much slower than it had for her in the past twenty-four hours.

"Not exactly. Carter was part of the rescue. I just met him yesterday, but I might be moving into his place since I can't stay where I am with Dudley. This all happened within hours, which is why I haven't had a chance to talk to you."

"Have you lost your mind? You can't move in with a guy you've known for one day!"

She laughed. "I'm not. I'm renting his guesthouse."

"Okay, stop," Rachael said. "You need to start from the beginning and fill me in on everything."

"I will, but not now. I've got to go."

"You better call Mom. She'll want to hear this from you."

"I will. Talk soon."

Sydney hung up and checked her texts. They were from friends who had also read the article. She had to see it for herself and pulled it up online. There were two photos taking up the entire front page. One was of Zachary and his mom reuniting, and the other was of the rescue team. She was closest to the camera, looking worried while holding her dogs, as Zachary was being carried up the embankment by the paramedics. Carter was barely visible in the photo, which was disappointing. She definitely needed to call her mom before she got in the shower, only her phone wouldn't stop ringing.

"Hey, Jacqui. How's Taffy?" She glanced at the time and moved on to breakfast.

"She's doing really well, thanks to you, and I'm glad to see you took my advice on doing more animal communication."

"You saw the article?"

"How could I miss it? You're on the front page!" Jacqui squealed. "That's serious celebrity status in Pinecrest. You have such an amazing gift, Sydney."

"Actually, Dudley, the dachshund in the photo, is the one with the gift. He can talk to all sorts of animals."

"Can't all animals talk to one another?"

"Not like Dudley. In fact, he helped Taffy. He was the one who gave me so much information."

"That's incredible," Jacqui said. "Please tell me you'll continue to do this type of work."

"I want to. I've just got to figure out a way to make a living too."

"It's called session fees. We've talked about this. In fact, I'm sending you money through PayPal as we speak."

"For what?"

"Your very successful session with Taffy."

"That wasn't an official session."

"If that wasn't one, I don't know what is. No arguments. Everyone needs to make a living."

"I know." Sydney sighed. "But I feel horrible charging."

"Do you think a surgeon looks at a very sick patient and says, 'It's on me today?'"

"I never thought of it like that."

"Well, now you can, and soon you'll be hearing a lot more people say, 'Thank you, Ms. Elder, for your spot-on session with my dog. I'll be recommending you to my friends.'"

She chuckled.

"Drinks soon?" Jacqui asked.

"Absolutely." Sydney heard another call come in and glanced at her phone. "That's my mom calling."

"Call me later, and we'll make plans. Talk soon, hero."

Sydney switched over. "Hey, Mom." She poured herself a bowl of cornflakes and milk.

"Did you hit your head while rescuing that little boy?"

"Uh, no. Why?"

"Because you obviously must be suffering from amnesia. That's the only logical explanation I can come up with as to why I wasn't your first phone call when it was over."

"I've been trying to call you, but my phone keeps ringing," she said with her mouth full.

"That's your excuse for this morning. What happened yesterday?"

"It was nonstop. I didn't get home until late last night. In fact, I had to meet with one of the paper's reporters for an in-depth interview, which will be out tomorrow morning, by the way."

"You'll be in the paper two days in a row?" Her voice suddenly sounded very sweet and proud.

"Yes, and you're the first to know."

"My youngest daughter is a local celebrity." Her mom sounded downright giddy. "Just look at this photo of you! And the article is very good."

"I haven't had a chance to read it."

"Why not?"

"Because my phone started blowing up before my alarm went off."

"Oh, then don't let me keep you, but I want to hear every detail very soon."

"I'll call you in a few hours."

"I'll be here."

As soon as Sydney got off the phone, she had three more voicemails. She couldn't believe what was happening. Needing to ignore her phone, she got ready for work, then ran out to buy a copy of today's paper.

"Is this you?" The vendor at the convenience store asked as he rang her up.

"Yeah."

"Good job rescuing that kid."

"Thanks."

She took the paper and sat down at a nearby bench to finally read the article. It was weird to read about herself. She glanced at the time and realized she needed to get going. As she hopped in the car, her cell rang again. "Hey, Carter."

"Hope I'm not calling too early."

"Not at all. My cell hasn't stopped ringing."

"I figured it would once your family and friends saw your photo in the paper. Have you had time to read it?"

"Yeah. I just picked up a copy. I liked it, though I would have liked it better if you had been more visible in the picture, and if Shep had mentioned you more than twice."

"The article wasn't meant to be about me," he said. "But I'm glad you liked it, and don't forget that mine comes out tomorrow."

She suddenly sucked in a lot of air, remembering how long the interview was and how much they'd been drinking. "Please tell me I didn't say anything embarrassing last night. We were drinking after all."

He chuckled. "I think you'll be pleased."

"Since you wrote it, I already am," she said. "Thanks again for dinner."

"We'll have to do it again soon."

"I'd like that." There was an awkward pause. It was time to hang up, but neither one was moving in that direction.

"Oh, Grace called to let me know that your credit report looked great and that she'd be sending the contract over today."

"I'll be on the lookout for it."

"Great," he said. "Well, uh, I guess we'll talk later?"

"Yes. Definitely." There was another awkward pause.

"Say hi to Dudley for me."

"I will," she said through a light chuckle.

"Bye."

"Bye."

Sydney couldn't stop smiling after they finally hung up. Even after she picked up Dudley and her morning clients, she found her mind wandering to Carter. She'd felt so comfortable around him and couldn't wait to move into his guesthouse where she hoped to see him on a daily basis.

The morning had flown by. She dropped off Pupperton, then loaded Dudley into the car. "We have two hours before we need to pick up the afternoon crew. How about we grab a turkey sandwich in town?" She glanced at Dudley, sitting calmly in his doggy car seat, as she drove through the neighborhood.

Do you really need to ask? When it comes to food, always count me in.

Sydney turned the corner and saw a crowd gathering in a homeowner's front yard, around what looked to be a hundred-year-old pine tree. A forestry bucket truck was right next to it, with a ladder extended high into the tree.

"I wonder what's going on?" She slowly drove by, noticing that everyone was looking up at the forestry employee who was close to fifty feet off the ground. He was reaching for something on the trunk of the tree. She gasped when she saw what it was and quickly pulled over.

I'm sensing our lunch is about to be postponed.

"Our services might be required." She turned off the car and helped Dudley to the ground. "If this takes longer than expected, I promise you'll get more than the tiny nibble of turkey I had planned on giving you."

I wasn't getting half?

"Not when the dachshund breed is prone to obesity."

I clearly don't fit the norm.

"We'll negotiate lunch later."

They walked over just as the truck's ladder was extended even higher.

"Hang on, Pepper!" someone yelled.

There were gasps as the employee tried to reach the cat, but he scrambled up the tree another five feet.

"He's really up there." Sydney shielded her eyes from the sun.

I'm sensing the little bugger is terrified and isn't going to allow anyone to touch him.

"Can you talk the poor thing down?"

Without a doubt, however, the forestry service must get out of the way.

Sydney scanned the crowd, looking for the owner. She saw an older woman wringing her hands. "Excuse me, are you Pepper's mom?"

The woman's frightened eyes met hers. "Yes?"

"I'm an animal communicator, and I can help."

"By doing what?"

"By talking him down. Actually, my dog can talk him down." She picked up Dudley.

"What is wrong with you?" The woman frowned. "You obviously know nothing about cats. They can climb up, but they can't climb down. And even if they could, my sweet Pepper despises dogs, so please leave. You'll only make matters worse."

Before Sydney could respond, there was a collective groan as Pepper moved higher and disappeared into the canopy of the tree. He was now permanently out of reach of the forestry employee.

The workman descended out of the tree. "I'm sorry, ma'am, but our ladder can't extend any farther. We'll need a crane to reach him now, and we won't have one available until next week."

The woman started crying.

"Please, let me help," Sydney said. "Dudley and I found the missing boy in Mulberry Park."

The woman looked at her again, studying her face.

"She did," a male voice said behind her. "I was right there."

Sydney whipped around to see Carter approaching. "What are you doing here?"

"My job. Someone here contacted the paper, and Russell always sends me to cover any situation dealing with animals."

"I heard about Zachary," the woman said, softening. "I'm sorry to have questioned you." The woman grabbed her hand. "Please, do whatever you can."

Sydney patted the woman's hand. "We'll do our best." She walked with Dudley over to the base of the tree and stood in front of the forestry truck.

Tell them to stay, just in case we need them again.

"Sir, we might need you," she said to the employee. "Can you stay?"

"Oh, we're not going anywhere." He took off his hard hat and leaned against his truck, seeming interested in seeing what a petite woman and a dachshund could do that he couldn't.

"Let me introduce myself to Pepper first," she told Dudley. She closed her eyes and tried to make a connection, and as soon as she had one, she could feel his fear. "You're right, Dudley. He's scared to death, being so high off the ground."

Typical cat. Leap first, think about it later. Dudley grumbled, then got closer to the tree. He looked up, spotted Pepper, and started whining with long guttural sounds.

A few people laughed behind them at the strange sounds he was making.

Dudley glared at the crowd. *Do tell the onlookers to be silent. I need to hear Torkahndor.*

"Quiet, please," Sydney said, and everyone stopped talking.

Dudley whined again, and at last, Pepper meowed back.

Everyone cheered, and Sydney quickly silenced them with her finger to her lips.

I'm instructing him to climb down using the branches. Dudley continued to talk to Pepper, but the cat wouldn't budge.

"What's going on?"

He's afraid to move. Dudley began barking aggressively, and at last, Pepper gingerly took a step onto a tree branch directly below him.

A few people whispered in excitement.

"What did you say to him?"

I simply reminded him that "Torkahndor" means fearless in the feline language, and that he needs to live up to his name.

"Good job," she said to Dudley, and psychically sent Torkahndor, aka Pepper, feelings of strength and courage.

Dudley barked and continued to whine as the young feline slowly made his descent out of the canopy.

Pepper cried a few times and Dudley whined back. Several minutes later, he'd descended to the last remaining branch.

"Now what?"

The hard part. He's going to have to back down the trunk.

"Can he?"

That's up to him.

Dudley barked and whined but Pepper wouldn't move. He barked again, and still, the cat wouldn't leave the safety of the big branch.

"Come on, Pepper, you can do it," Sydney said under her breath as she telepathically sent him a picture of chicken on a plate, waiting for him if he came down. At last, Pepper hooked his nails into the tree trunk and took one small step back down the tree.

The crowd let out a collective gasp of amazement as all of their cell phones were poised in the cat's direction. Sydney glanced at Carter who was snapping away, capturing it in still photos.

Pepper took a few more backward steps, then began crying.

He's too exhausted to continue, but now he's low enough for the forestry human to reach him.

She quickly turned. "Sir, we need you up there now!"

The man hesitated. "He'll just climb into the branches again."

I've told Torkahndor to trust the man who will be coming up to help him to safety.

"No, sir, he won't. He's too tired. Please hurry. He's very weak."

The man got back into the bucket, and his coworker began raising the ladder toward Pepper. As the man got closer to Pepper, Dudley started talking with guttural whines again. Pepper was crying louder, desperate to move away, but he didn't this time. The man was five feet away, then three, then right on him. He grabbed Pepper, set him in the bucket, and the crowd went wild.

"You did it!" Sydney picked up Dudley and gave him a bunch of kisses.

Perhaps I can have my own sandwich now.

She laughed. "You've earned it."

"Amazing job." Carter took a few more photos of Sydney and

Dudley, then moved on to the woman who was crying with relief as Pepper was handed back to her.

"That was the most incredible thing I've ever seen," a female voice said behind Sydney. "How did you do that?"

She turned to see a young woman, only a few years younger than herself, admiring her with big brown eyes.

"The credit goes to my dachshund," she said. "Dudley literally talked him down."

The young woman gazed at Dudley. "I knew animals communicated with each other, but I had no idea how well. Can I get your contact info?"

"Sure." She set Dudley on the ground and fished out a business card from her fanny pack.

The young woman looked at the card. "Thank you, Sydney. I'm getting a puppy next week, and I might need your help in the future."

"Call me anytime."

Carter came back over and gave Dudley a scratch behind his ear. "You two are becoming daily Pinecrest heroes."

She glanced at the forestry employee who seemed to be taking credit for the save. "It was a team effort."

The older woman approached Sydney with Pepper in her arms. "I should have never doubted you. Thank you for helping us. How can I ever repay you?"

"No need. Just hold on to that cat of yours."

"I'm not letting go." She rubbed her face against his, but the cat jumped out of her arms anyway. The woman yelped, startled, and tried to catch him to no avail.

Pepper pranced around Sydney to meet Dudley. Nose to nose, the cat and dog stared at one another without moving.

Carter quickly took several pictures of them. "I wonder what they're thinking?"

"I imagine Pepper is thanking Dudley for helping him to the ground," Sydney said.

Pepper's owner instantly scooped him up. "I thought you hated dogs?" The woman eyed her cat curiously.

He still does, but he loves me, for I, Durlindemore, King of the Dachshunds, am now his hero.

"Should we get you a playful doggie to be your companion?" the woman asked, snuggling into Pepper.

For the love of God, no.

"I think he only likes Dudley," Sydney said, suddenly seeing Pepper's introduction to a new dog going seriously wrong. "Cats are smart. Pepper knew he was in trouble, which is why he accepted Dudley's help."

Pepper meowed, and she wondered if he understood English as well as Dudley.

He does not, if that's what you're thinking. Dudley seemed to have read her expression. *Torkahndor's human servant is currently smothering him with too much affection—hence the verbal protest.*

"Come on, Pepper," the woman said. "You must be hungry."

At least she got that right.

"I think I owe you some turkey," Sydney said to Dudley. "Carter, would you like to join us for lunch?"

"I'd love to, but I'm still on the clock and need to do a quick interview with Pepper's owner and the forestry employees."

"Another time, then." She tried to mask her disappointment.

Cheer up. We'll be living near the guy in a matter of days.

"I got some great photos of you two." Carter held up his camera. "Do I have your permission to use them?"

"Of course."

I'll agree only if I get treats of my choosing for payment.

She nodded but didn't verbally respond, attempting to stay focused on what Carter was saying.

"With yesterday's story on the rescue, my upcoming interview with you, and now this cat rescue, *The Pinecrest News* is practically becoming your paper," he said.

Then it only stands to reason for the name to be changed immediately to The Dudley Daily.

Sydney laughed. "I think celebrity Dudley wouldn't mind your paper being called *The Dudley Daily*."

Carter chuckled. "I'll run it by my boss, little man, but he might not agree with your idea."

His loss. I suppose not everyone can be a genius.

"Well, I'll let you get back to work," she said.

"Don't forget to pick up tomorrow's paper," he reminded her.

"Our interview will be in there, as well as a write-up on what just happened here."

"I can't wait to read them." She held his gaze, smiling.

Are goodbyes always going to be this long? Dudley gave her an impatient whine.

"I hear you, Dudley, time to go."

I'm going to need some ice cream to go along with that turkey sandwich.

"We'll see about that."

Did I not crush the forestry chap and win the day once again?

"You did."

Then turkey and ice cream it is!

Carter watched her walk away with Dudley, talking to him as if they were carrying on an actual conversation. What did she mean by, "We'll see about that" and "You did"?

Those two were very curious. He could swear Sydney had been discussing the rescue with Dudley, as if he wasn't a dog. And as far as any so-called signals she was giving him, they didn't exist.

How were they doing it? How were they communicating? And how had they not only talked to a cat, but instructed him to back out of a tree sixty feet in the air? Even he knew cats didn't naturally know how to do that, which was why they often got stuck in trees.

Carter finished up his interviews and got back to the paper to write up today's story. He had to admit, the rescue had been heart-stopping. One false move and it would not have ended well for Pepper.

But who should Carter credit for the save? Would Pepper still be up in that tree if Sydney and Dudley hadn't shown up? The cat kept climbing higher, moving away from the forestry employee. Only after Sydney and Dudley started interacting with Pepper had he changed his course of action. Clearly, they were critical to the situation and had to be credited for the rescue.

However, if he were to look at the facts with an objective eye, Pepper could have decided to come down on his own accord once he saw that he was stranded. The forestry employee had backed off, allowing the cat to move freely.

He could also argue that the reason Pepper finally accepted help from the forestry employee was because he was exhausted and couldn't hold on any longer. What Carter couldn't explain was how Pepper had suddenly decided to back down the tree far enough so that the forestry guy could reach him. Pepper's behavior was not natural, and it was as if Dudley had told him to do it.

Impossible.

He wrote up the story exactly as it happened and let the reader decide. Had Sydney and Dudley's special communication skills saved the day, or had it been Pinecrest's forestry crew?

If Carter ever had the opportunity to watch Sydney and Dudley in action again, he needed to film them. Whatever they were doing went well beyond the ordinary, and if they kept being called upon to rescue lost kids and careless cats, it was only a matter of time before news stations would hear about them and want to see footage. When that happened, he'd be more than happy to supply it.

For the rest of the afternoon, he couldn't stop thinking about Sydney, and he found himself adding to his to-do list for the guesthouse. He wanted to mount two small shelves in the bathroom and plant flowers in the window boxes.

After work, Carter stood in the nursery department, overwhelmed by the massive selection. The petunias were vibrant and had great colors, so he loaded several into his basket.

"Hey, hero."

He turned around to see one of his good friends. "Nathan. When did you get back in town?"

"Last night. I see you've been busy finding missing kids."

"Yeah, it's been an interesting week. The dog walker who found the boy is moving into my guesthouse."

"What? You're finally allowing the opposite sex to get within a hundred yards of you? She must be something special. When do I get to meet her?"

"She's just a tenant moving into my rental."

Nathan eyed the items in Carter's basket. "When I stayed at your place, you never bought me flowers."

"That's because you lived on my couch for almost two months."

"Those were good times." He sighed. "Now I'm married with dogs."

"You love it, and you know it."

"I do." He chuckled. "What are you doing this weekend?"

"Cleaning out the guesthouse and fixing it up for Sydney."

"Sydney, is it?" He smiled, lifting a brow. "I can lend you a hand if you need it."

"Thanks, man. I might take you up on that."

"In exchange, I want to hear all about Sydney. I know you too well. She's not just a tenant."

Carter glanced at his shopping cart and realized Nathan was right. Everything he planned on buying was for Sydney and Dudley.

By the time Sydney got home, she was feeling pretty good about her employment opportunities. She and Dudley had accomplished another successful impromptu rescue, and four more potential clients had asked for her card as they were leaving. Her pet care business had always been word-of-mouth, but maybe it was time to put a professional website together.

With so much positive response from people she didn't even know, she thought it might be a good time to speak with her landlady about getting out of her lease—especially since she knew Mrs. Seidleman got the paper. She knocked on her door and waited.

"Who's there?" barked Mrs. Seidleman.

"It's Sydney Elder."

Mrs. Seidleman immediately swung open the door. "Sydney!" She was wearing a housecoat and slippers but was all smiles. "I read about you this morning. Please, come in. Do you want some tea?"

"No, thank you."

Her landlady's apartment was shockingly dirty for someone who gave everyone else so much grief. She had piles of old newspapers sitting by the front door, dirty dishes by the couch, half-dead house plants around the kitchen table, and cobwebs decorating the light fixture over the table.

"Congratulations on finding Zachary." Mrs. Seidleman held up a copy of the paper.

"I was happy to do it."

"Seems you have quite a way with dogs." She studied the photo again.

"Yes, in fact, that's why I'm here. Do you see the little dachshund there?" She pointed to Dudley. "A woman I know had recently found him on the street, but she can't keep him, and has asked me to adopt him. I know you have a strict—"

"Yes, you can keep him. I'd never toss out two local heroes." She heated up water for her tea in the microwave.

What? Never in a million years had she expected to hear that from her landlady, and while it was nice to know Mrs. Seidleman would have made an exception for her, it was too late. She'd already signed Carter's rental agreement, and she didn't want out of it. She was looking forward to living in his guesthouse. It was beautiful. Plus, living on the ground floor with a dog would be much easier than living on the second floor. And if she was being perfectly honest with herself, she wanted to be near Carter.

"Thank you so much for the offer, Mrs. Seidleman, but knowing the no-pet policy has been strictly enforced here, I found a place yesterday, and I need to move as soon as possible for the sake of the dog. I was hoping you'd allow me to break my lease early."

"Why would you look for another place to live without speaking to me first?"

"Like I said, with the strict no-pet policy you've reminded me of every day, I assumed the answer would be no."

"You assumed wrong—except for now. The answer is no."

"You won't let a local hero out of her lease?"

"Not when I plan on using your celebrity status to attract other renters."

"But won't they be upset if I can have a dog and they can't?"

"That's life. Celebrities always get preferential treatment."

"Mrs. Seidleman, I truly appreciate the offer, but I really need to move *now*."

"No problem. You can move anytime you like, but you'll still be responsible for the rent. As your rental agreement states, you must give me a thirty-day notice in writing."

Sydney let out a long, disappointed sigh.

"As a celebrity, I'm sure you can afford to pay for an extra thirty days."

"But I can't, Mrs. Seidleman. I wasn't handed a big fat check from the city for helping to find a missing boy. My financial status hasn't changed."

Mrs. Seidleman stuck a tea bag in the mug of hot water and let it steep. "Tell you what I'm going to do. I'll try to get your apartment rented as soon as possible, and if I do, then I can refund a portion of your rent."

"I'll bring you the notice in ten minutes."

"No, dear. It must be mailed. I'll need the postmark for legal reasons."

She wanted to scream and tell her landlady exactly what she thought of her but held her tongue. She had to picture herself living in Carter's serene backyard to calm down. "Of course. Thank you for your time."

She walked out, headed up to her apartment, and immediately started packing. Moving day couldn't come fast enough.

CHAPTER ELEVEN

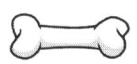

Sydney had been so irritated by Mrs. Seidleman that she ended up packing a quarter of her belongings before she was able to fall asleep. The moment her alarm went off the next morning, she was back to worrying about whether it was smart for her to move so soon and lose money. She'd picked up new clients, but they were for pet sitting dates weeks away—not next week when she needed the extra cash.

As much as she couldn't afford to lose the money, she wouldn't be able to handle living another month in her apartment. She wanted to get on with her life, and she knew that included both Dudley and Carter.

She got in her car and was driving to Dana's to pick up Dudley when she realized she'd forgotten to get the paper. She just hoped Carter didn't call her before she had a chance to read his interview and article on Pepper's rescue.

She knocked on the door, and it whipped open. "You're famous!" Dana excitedly shoved *The Pinecrest News* in Sydney's face. "The paper dubbed you 'The Dachshund Whisperer.'"

"What?" She could barely catch a glimpse of the front page before Dana set it on the table. "I'm on the front page again?"

"Yes, in two different articles. You and Dudley also rescued a cat yesterday? I knew you were meant for each other." Dana closed her laptop and slid it into her bag. "It certainly didn't take you very long to figure out how to talk to him."

Sydney hovered over the newspaper, anxious to know what Carter had written. "What do the articles say?"

"All good things. Go ahead and keep the paper. I've already read it."

"Thanks."

"Have you found out if you're able to break your lease?" Dana asked, gathering up several interior design sketches.

"I did, and it's a big no." Sydney let out a long sigh.

"That's terrible." The look on Dana's face was strained. "So you won't be moving for another month?"

"No, I'm taking the financial hit. I'll be moving as soon as I can."

Dana let out a relieved breath. "That's great. Do you need help? I'm very good at packing."

She smiled, recalling what her sister once said, that Dana went on mini vacations almost every weekend and practically lived out of a suitcase. "Thank you, but Rachael and her husband will be helping me."

"Wonderful." She tamped down her enthusiasm as Dudley trotted into the room. "Not that I don't want you here, Dudley, but I know you'll be much happier with Sydney."

That goes without saying, though I fear you won't fare as well. Your fiancé is too fussy to make you happy long term.

Sydney's eyes shot wide, but she quickly recovered before Dana noticed the look of horror on her face. "I'm sure Dudley is very happy you rescued him. I know I am."

"Aww. You're very welcome," Dana said to both her and Dudley. "You two are a perfect match. This interview about your special communication is very interesting." She tapped her finger on the paper. "I have a good feeling 'The Dachshund Whisperer' is going to get very busy with new clients."

She smiled. "I sure hope you're right."

Dana picked up her workbag. "Speaking of new clients, I better get going. Keep me posted about the move. Enjoy your walk."

As soon as Dana left, Sydney grabbed the paper. It seemed surreal to see photos and articles about herself for a second day in a row. Carter's interview was front and center, while the article on Pepper's rescue was at the bottom and off to the side. "I wonder why they didn't make Pepper's rescue the bigger story?"

Because we're a bigger deal. A cat getting stuck in a tree is nothing new.

"I suppose you're right."

Carter had chosen a picture of her holding Dudley in her arms, talking sweetly to him—telling him how exceptional he was, and the expression on Dudley's face was pure joy.

Yesterday's article had not only gotten her a lot of attention from family and friends, but also from Pinecrest residents. Now that Carter's interview was out about her and Dudley, she couldn't imagine how many more locals would be seeking her out.

Don't keep me in suspense. What does it say?

Her eyes flew over the interview, reading it as fast as she could. "It's a lot about me—how I've been in tune with animals all my life, specifically dogs, and how we—" She frowned.

What?

"Carter wrote that we work so well together, without standard dog-training signals, that he couldn't figure out exactly *how* we were communicating. He says, and I quote, 'It's almost like the pair talks telepathically. But we all know that's impossible.'" She set down the paper, expelling a disappointed sigh.

He's half right. Aside from not making the article exclusively about me, what don't you like about it?

"He thinks telepathy is impossible. After everything he's witnessed, how can he believe that?"

He wrote that before we rescued Pepper.

She began reading the article on Pepper out loud, and Carter had described everything as it unfolded. "Listen to this." She sat up, excited. "'Though the incredible rescue was a team effort between the forestry crew and the Sydney-Dudley team, it was clear to all who witnessed it that the Dachshund Whisperer's talent was something we've never seen. How else are we to explain that a scared, terrified cat suddenly knew how to back down a tree?'"

I'd say he's a skeptic who's open to persuasion.

She held the paper in her hand, rereading some of his paragraphs, trying to get insight into what he believed.

Why is it important to you that he believes in telepathy?

"I want him to respect what I do, and I don't want him to think I'm a crazy dog lady."

It's all relative, Sydney. I find people who love to swim in public pools completely mad, with all those germs and the unhealthy level of chlorine used to kill those germs. But would I hang out with those mad pool people if they were sharing their food with me? Absolutely. I don't think Carter would think less of you if you believed in telepathy and he didn't.*

"You're right, Dudley. He wouldn't. But this isn't entirely about telepathy. This is more about you. How will I explain your incredible ability to him when I've never come across anyone like you?"

Quite simply. Don't.

"But we're going to be living so close to him. What are we supposed to do? Only speak to one another when we're alone? I'll constantly be talking to you in front of him, which is extremely difficult to pull off without looking like I'm crazy."

He's already spent enough time with you to know you're of sound mind. Do you think he'd be renting to you if he thought otherwise?

She was in awe at how smart her dog was. "Maybe I *am* making too much of it." She grabbed his harness out of the utility closet and put it on him.

Humans always do. Perhaps we should think about creating a blog or an advice column on our new website. It could be titled, "Dear Dudley." I could cure most of mankind's neuroses in one day.

She chuckled at his imperious way of thinking. "I've no doubt you could."

If only she could change Carter's belief about telepathy in one day…

Russell seemed very pleased with Carter's in-depth interview on Sydney. Even Shep had given him a backhanded compliment—something about how Carter's front-page interview read so well that residents would think Shep was the one who had penned it. For Shep, that was a step forward, so Carter considered it a win.

He checked his phone for the umpteenth time and frowned. He was happy to be receiving praise on an article he'd spent half the night writing, but he still hadn't heard from the one person who mattered. Had Sydney not seen it yet—or his article on the cat rescue? He took a sip of coffee and winced. It was stone-cold. He snagged his phone off the desk and headed toward the employee lounge where Jamie was making herself a cup of tea.

"Great interview," she said as he entered.

"Thanks." He threw out his stale coffee and poured himself a fresh cup.

"The Dachshund Whisperer is a dog walker, a pet sitter, a child and animal rescuer, but she's not a dog trainer?"

"Sydney planned on being a trainer at one time, but she took a different path," he said. "Though, as you read, she definitely has a way with animals."

"She sure seems like it," Jamie said. "Do you think she'd be interested in meeting my Rottweiler? He's got all kinds of issues that I can't figure out."

One of Carter's high school friends had owned two Rottweilers. Bear was a sweet, lovable dog, while Brutus was an unpredictable handful. "What kind of issues?"

"He's destructive, anxious, and paces when it gets dark outside. He's a big, scared baby."

"Any aggression?"

"Not in the least."

That put his mind at ease. "Sounds like he could use Sydney's help. Let me give her a call."

"Thanks, Carter."

After Jamie left, he leaned against the counter and shot Sydney a text to see if she could talk—happy that he now had a legitimate excuse to contact her. While he waited for a reply, he pulled up the pictures he'd taken of her and Dudley. The way the dog was looking at her as she talked to him was comical.

"I haven't seen that type of smile on your face in months."

Carter glanced up and saw his sister standing in the doorway. "Hey, what are you doing here?"

She held up a pink bakery box. "Thought I'd bring you a few of your favorite chocolate chip cookies from Aunt Joan's bakery."

His mouth began to water. "What did I do to deserve this?"

"You've been working hard." She eased herself into the nearest chair. "Besides, I was already there, taking care of my own cravings."

"Is it still carrot cake muffins?"

"That was last month." She rubbed her well-rounded belly. "Baby is now into banana walnut bread."

"I see culinary school in your child's future." He opened up the box, pulled out a cookie the size of a teacup saucer, and bit into it with a moan of pleasure.

She laughed. "So what was that smile all about?"

"Nothing." He shrugged.

"You're talking to the person who knows your every incremental expression, little brother. Please tell me you're dating again."

Could he actually say he was dating? It was only one dinner—and a working dinner at that. "I was just looking through some of the photos I took of Sydney and her dachshund, Dudley. He's pretty funny."

"And Sydney? What's the Dachshund Whisperer like?"

"Nice, sweet, smart, funny, and she's my new tenant."

Lorelai's face lit up. "What's this?"

"A weird coincidence. I called my real estate agent about getting the guesthouse listed, and she happened to have Sydney with her, who was looking for a new place to live."

"That's serendipitous," his sister said, watching him carefully, waiting for any morsel of information he'd drop on how he felt about Sydney. When none came, Lorelai changed tactics.

"Great interview, by the way. I loved your story on Pepper as well, but your interview with Sydney was different. It drew me right in."

"Thanks."

"Is she single?"

He stifled a laugh. His sister was slipping. Her tactics used to be smooth and subtle.

"Yes," he said reluctantly, knowing that twenty questions were coming.

Lorelai reached for a copy of today's paper lying on the table, and studied the photo. "She's pretty. I can see why you decided to rent to a woman with a dog."

"They rescued a boy, his dog, and a cat. How could I say no?"

His sister narrowed her eyes at him. "You like her."

"I like a lot of people." He broke eye contact, which was useless. He could never hide anything from his sister.

"You know exactly what I mean, and I'm happy for you. She sounds great—especially her loving dogs so much. That will make Mom happy."

"She'll be even happier when Sydney and Dudley figure out the reason for Penelope's aggression toward me."

"If they can get a cat to back out of a tree, I'd say Penelope's problems will be a snap," Lorelai said. "How *did* they accomplish that, and find a missing boy when bloodhounds couldn't?"

"It's a mystery," he said. "Maybe they just got lucky."

"Sounds like it's a story for an investigative journalist. And now you'll be able to keep a close eye on them."

"I'm not renting to her so I can spy on her. Besides, we have already printed three stories about her. There really isn't much more to say."

"Maybe not to the town of Pinecrest, but I have a feeling her story is just beginning with you." She raised a brow.

"You never give up."

"What are sisters for? Now what can I do to help you get the guesthouse in shape?"

"In your condition, nothing—though do you happen to know what kind of treats dogs like the best?"

A big grin spread across Lorelai's face. "You've fallen farther than I thought."

"I have not. I figured I'd buy some dog treats so when Dudley ends up barking all night while she's out on a date, I can bribe him to be quiet."

"Somehow, I'm not seeing that scenario happening. But to answer your question, it depends on the dog." She studied his photo on the front page. "Is Dudley on a diet?"

"I don't know. He looks okay to me."

"I'd go with turkey or chicken jerky, just to be safe," she said. "He's very cute. I can't wait to meet them." She pushed off the arms of the chair and staggered to her feet. "I'm really happy for you, little brother. Change is good, and in your case, I think it might be great."

"Whoa, Pupperton. Heel!" Sydney kept sending him a mental image to slow down, but he was ignoring her. It was like her telepathic messages were being bounced back. "A little help here?"

Dudley barked at him in the canine language and the energetic Mountain Cur instantly slowed to walk beside her.

"Thank you." Sydney let out a heavy breath, then directed Pupperton, Finn, Cocoa Puff, and Dudley to a bench under a beautiful blooming crab apple tree. She unfolded her travel dog bowl and poured water into it for them to get a drink before she checked her phone. Carter had texted a while ago, asking if she could talk. She replied that she was available and her phone rang instantly.

"Hi, Carter." She couldn't hide the smile in her voice.

"Are you out walking dogs right now?"

"I am. Dudley and I just got the gang to the park, and we're taking a ten-minute water break."

"Tell the little guy I said hi."

"Dudley, Carter says hi."

Tell him I expect a treat from him the next time I see him or we're no longer friends.

"He's sending you a very happy 'hi' back."

Carter chuckled. "Not sure if you saw my articles today, but I already have a colleague asking if you'd be interested in meeting her non-aggressive Rottweiler. She said he's a big baby with a lot of anxiety issues."

She'd helped several anxious dogs over the years, but never a Rottweiler. She eyed Dudley.

They look scary but are teddy bears. I'll have the thing whipped into shape in ten minutes.

If Dudley was confident, she was too. "Sure. Send me her number. And, yes, I loved both of your articles. I only just read them a little while ago, which is why I hadn't called you. The interview was very flattering, probably too flattering."

For you, but not for me. He could have mentioned me a lot more.

"Did I get everything right?"

"More than you know," she hinted, hoping to make a believer out of him. "There was only one little thing."

"Uh-oh." He sounded nervous. "What?"

"You might want to rethink your stance on telepathy. It's a great communication tool."

"I imagine it would be." Which meant he believed telepathy was as real as teleportation.

"It *is* a great communication tool. I speak from experience."

There was silence on his end, and she assumed he was figuring out what to say. She was about to change the subject when he said, "Do you know what I'm thinking right now?"

"Just to be clear, mind reading is about interpreting another person's emotions or thoughts through physical interaction, while telepathy is direct communication between two minds. That said, are you sending me a telepathic message right now?" she asked.

"You tell me."

It's sexual in nature. Trust me on this.

"I'm blushing," Sydney said, and Carter went silent. She smiled at Dudley, surprised he was right. "Are you still there?"

Carter cleared his throat. "Lucky guess."

She stifled a laugh.

"Is your landlady going to let you out of your lease?"

"Of course not," she huffed. "I'm on the hook for another month's rent, but Dana is anxious for me to take Dudley, so I'm not waiting."

"I'm really sorry to hear about your difficult landlady," he said. "Let me at least help you get out of there as soon as possible. I can have your place move-in ready by next weekend."

"Thank you, Carter. I really appreciate it. And Dudley also thanks you."

He chuckled. "I imagine Dana will be happy too."

"Yes, she misses having her fiancé over. It's a good thing she isn't a huge dog person like I am. Not being able to have a dog would be a deal-breaker for me."

"No, really? I would have never guessed," he said teasingly, and she laughed.

"Pupperton, hold on. Sorry, but I've gotta run. Literally."

"Okay. Take it easy out there."

"Talk soon!" She hung up as Dudley got Pupperton back under control again.

"One more week to go, Dudley, and then we'll be living the good life in Carter's guesthouse."

I do hope he knows how to make delicious snacks. I might need to order room service while I'm sunbathing in the backyard.

"Yes, I'm sure Carter lives and breathes to wait on you hand and foot."

That's the life of a manservant.

"How did you know what Carter was thinking, anyway?"

He's a man. Men are very simple and easy to figure out.

"I haven't had an easy time figuring them out."

That's because you overthink it.

"I do not," she said defensively. "And how would you know anyway?"

Not you specifically, but women in general. As an objective third-party observer, I note that women tend to overthink situations or problems while men underthink them, or don't think at all.

She let out a big laugh. "For a canine, you have incredible insight. You might have just explained the biggest cause of disagreements between our genders."

Yes, well, all the more reason I need an advice column.

"I couldn't agree more."

CHAPTER TWELVE

Carter headed back to his desk with cookies and coffee in hand. He was having a difficult time concentrating, not that there was anything to concentrate on. Even Shep hadn't been sent out in the field, which meant the town was blissfully quiet.

The second he sat down, Chester jumped on his lap. "I've got a dog moving into my guesthouse, Chester. What do you think about that?"

The cat instantly jumped down and ran off, leaving Carter to wonder how much animals really understood.

He checked his email and realized that he had over twenty messages asking about how to get in touch with Sydney. The first one asked if they could help find a cat who hadn't come home in two days. The next one was asking if the dynamic duo knew how to pick out the perfect puppy for three young girls, and another wanted help locating a coin collection. He was about to text Sydney when Russell motioned him inside his office.

"Yes, ma'am," Russell said to the woman on the phone as Carter walked in. "*The Dachshund Whisperer* column will be appearing every Friday both in print and online. Wonderful. Let me connect you with someone who can take your subscription information." He transferred the call before giving Carter his full attention.

"Your article did better than I expected." Russell sat and rocked back in his chair. "Our readers have Dachshund Whisperer fever, which gave me an idea—one I hope you'll agree to since I've already sold it to new subscribers."

"I heard. *The Dachshund Whisperer* column?"

His boss nodded. "I know you wanted to get away from animal stories, but my inbox is getting flooded by residents asking if Sydney and her dog can help find lost pets and missing valuables. One woman even wants to know if they can help catch a cheating husband."

He stiffened. "Sydney isn't a sideshow."

"Obviously, but you intrigued our readers, both with the interview and the story about the cat backing down a tree. Everyone wants to know how Sydney Elder and Dudley the dachshund talk to each other." He turned around his computer to show Carter the sheer number of emails regarding The Dachshund Whisperer.

"Look, I know she won't be interested in some of these requests," Russell said. "But here's a woman whose corgi ran away from home two years ago, and she hasn't stopped searching. Another has a dog that won't stop barking. What if you were to accompany Ms. Elder on these sessions and document them? Then, with her and her client's permission, you can tell our readers all about it."

He had to admit, Russell had come up with an interesting idea for the paper, and he certainly wasn't going to complain about spending more time with Sydney. Besides, if he was there to document her work with Dudley, he'd be able to see every step of their process. "I'll have to talk to Sydney first."

"I assumed you would, but don't take too long. Since I'm selling subscriptions on this, I don't want to have to refund everyone's money."

"Don't you think you should have waited until I got her approval?"

"The electric bill is due in three days."

"Understood." Carter sighed, then dialed her number. "Hey, Sydney. Got a minute?"

"I'll see you there. Thanks, Carter." Sydney disconnected the call and slid her cell in her back pocket. "Be good, Pupperton."

She blew him a kiss, locked her client's front door, and headed toward her car with Dudley.

Sydney hoisted him into the car seat that Dana bought him, and buckled him up. He gazed out the window, ready for the car ride, but the car wasn't moving. *What are you doing?*

"I'm adding a new address into my phone."

Aren't we going to pick up Jammer and Nellie for their late morning walk?

"No, their mom and dad took them out of town." She started the car, then followed the directions that her phone was giving her.

Where are we going?

"We're about to meet our first client. Carter said the paper has been inundated with people needing our services."

What's the job?

"A missing cat."

Dudley groaned. *Male or female?*

"I don't know. Why?"

If it's a male, he's most likely gallivanting around the countryside, prowling around for some tail.

She laughed. "I guess we'll soon find out."

A few minutes later, she arrived at the address and saw Carter already there waiting for her.

"Hey Sydney, Mr. Dudley."

It's Sir Dudley to you.

"He's very happy to see you."

Honestly, Sydney, you need your ears cleaned out. That's not at all what I said.

Carter gave him a rub on the head. "I'm happy to see you too, little man." He glanced at Sydney. "Thanks for doing this, and for being so cool about my boss wanting to document it."

"Of course." She hooked Dudley's leash onto his harness, then took him out of the car.

Carter double-checked his equipment to make sure he had everything. "I've decided to film the session instead of taking photos. That way you'll have something to put on your website, if you choose to have one someday."

"Are you sure you don't believe in telepathy?"

He gave her a cautious look. "Why?"

"Because I picked up four new clients, thanks to you, and I've decided that Dudley and I need a website."

He smiled. "I can help you with that. I used to build them to make some extra cash."

"I'd love that. Thank you, Carter. I really appreciate everything you're doing for me. I still can't believe people actually called the paper."

"Why not? You two have a unique talent."

"A talent that has only been put to the test twice." She walked with him and Dudley up to the house. "Let's hope we can find her cat."

Carter rang the bell, and they heard footsteps hurrying to the door. A moment later, it was opened by an older woman in her sixties with stark white hair and a grateful look on her face. "Oh my gosh. I got the rescue team. Please, come in."

The trio stepped inside.

It definitely smells like cat.

"I'm Marjorie, and this is my daughter, Helena."

A woman in her forties got up from the couch. "You must be Sydney."

"Yes, and this is Carter, who's with the newspaper."

"Hi." He shook Helena's hand. "As I mentioned over the phone, I'll be filming today's session, if the both of you are still okay with that."

Helena nodded.

"That's not a problem at all," Marjorie said.

"Great." Carter gave them a short release form to sign, then stepped back. "Pretend I'm not here." He slated the date and session number, then began recording.

"Is this Dudley?" Marjorie asked, bending down.

"The one and only," Sydney said.

Dudley wagged his tail. *Do they have any treats? I'm hungry.*

"Thank you for coming on such short notice," Helena said. "My mom has been beside herself. Norma Jean, my mother's Persian cat, has been missing for two days."

"It's so unlike her." Marjorie put a hand to her heart. "She loves to sunbathe on the backyard deck. I always go out there with her, and she's never strayed from it. I had a package delivered and was at the front door for less than two minutes. When I returned, she was gone."

"Do you have a photo of her?" Sydney asked.

"Of course." Marjorie took a framed picture off the bookshelf and handed it over.

Sydney stared into the beautiful blue eyes of Norma Jean and introduced herself telepathically, then said she wanted to ask the cat some questions about her whereabouts. Sydney waited for a response and didn't hear anything. That had never happened before. Sometimes pets were reluctant to talk, but she always felt their energy. Why wasn't she hearing or sensing her?

She told Norma Jean that she was a friend of her mom's and was contacting her to help her find her way home. Still nothing, and Sydney's pulse quickened. She at least knew Norma Jean was still alive because from past experience, she found those who had passed were usually very chatty. Sydney suspected the cat was too scared and freaked out to speak, which made her heart race even faster. Having desperate eyes on her, along with a camera, wasn't helping, either. Anxiety took over, and she began to shut down.

Where are you going?

She instantly heard Dudley and focused on him. Her stress level had almost closed him off too. "Still trying to get a solid connection," she quietly said to him, even though everyone else could hear her.

She took a deep breath and closed her eyes to calm down. She couldn't fail now. She tried to connect again, but no one was talking back. She opened her eyes, stared at Dudley, and marginally shook her head.

It was all up to Dudley now. She showed Norma Jean's picture to Dudley, hoping he understood that she hadn't gotten a connection.

"This is who we're looking for," she said to him, buying time, hoping one of them could pick up on something.

Too pretty for her own good. Time to take a look outside.

What did that mean? Could he not pick up on her energy, either? "Can we see where she was last?"

"Right this way." Marjorie led Sydney, Dudley, and Carter out to the deck.

The moment Sydney stepped outside, she finally heard from Norma Jean. "Wood with holes?" She looked to Marjorie. "What does that mean?"

"I don't know. Do you, Helena?"

She shook her head. "I'm afraid not."

I heard the feline's description of her whereabouts as well. Dudley stared at Sydney. *I suppose I must do some investigating.* He began sniffing around the deck. When he moved into the corner behind an outdoor barbecue, he jumped.

"What is it?" Sydney came over.

A bloody field mouse.

"Does he know anything?"

"Does who know anything?" Marjorie asked.

Sydney's mind was working overtime, trying to come up with a logical explanation for her question when Dudley started making super high-pitched whines at the corner of the deck, which, no doubt, was mouse speak.

"What's he doing?" Helena asked.

"Gathering intel," Sydney said.

Carter moved in closer to capture Dudley glued to the corner of the deck, making weird noises, but Dudley took off like a shot, chasing the mouse.

Carter, Marjorie, and Helena suddenly saw the mouse, and Helena screamed.

"Not good that a little mouse has already distracted him," Carter whispered to Sydney.

Sydney, on the double. Ziegengluber knows where she is!

"Right this way!" Sydney hurried after Dudley, who was following the mouse through the grass, then through a field, and onto the property next door.

"Is your neighbor friendly?" Carter asked Marjorie as she and Helena followed close behind.

"Yes," she said, "but I've already asked them if they saw her, and they haven't."

Dudley was zigzagging all over the place. Sydney knew what it looked like—that Dudley had no idea what he was doing, but he did. After another minute of zigzagging, he finally made a beeline toward a greenhouse, then came to a dead stop.

This is where Ziegengluber last saw her.

"When?" Sydney asked Dudley.

Two suns ago.

Marjorie thought Sydney was talking to her. "I came over here and asked them the day Norma Jean went missing."

Sydney groaned. Not what she wanted to hear from the mouse or Marjorie. She leaned in to Dudley. Carter was filming them, but Marjorie and Helena were hanging back. "Are you picking up anything on her?"

Dudley made eye contact. *Fear.*

"I sensed that too. Is she in this vicinity?"

Yes, but she's hiding.

Sydney turned toward her audience, who was intently watching the two of them. "Norma Jean is here, but she's scared and hiding. Marjorie, call to her."

The older woman stepped forward. "Norma Jean?" she called out. "Can you hear me?"

"No one move," Sydney said. She needed to hear any sound beyond them.

"Over there." Carter pointed. "White lattice."

Sure enough, there was a small structure with white lattice covering the foundation. "Wood with holes. Marjorie, over here."

The older woman followed. "Norma Jean? It's me, honey. You can come out now."

Carter got down on his knees with a flashlight and scanned the dark crawl space. "I think I see something."

"Is it her?" Marjorie asked anxiously.

"I don't know." He saw an animal's eyes in the light until it turned and moved farther away.

"Is it Norma Jean?" Sydney asked Dudley.

Obviously. I wouldn't have brought you out here on a wild mouse chase. Dudley sat down and stared at the lattice, as if he was waiting for Norma Jean to make an appearance.

"It's her," Sydney said. "Dudley, talk to her."

"No." Marjorie stopped him from coming closer. "She's terrified of dogs."

Please inform her that I'm most certainly no ordinary dog.

"Dudley can actually communicate with several species. He can coax her out."

Marjorie wrung her hands and stepped aside. "I sure hope you're right."

Must I do everything? I expect a steak for dinner tonight. Dudley trotted over to the lattice, lay down, then began making growling, gurgling noises similar to the ones he'd made with Pepper.

"What is he *doing*?" Helena gave Sydney a strange look.

"He's talking to her."

"I've never seen anything like this in my life." Marjorie couldn't stop staring at Dudley.

Almost. Dudley flipped over on his back, still making noises, before he got to his feet and turned toward Marjorie's house. He looked over his shoulder and gave one bark, as if to tell Norma Jean that it was time to go home.

Sydney was about to say something when a scared meow could be heard beneath the structure.

"Norma Jean!" Marjorie dropped to her hands and knees. "I see her! I can't believe it. Hi, precious."

Norma Jean's meows grew stronger and louder.

"How did she get in there?" Sydney asked Dudley.

No clue.

"She probably found a small opening somewhere, but no longer knows where it is," Carter replied, assuming she was talking to him. "Let's see if I can find her another way out."

He shook the lattice. Sydney hoped it would pop off, but it didn't. He tried another section, and then another. The last section was very loose, and it came down easily.

"Here." He set the lattice section aside. "Have her come this way." Carter backed up and continued filming.

Marjorie was sticking her fingers through the lattice that was still in place, in order to touch Norma Jean.

"Follow me, Norma Jean." Marjorie got up and moved toward the opening. "Come to Mama." She got on her hands and knees again and reached into the opening. A few seconds later, Norma Jean came running, and Marjorie scooped her up into her arms. "My sweet baby." She held her tight and cried, overjoyed.

"Incredible," Helena said. "Thank you."

"My pleasure." Sydney glanced at Dudley, ready to give him praise, but he was chasing a butterfly, or having a conversation with it. She honestly didn't know which one it was.

After Carter resecured the lattice, everyone headed back to Marjorie's, where Norma Jean ran to her water bowl. Marjorie spooned some cat food into a dish and set it in front of her.

"Sydney, I can't thank you enough." Marjorie gave her a hug. "And, Dudley, there are no words to describe your incredible talent." She ran a hand down his back, then gave him a rub under his chin. "May I give him a little piece of chicken for his efforts?"

Dudley yelped and patiently sat at her feet, licking his chops.

Marjorie bubbled with laughter. "You are one smart boy. You understood what I said, didn't you?"

Clearly. Now where's that chicken you promised?

"Yes, he loves chicken, and he can have one bite."

"Wonderful." Marjorie opened the refrigerator and took out a plastic container. "I made this for dinner last night, but I couldn't eat it without my Norma Jean."

Dudley whined, glued to Marjorie. *I'll take the whole thing off your hands.*

She pulled off the tiniest of bites and gave it to Dudley who swallowed it whole before he searched the floor. *Where did it go? Do you see it?*

"My mom is used to feeding a cat," Helena said to Sydney and Carter. "I think you can give him a bigger bite, Mom."

Dudley barked, looking excited.

"My apologies, good sir." She pulled off a piece three times the size, gave it to him, and it was gone in seconds. "Dogs are a lot less finicky than cats."

"Not necessarily," Sydney said. "I just happen to have a chowhound."

A starving hound is more like it. Honestly, Sydney, I'm doing all the work, burning an exorbitant number of calories. I deserve that whole chicken breast.

Sydney laughed out loud. "Oh, I don't think so."

"You don't think what?" Marjorie asked.

"Uh, I was just reading Dudley's face. He looked like he was expecting the whole thing."

Marjorie glanced at Dudley, then at Sydney. "I can give it to him if that's what he wants."

Yes!

"No, completely unnecessary, but thank you."

Why? It's right there!

"Sorry, Dudley. Your mom said no."

She always says no. Look, my mouth is open. Just drop it in.

Marjorie put the chicken back in the refrigerator. "What do I owe you, Sydney?"

"Oh, it's okay. I'm happy we could help."

"You brought my precious Norma Jean back to me. That's worth all the gold in the world. Please, let me pay you."

Sydney hated this part. She hated taking money for doing something that she'd gladly do for free. "Seriously, I'm fine."

"But you need money to buy Dudley chicken," Marjorie said, and Dudley barked. "See, even Dudley agrees, and I insist."

"I've got it, Mom." Helena took out her wallet and gave Sydney a hundred bucks.

"Thank you," she said. "That's very kind."

"No, thank *you*." Helena reached down and patted Dudley on the head. "We've always been a cat family, but you've won us over, Dudley. Maybe we should get a dog just like you."

Good luck with that. No dog comes close to being me.

"Bye, Norma Jean," Sydney called out to the cat who was licking her bowl clean.

Dudley whined and Norma Jean meowed.

"What did you just say?" Sydney quietly asked Dudley.

I told her to stay on the deck from now on or I'd be back to eat all of her food.

She laughed. "That cat isn't going anywhere."

As everyone walked to the door, Helena asked, "When do you think we'll be able to read Norma Jean's story?"

"It'll be in next Friday's paper," Carter said. "I'm starting a new column called 'The Dachshund Whisperer to the Rescue.'"

Marjorie laughed. "I love it!"

Oh, please. I'm the one whispering.

"More like shouting," she said to Dudley, then realized Carter and Helena were staring at her. "But saying I whisper works just fine. Don't you agree, Dudley?"

"Durlindemore, King of the Dachshunds and Expert Dog Trainer," is more precise, but I suppose "The Dachshund Whisperer to the Rescue" is a decent alternative. An inferior one, but an alternative nonetheless.

"He absolutely loves it." Sydney smiled. "Take care, and call me if you need us again."

She let out a satisfied breath as she watched Dudley trot back to the car.

"You and Dudley are extremely good at this." Carter seemed to regard her with new admiration.

Was there any doubt?

She gave him an easy smile. "I have to say, it feels good to be a part of happy reunions."

"You said the other night that you were still trying to figure out your career. Maybe you've finally found it."

"Maybe so." She opened the car door for Dudley. "But before I hang out a shingle saying I'm open for business, I'd like to see if we continue to have the same success rate."

"You're in luck." He set down his bag and pulled out his phone. "I have several more inquiries from readers asking for your help. Nine and counting."

"Seriously?" She couldn't believe how much she and Dudley were in demand. There was no doubt they'd been destined to find each other.

"When I get back to the office, I can forward them to you, if you'd like."

"That would be great. My afternoons are opening up, so I could schedule sessions then."

He studied her. "Are you still comfortable with me coming along to document the sessions?"

She didn't want to tell him the camera made her nervous, because she liked spending time with him. "If it helps you and the paper, I have no problem with it. Did you get what you needed today for Friday's column?"

He smiled. "The story will practically write itself."

She turned toward him. "Thank you, Carter."

"For what?"

"My new gig. Because of you, I might have found my place in the world."

"That credit is all yours." His eyes lingered on her, then seemed to reluctantly pull away. "Guess I better get back to work." He glanced at Dudley before he leaned into her car and gave him a quick scratch down his back. "Bye, little man. No distracting the driver."

Impossible. I'm a vision to behold.

"He said it was really great seeing you again and that he can't wait to move in."

Instead of putting words in my mouth, how about some food?

"Then you better help your mom pack," he said, before turning his attention back to Sydney. "If you need any human help just let me know."

She laughed. "I will."

As Sydney finally drove away, she saw Carter in her rearview mirror watching them go, and it tugged at her heart.

Is that smile for me? Dudley eyed her.

"For you, Carter, the whole day. You are amazing, Dudley. I'm seriously thinking we could do this as a successful business."

I tried to tell you that moments after we met.

"My apologies. Humans are a little slow sometimes. And speaking of which, I think Carter will definitely believe in telepathy after he observes a few more of our sessions."

He's a bright lad. I'm counting on it, along with the treats I'll be training him to feed me.

"And how exactly are you going to do that?"

Humans are astonished by pet tricks. They obviously won't work on you, since you can hear me, but everyone else will be throwing me treats when I dazzle them with my brilliance. I could have had that entire chicken breast.

"Could and should are two different things."

I should have been a Great Dane. Then I could receive a properly sized meal.

"You are seriously food obsessed."

I'm afraid it's a dachshund trait.

"I suppose I can add a little poached chicken to your diet once you move in with me."

He thumped his tail wildly. *A truly brilliant idea!*

"Of course, that means you'll need to get more exercise." She pulled up in front of a house he didn't recognize.

Aren't we going to lunch?

"We've got to get in a quick walk with a new client."

How quick?

"Twenty minutes."

Your definition of quick is as inaccurate as your idea of a large food portion.

She laughed. "C'mon, grumpy. It's time to get in shape."

Sydney and Dudley filled Carter's thoughts all the way back to the paper. Admittedly, he was thinking mostly about Sydney—how she was so positive and bright-eyed. How she seemed content with the little things in life, like walking dogs, or a beautiful spring day. She wasn't into fashion or social media or wanting to make a big splash in a high-profile industry. She appeared to be content in the here and now. She was probably the most selfless woman he'd met, and that was very appealing.

With past relationships, he never seemed to rank first in his girlfriends' lives. Their future career or their social calendar seemed to take precedence. In truth, Dudley ranked first in Sydney's life, but Carter could understand that. She was moving so the dog would have a home, plus they worked beautifully together.

And it wasn't as if he'd been excluded. Quite the opposite. Sydney included him whenever she pretended to be carrying on a long conversation with Dudley, by thinking of funny things Dudley might say if he could actually talk. It was amusing and clever. Did she entertain all of her clients with what their pets might be saying, or was it for his own enjoyment?

Having her move into his guesthouse was the best thing that could have happened. With her living behind him, there would be plenty of opportunities to hang out with her and really get to know her without feeling the pressure of an actual date. And now that they would be working together, they'd soon know a great deal about one another.

When Carter finally got back to work and sat down at his desk, Chester immediately jumped on his lap. "Hey, Chester." The cat didn't seem to be his usual relaxed self. He wondered if Chester could smell Dudley on him. "I had an assignment with a dachshund, and it will be a recurring thing, so you'll have to get used to it."

Chester gave a short meow, turned his back on him, and hopped down. He wouldn't have given it a second thought before he met Sydney. But now he continually found himself questioning how much animals understood.

He uploaded his video from today's session for review and to select which frames would be best to grab for the paper. As he began watching the playback, he was pleased he could hear what everyone had said, especially Marjorie, who had a softer voice.

He could also see Sydney's interactions with Dudley very clearly. Had they been carrying on an intelligent conversation throughout the search for Norma Jean? Dogs were smart, but how much did they really know? How much could they understand? He'd read that German shepherds were considered one of the smartest breeds around. Was that because they were incredibly trainable? An Afghan hound was considered to be one of the least trainable canines. Did this mean they were dumber than German shepherds? Or maybe they were outsmarting everyone by pretending they couldn't be trained. How complex was a canine's cognition?

Keeping all of this in mind, he started the video over and watched it as if Dudley *could* understand everything Sydney said. He reacted every time she spoke to him, like when Dudley had cornered a mouse and Sydney asked if he knew anything. Even Marjorie wondered what she was talking about. Sydney said Dudley could communicate with different species. Carter knew animals had their own innate way of communicating with each other, but to what extent?

Later Sydney told Helena that Dudley was gathering intel when he was making all those odd noises. Carter thought she was apologizing for Dudley's strange behavior. Or was she? Those noises were very similar to the ones he made the day before.

If Dudley didn't know English and Sydney didn't use telepathy, then how could Sydney have declared victory before there was one? She said they knew where Zachary and Scout were before they found them in the park. And today, Sydney insisted that Dudley knew the whereabouts of Norma Jean, when it looked like the dog just wanted to kill a mouse. Only he hadn't killed the mouse.

That funny little wiener dog had found a missing cat.

CHAPTER THIRTEEN

Sydney had been packing up her things every night after work, and now it was moving day. She had everything boxed up, except for the kitchen, when she ran out of boxes.

"You arrived just in time," she said to her sister, who entered her apartment with packing material and a dozen flattened boxes.

"With all the deliveries we get, I have an endless supply." Rachael dumped them in the middle of the living room, then took a look around. "How did you pack up so quickly?"

"It's easy when you don't own much." She took her plates from the kitchen cabinets and wrapped them in paper. "Still, I worry if it's all going to fit."

"I'll help you find a place for everything, and if some of your furniture is too big, I can always store it for you in my basement." Rachael started at the other end of the kitchen and boxed the pots and pans. "Where's Dudley?"

"With Dana. She'll bring him over later today."

"It's nice that Carter's allowing you to move in early without charging you extra."

"I offered, but he's good with it, which really helps, since I'm losing money."

"Your landlady still won't give you a break?"

"She's an unhappy woman."

"I gathered that," Rachael said. "She was watching me like a hawk from the moment I stepped out of my car."

"Did she give you the third degree and ask who you were visiting?"

"Yes. I almost told her it was none of her business, but instead I said, 'I'm seeing my sister, the famous dachshund whisperer.'"

Sydney laughed. "I'm not famous yet, and I don't want to be. It's weird to read about myself."

"But look how much good is coming from it. You're not only reuniting pets with their owners, but you're getting a lot more work."

"Yeah, you know, I never thought there'd be so many animal issues in our town."

"Have you figured out why your psychic abilities are so incredible with Dudley?"

"Not yet, though I have a feeling Dudley knows more than he's willing to share. I've asked him about his past, and he's very guarded about it."

"I never knew dogs could come with baggage."

"Of course they can, especially with rescues. If you think about it, their baggage is often the reason for their behavioral issues."

"What's he like as a telepathically talking dog?"

"He's funny. He's got a very colorful personality, and he speaks with a British accent."

"Seriously?" Rachael gave her a skeptical look.

"I couldn't believe it myself."

"Maybe all UK canines can do what he does."

She laughed. "Now that's an interesting theory."

"What does Carter think about you and Dudley?'

"I think he's fascinated by our relationship. He's the one who got everything going with the in-depth interview, and now he's filming the sessions for the paper's weekly column. He's been an integral part of all of this, only I'm not sure he believes that psychic connections are real."

"If he goes to enough sessions with you, I think it will become very apparent what's really going on."

Sydney nodded. "That's what I'm hoping."

"What does he think of Dudley?"

"He seems to like him a lot."

"Is he single?"

She laughed. "Yes."

Rachael gasped. "Are you two already dating?"

"I barely know the guy."

"You saved a kid together and are moving into his guesthouse."

"True. But it's not like I know a lot about him."

"Well, you *do* know if you find him attractive, or funny, or—"

"I just agreed to get a dog. I'm not sure if I'm ready to commit to a boyfriend too."

Rachael stopped packing and studied her. "You've got to get over your relationship phobia."

"It's warranted."

The last guy she dated was Anthony Facinelli. Sydney met him at the gym when they'd both walked to the leg press machine at the same time. She'd stepped back, not wanting to get into a conversation, but he'd noticed that she'd been crying and asked if she was okay. She'd been dumped the night before. It turned out he'd been dumped the previous week, so their shared experience had them exchanging numbers. One date led to another, and she soon found him moving in with her.

Everything had been going well for a solid year. She'd actually thought he'd propose to her on her upcoming birthday. Instead, she came home early from work to find him in bed with his ex. Right then she'd convinced herself that she didn't need a guy in her life, especially when she received unconditional love from dogs.

"What happened with Anthony sucked, but not all guys are like that," Rachael insisted.

She shrugged. "I wouldn't know."

Her sister opened her mouth to object, but couldn't. Sydney always managed to choose the worst guys. Looking back, none of them had liked dogs, which should have been her first clue.

"Are you okay with losing two hundred square feet?" Rachael asked, changing the subject. "I only ask because I'm the one who brought you and Dudley together."

"If I wasn't happy with moving, I wouldn't be doing it. Besides, what I love best about the guesthouse is having access to a private backyard—especially if Dudley needs to go out in the middle of the night."

"Yeah, that's definitely an incentive to move there."

Carter was a bigger incentive, which she wanted to share

with Rachael, but she decided to wait and see what her sister's impression was of him first. She hoped Rachael would get good vibes from him in the way that she had. In truth, Sydney had never wanted to give up on dating, but the time and effort she'd put into trying to get to know someone hadn't ever panned out.

Yet there was something special about Carter. He seemed different than the others—more present and in the moment. He hadn't given her an odd look when she told him that she liked being a dog walker. He didn't appear to judge her for not having a loftier career goal. *Give it time*, the pessimistic side of her said. Whether he would simply remain the owner of her guesthouse or become something more, she didn't know. And to assume they'd end up together was premature and reckless when her heart had been broken more times than she'd ever care to admit.

"I think this move will be good for you, Syd. And I hope you keep yourself open to possibilities. Any guy who breaks a pet policy has a heart."

"He gets two points for that."

"I knew it!" A grin spread across Rachael's face. "You've already put him on Sydney's Sliding Scale. You do like him."

"I like my dentist, too, but I wouldn't date him."

"No, but you just might date your new landlord."

Sydney and Rachael made short work of packing up the kitchen while Rachael's husband, Todd, and his friend Ian loaded the U-Haul truck she'd rented for the day. Rachael rode with her across town while the guys followed in the truck.

"I've always loved this neighborhood." Rachael checked out the modest but pretty homes as they drove past them.

"Yeah, it really is a nice area." Sydney turned onto her street. "One of my clients lives three streets over. Lots of young couples seem to be moving here." She pulled up in front of Carter's house. "This is it."

Her sister looked it over. "Seems nice. He keeps his lawn and flower beds well-manicured."

"The guesthouse is even prettier," Sydney said as they got out of the car and walked up to the front. "My key is supposed to be here somewhere." She searched around the planter box.

The front door opened, startling her. "I bet you're looking for this." Carter held up a key and handed it to her. "Sorry. I forgot to set it out."

"No worries. I hope I'm not interrupting anything."

"Paying bills, so the interruption is welcome." His smile lingered as his attention remained completely on her until he heard the metallic rattle of the tailgate opening on the back of the U-Haul truck. "Let me help you get moved in."

"I'm sure you have more important things to do."

"Not really."

"Okay, well, thanks." Sydney introduced him to Rachael, who'd been hanging back, before they headed down to the truck.

"He's totally hot," Rachael whispered.

She watched Carter introduce himself to Todd and Ian. "He kinda is."

"Kinda? If you don't tell him you're available, I will."

"Would you stop? He already knows that, and please don't grill the guy in the first five minutes."

There was an explosion of laughter at the truck. "Sydney, I know this dude," Ian called out.

"Look who's racking up the points on your sliding scale," Rachael said before they joined them.

"What's this?" she asked.

"We were in the same English class in high school," Ian said.

Which meant Carter was two years older than she was. "No way." She glanced at Carter. "Were you in any of Rachael's classes?"

He studied her face. "I don't think so."

"No." Rachael tilted her head, scrutinizing him. "I would have remembered you."

"Did you go to Clearview High, too?" Carter asked Todd.

"No, Rachael and I met in the grocery store."

"I took pity on him when I saw him pick out the worst fruit."

"It was a ploy to get her to talk to me," Todd said.

"Don't believe him." Rachael rolled her eyes. "The guy knows nothing about what goes on in a kitchen. He doesn't even know how to turn on an oven."

"I do too. I just choose not to."

"I'm right there with you." Carter high-fived Todd.

"I guess that means you eat hot dogs more than you let on." Sydney's mouth twitched, teasing him.

"I'm not admitting anything," Carter said. "Though they are my go-to meal when I don't have time to cook something complicated."

"Syd's is spaghetti," Rachael offered.

"Hey! No tattling." Sydney scowled at her sister, who just laughed in return. Sydney then grabbed two boxes and led the way to her new home. As the guesthouse came into view, Sydney gasped, gazing at the stunning pop of color under her windows—petunias in a mixed arrangement of pinks, purples, reds and whites. "Carter, the window boxes are gorgeous!"

A big grin took over his face. "I thought you might like them."

Rachael was in awe, taking in all the pretty trees dotted around the property. "It's so serene back here."

"Does this mean keggers are out?" Ian asked, bringing up the rear.

"Just what Carter needs, a bunch of beer-drinking guys messing up his beautiful backyard." Rachael gave Ian a disapproving look.

Sydney opened the door and felt like she was home.

"Very cute," Rachael said, taking a box of dishes into the kitchen.

"I've scrubbed this place from top to bottom, so you don't have to waste time doing it again." Carter set his boxes just outside the kitchen area.

"Dude, you're an awesome landlord," Ian said. "Got any other rentals? My place hasn't been cleaned in months."

"Yeah, we know." Todd put a hand to his nose, which brought a protest by Ian.

Sydney caught Carter's eye. "Thank you. I really appreciate everything you've done for me."

His mouth rose into a half-smile. "It was nothing."

She knew how long it took to plant flowers and to clean a home, no matter how small. It was more than nothing.

The guys moved in the furniture, and everything fit nicely except for a table and an armoire, which Rachael and Todd said they'd store in their basement. They took a break for lunch, and Sydney bought everyone pizza and cold drinks. Carter seemed to fit right in. After lunch they unloaded the remainder of her belongings before Ian's girlfriend texted, reminding him of their early dinner plans.

"Are you sure you don't want Todd and me to stay to help you finish unpacking?" Rachael asked.

"I think I can manage. You all went above and beyond. Thank you so much."

"Anytime." Rachael gave her a hug. "Enjoy. Hope we see you again, Carter."

"You will."

"Yeah, Carter, hit me up next week, and we'll catch a game or something," Ian said.

"Sounds good."

After they left, she closed the door and turned toward Carter. "You, in particular, went above and beyond. You made this quaint little guesthouse feel like home."

His mouth curved into a soft smile. "That was the goal—to make you feel comfortable."

She took a step closer to him. "I may never want to leave." She touched his arm, and he held her gaze. He moved into her as if he was about to kiss her when her phone rang, making her jump. Carter chuckled, equally surprised.

"It's Dana," she said. "I'll only be a minute." As she talked to Dana, she stole a quick glance at Carter. He was fidgeting, no doubt wondering, like she was, how they were going to get back to the moment.

"Yes, I'm here," Sydney said into the phone. "Do you still have the address? Okay, I'll see you in a few." She hung up and her shoulders fell, knowing their moment was lost. "Dana is on her way with Dudley."

She saw disappointment in his eyes, but he covered it quickly. "Then we better get moving. Which box has his stuff? I can get him set up."

In that moment, he warmed her heart more than he'd ever

know. Any guy who thought of her dog as a priority would always be at the top of her list. "That's sweet of you, but Dana's bringing all of it with her."

"Oh." He looked around. "How about I start on these boxes marked for the living room?"

This guy was so thoughtful. How was he still single? "I don't want to blow your *entire* Saturday."

He shook his head, dismissing her comment. "Two can unpack faster than one."

"Okay, but dinner's on me—though it might have to be delivery."

He flashed her a big smile. "Deal."

CHAPTER FOURTEEN

Sydney felt giddy knowing that she and Carter would be spending the evening together. "Guess I better unpack my kitchen or we're not going to have any dishes to eat off of."

"We can always use mine," he said.

She didn't know how to respond. Not only was she feeling comfortable in her new home, but she was feeling incredibly comfortable with him being around. Was it too fast? Was he thinking the same thing or was he just being nice? Was he about to kiss her before Dana called, or had she imagined it? He was so focused on the task at hand that she couldn't tell.

He pulled the tape off one of the boxes and began unpacking her books and knickknacks. He unwrapped the first two items and laughed. "Did you get these because of Dudley?" He held up two bookends in the shape of a dachshund.

"Aren't those cute?" She found the dish box and began unpacking them. "One of my clients gave them to me for Christmas."

"I'm sure Dudley will approve."

"No doubt."

Carter's Ring app alerted him that someone was at his front door. "I think you have a delivery." He hit speaker and passed it to Sydney who saw Dana standing at the door holding Dudley.

"Hi, Dana. I'm in the back. I'll be right there." She hurried out the side gate to the front door. "Welcome!"

Finally! I was beginning to think you abandoned me.

"Never." She picked him up and gave him a bunch of kisses, which made his tail wag feverishly.

"Never what?" Dana asked.

"Oh. Never did I see a happier dog," she said as Carter appeared from around the corner. "Dana, do you know Carter?"

"Nice to meet you." Dana set Dudley on the ground. "I'm happy to know that my mom was able to help both you and Sydney."

"She did a great job finding me the perfect tenant," he said.

Dudley barked.

"I stand corrected," Carter replied. "I meant to say two perfect tenants."

Dudley wagged his tail, then rolled over in the grass with a toothy smile on his face.

"He is one happy dog." Dana chuckled. "Sydney, I brought everything I bought for him, but you don't have to take it all if you don't have room."

"Let's have a look." Sydney motioned for Dudley to follow them.

Dana opened the back of her SUV. There were two small beds, his wire enclosure, and a couple of large boxes. Dana opened one of the boxes. "He's got food, bowls, an extra leash and harness, a hairbrush, a toothbrush, and some other little things. The other box has his toys and blankets."

"You hit the jackpot, Dudley. This is all great," Sydney said. "I can use everything."

Not the prison. You can let her keep that.

"I might not need the enclosure though, since my place is a studio."

"Then I'll donate it to a rescue organization," Dana said.

Carter reached in and grabbed both boxes, while Sydney and Dana took the beds. "Let's get you settled in, little man." Carter led the way.

"Oh, how lovely." Dana admired the idyllic backyard and the cottage-like guesthouse.

Dudley immediately went running after a squirrel.

"Dudley, be nice," Sydney called out, not sure if his natural instincts would suddenly take over and he'd try to kill it.

Dudley looked back at her. *I'm just going to say hi and tell him I'm the king of my people.*

"Okay, well, speak quietly. That means no annoying barking."

When I speak, all wish to listen, therefore my voice could never be annoying.

Dana set the box of toys down on Sydney's porch. "He looked like he actually understood you."

"Dogs understand a lot more than we think they do."

"I'm so glad this worked out," Dana said. "Thank you for taking such good care of him. Call me if you have any questions."

"I will. And congratulations on the new account. Rachael told me you got it."

"Thank you. It will keep us very busy for the next few months. Bye, Dudley," Dana called out, but he was too busy talking to the squirrel.

"Dudley, Dana is trying to say goodbye."

Tell her bye for me. Freedolin is telling me a joke.

Sydney eyed the squirrel who was chattering away two feet above his head. "Dogs. They have a one-track mind." She shrugged, a little embarrassed.

"I'll walk you out," Carter said.

As soon as they headed out the gate, Sydney went over to Dudley and stood in front of him. "We're going to have to lay down some ground rules. You need to be on your best behavior, and you've got to give me a break with your incessant chatter when I'm trying to talk to someone."

It isn't incessant. I'm merely engaging in conversation. You need to work on dividing your attention better.

"Come again?"

Think of me as a child trying to talk to his mother when she's on a conference call with her boss.

"You're admitting that you can be annoying."

I'm admitting that it can be a challenge to split one's focus.

"Then you can help me out. I haven't told Carter yet."

"Told me what?" Carter asked hesitantly.

She whipped around and wasn't sure if his look of concern was because he caught her having a conversation with Dudley, or that he was worried about what she was hiding from him.

Awwwkward.

"Thanks to you," she said under her breath.

We're living here now, Sydney. We can't play charades forever. The sooner you tell him the better.

"Fine." Sydney sighed, then set her gaze on Carter. "You've wanted to know exactly how Dudley and I communicate with one another? Well, the official term for what I am is an animal communicator, and though my ability is so-so with most animals, my connection with Dudley is exceptional."

He shrugged. "Isn't that another term for a dog trainer?"

"No. The way we communicate is not at all like a typical dog trainer." She paused, wondering how she was going to explain it to him. "For one, we don't use hand signals."

"I gathered that. I studied the recording from Norma Jean's session, and I never saw any signals of any kind between you and Dudley. So how *do* you communicate with each other?"

She glanced at Dudley who was also staring at her. *Just tell him. It's not a big deal.*

"Okay." She put her attention back on Carter. "An animal communicator is an intuitive. He speaks to me telepathically."

Carter laughed, but she only glared at him. "Oh. You're being serious," he said.

"Very."

His eyes widened as he took a step back. "You're telling me you're a pet *psychic?*"

The way he said it meant he didn't believe in psychic ability one bit. "Sort of." She shrugged, as if it wasn't a big deal, and then she was quick to say, "We are all born with psychic abilities. Anyone who is open to it can do it. I learned how to communicate telepathically, and you can too."

"Who told you that? The person who took your money?"

She refused to take offense. At one time, she'd thought the same thing. "Look it up." She motioned to his phone. "Go on. See what the internet says about animal communicators."

Carter pulled out his phone and typed in a search. His face registered surprise as he scrolled through a list of articles and pet psychic businesses. "An animal communicator, also known as an animal intuitive or pet psychic, will telepathically connect to your beloved pet, even over the phone." He gave her a skeptical look.

He's not buying it.

"It involves working with energy," she said, "so yes, it does work over the phone."

Tell him about Taffy, and how you helped her over the phone.

"How long have you been playing Dr. Dolittle?"

She ignored the dig. "I haven't been doing animal communication for that long. As you already know, I've never charged money for it, like the pet psychics you see online."

"Why not? If it's legit?"

"Because it's stressful to have someone crying and begging you to find their dog that ran away from home, or to find a miracle cure for their cat who's been diagnosed with cancer."

"Someone actually thought you had a cure for cancer?"

She nodded, and thinking back on it made her eyes water.

Carter noticed, and the smile fell from his face. He shifted, finally seeming to take her seriously, and shoved his hands in his pockets. "Were you able to find the lost dog?"

"I psychically connected to him and asked him to send me mental pictures of what he was seeing. I received images of trees and dirt, so no, I didn't find him."

"Sorry to hear that. I can see why that would be stressful," he said, sympathetically.

"If I'd known Dudley then, the outcome would have been different, like it was with Norma Jean."

"How so?"

"Because Dudley is an exceptional dog. Our line of communication is as clear as you and me speaking. He can retrieve more vital information than I can, and is able to pass it to me. When I tried to telepathically speak to Norma Jean, she didn't respond because she was too scared. I tried a few times but was shut out. I thought the whole session was going to be a complete failure. Then Dudley suggested we step outside, and in doing so, I finally connected with her. I asked her what she was seeing. That's when I got a message from her. She was seeing wood with holes."

"The lattice."

She nodded. "A bit easier to find than trees and dirt, but would we have seen the lattice without Dudley's help? Probably not. Marjorie already said she'd gone over to her neighbors, so I wouldn't have started the search there. It was Dudley, not me, who led us to her."

"How did Dudley know where she was?"

She hesitated before answering. Should she simply tell him that all animals communicate with each other and leave it at that? She could, but he'd already asked about Dudley's strange noises. Now was the time to tell him the whole truth, not just half of it. "He talked to the mouse."

Carter shook his head, chuckling to himself.

"I know. It sounds even crazier than me being a pet psychic, but it's the truth. Dudley is fluent in a thousand languages. He spoke to the mouse, who had seen Norma Jean, and then Dudley spoke to me."

Carter scratched the back of his head. "From an impartial observer, he looked like he wanted to kill it."

I'm far above such vulgarity.

"But he didn't, did he? The mouse led Dudley and all of us to Norma Jean."

Carter took a deep breath, switching his focus between her and Dudley, vacillating between wanting to believe what she was saying and dismissing it completely. "How did Pepper back out of the tree?"

"Dudley talked him down to where the forestry crew could retrieve him."

Carter studied Dudley. "Was he the one who found Zachary so quickly?" She nodded. He ran his hand over his mouth, as if he were coming to terms with the truth. "How exactly does it work?"

"For me, I need to see the animal, either in person or in a photo. If it's a photo, it must only be of the animal and no one else, so I don't mistakenly pick up on another's energy. I introduce myself to the pet if we've never met. Once he or she feels comfortable talking to me, I begin to ask questions."

"And they answer?"

"Yes."

"How can you hear them by looking at a picture?"

"Usually, I get images that pop into my head, or I hear a few words from them."

He suddenly stiffened. "Did you do this to me the other day when we were discussing telepathy?"

She laughed. "No. It was just a guess. I don't psychically read people. I tried a couple of times, but I didn't have much success."

"Why not?"

"People hide their emotions or lie. Some block what they're really thinking or feeling while animals don't. I have no desire to try to read people's minds. Animal communication is already draining enough. I imagine it would be worse with people."

"How is it draining?"

"Because it's energy work. It's like I have to work outside of my body, from the top of my head."

"I don't follow."

She paced a few steps, figuring out how to explain it so that he could understand. "You know the feeling you get when you're trying to remember something, and you're wracking your brain attempting to retrieve it?"

"Yeah."

"It's like that—a feeling of heavy, intense concentration. Try it for an hour and see how it feels."

"That would definitely be exhausting."

"I sometimes get lightheaded."

"Did you connect to Scout in the park?"

"Yes. I asked him where he was, and he sent me pictures of trees. I asked for more information, and all he said was 'up and down.'"

He squinted at her. "Up and down?"

"It didn't make sense to me, either. That's also part of the problem. A lot of animals only give a portion of the information, so I don't have the whole picture. But now that we found him, what Scout gave me makes perfect sense. They went up the trail and down the side of the embankment."

"Interesting."

I think he's starting to believe you.

Carter let out a long exhale. "Did you ask Scout anything else?"

"I asked if Zachary was with him, and he sent me an image of Zachary, so I assumed he was. I asked if he could tell me what was around him, and he sent me more pictures of trees."

"Not exactly detailed information."

"Not in the least, so you can see why I decided not to pursue a career in animal communication. But then I met Dudley. He's like nothing I've come across. He understands English perfectly. It's not a struggle with him. I can telepathically hear him, in his own voice, so there isn't any ambiguity."

"You actually hear a dog speaking English?"

"Yes."

"So when I said it looked like he understood everything you were saying, I was right?"

"He understands everything you're saying now. Go ahead. Test him."

"What?"

"Talk to him like you're talking to me."

"Okay." He made eye contact with the dachshund. "Dudley, turn around three times and bark once."

I'm not a show pony.

"Dudley, seriously. Now is not the time to be stubborn."

"What did he say?"

"He says he's not a show pony."

"A dog with a sense of humor."

More like an evolved sentient being who finds humor in the simplicity of man.

"Yes, he does have a sense of humor and quite the personality."

Carter cracked a smile. "Of course, you can just be saying that to cover for him not understanding."

"Dudley. Come on. You wanted me to tell him, so you need to participate in proving to him that this is real."

Oh, all right. Just know that this is beneath me.

"He said he'll do it, but it's beneath him."

Dudley turned around three times and barked once.

Carter let out an explosive laugh. "Look at that! Wait? Did you signal him?"

Sydney groaned. "How? I didn't know what you were going to ask."

149

Carter eyed Dudley. "Run to the stacked firewood and back."

What do I get out of this?

"He wants to know what he gets out of this."

"I bought a package of healthy beef hot dogs and can make you one, if it's okay with your mom."

Dudley charged to the firewood and back before Sydney could respond.

He threw his hands on top of his head. "I can't believe I'm seeing this. He really understands English."

"Some experts believe dogs can understand as much as a five-year-old child, but Dudley is far beyond that. He's fluent."

Where's my hot dog?

She let out a huff. "You need to watch your weight."

I just burned off what I'll be eating.

She laughed. "Not even close."

"Mind putting me in the loop?" Carter asked.

"Right. Sorry. He's looking for the hot dog you promised."

"Can I give him one?"

"Yes, but Dudley, you can only have half, and we'll save the other half for later."

I knew I was going to get shortchanged on this deal.

"C'mon, little guy. Let's get you that treat."

Sydney and Dudley followed Carter into the kitchen where he filled a small pan with water and set it on the stove to boil. He seemed calmer now. Did this mean he believed her?

"How exactly did Dudley know where Zachary was?" he asked. "Did he have a conversation with Scout, too?"

"No. He actually spoke to the wildlife about their whereabouts. Dudley can hear other animals telepathically, but it's much easier for him to speak to them verbally, in their own language."

"Are you trying to tell me that all those weird noises he was making with Pepper and Norma Jean actually represent a language?"

"Yes. He spoke to them in their feline language, and the mouse in, well I guess, mouse language."

"Are you messing with me?"

"No, I'm being serious."

Carter went silent as he waited for the water to boil, and she wasn't sure what to make of it. He studied Dudley, then said, "You can hear his thoughts, but he can't hear yours?"

"It seems strange to me, too, but that's what he tells me. That's why I have to answer him verbally."

"Are you able to speak to wildlife as well?"

"I've tried a couple times, but I haven't had much luck with it. Dudley loves talking to everyone. Earlier today, he was introducing himself to a squirrel, apparently in squirrel language."

Carter laughed, pinching his nose. "I'm being punked, aren't I?"

"No. I'm telling you the truth. Look, I know it's a lot to take in. Like I said, I was shocked myself. Dudley is the only animal I've met who can do this. In the park, he talked to a squirrel who told him he'd seen a boy and his dog run up the trail. Dudley then talked to a bird and asked her to go search for him while he relaxed in the grass. When the bird came back and told him where they were, we took off."

He went silent again, as if he was replaying the whole thing in his head. "And that's why you told Dudley to tell Pupperton what to do."

"Yes. Communication with Pupperton takes time for me, but with Dudley, it's as instant as you and me talking."

"Maybe you should learn how to speak English, Dudley."

"Hello," Dudley said with a rolling whine.

Carter's mouth dropped open.

Sydney stared at him, equally shocked. "Can you speak full sentences?"

I'm afraid not. Believe me, I've tried.

"He said no," she told Carter. "Can you say anything else?"

"I wuv you," Dudley vocalized.

"Aww." Sydney picked him up. "I wuv you too."

Carter shook his head, staring at Dudley. "I have a pet psychic and a talking dog as my new tenants. No problem."

A least I'm not a snake.

Sydney laughed. "Dudley said, at least he's not a snake."

Carter shuddered. "You wouldn't be moving in if you were." He dropped the hot dog in the boiling water but appeared to be lost in thought, and she wondered if she should be worried. He shot her a quick glance and caught her staring. "Were you just reading my mind?"

"No." She raised a brow. "But I *was* wondering what you were thinking."

A tiny smile played on his face before he broke eye contact. "I was thinking that I was already getting hungry."

He'd clearly changed the subject, so she let it go. "I can fix that."

While they waited for their food delivery, Sydney showed Carter a video of two German shepherds teaching a deer how to go through their doggy door. Carter laughed, and his arm brushed up against her, awakening her senses.

Dudley barked. *Might I have my hot dog before you two get cozy with one another?*

Sydney cleared her throat and set aside her phone. "That's not going to happen."

"What's he saying?"

"Uh…he's afraid you forgot about his hot dog."

You make a lousy interpreter.

"You might speak a lot of languages, Dudley, but you apparently don't know how to tell time," Carter said. "You've got one more minute to wait on the dog."

Ha-ha. He's already my manservant and doesn't even know it. Who's the dummy now?

"He said, 'Thank you for making it for me. I can't wait.'"

Carter bent down. "You're very welcome, little man."

That's not what I said. I— Dudley involuntarily pulled his mouth back as Carter gave him a scratch up and down his back. *That's the spot, yeah. Good boy, Carter.*

It didn't take long for Dudley to weasel his way into Carter's heart. He was smiling the entire time he watched Dudley wolf down half of his hot dog. When Dudley finished, he looked up at Carter with his big brown eyes, and Sydney knew she'd be battling both of them on what and how much Dudley could eat.

"Can he have the other half?" Carter asked as Dudley whined in agreement, wagging his tail.

She gave the dachshund a stern look. "Hot dogs are not meant for canines. You only got one tonight because it was a special treat."

Then allow me to have the entire thing, not a mere morsel.

"You're overweight."

Quite uncalled for. I don't possess a lovely coat to keep me warm during the cold Minnesota nights.

"It's May."

Need I remind you that I was out on the street? This is my winter fat.

The doorbell rang, which set off Dudley barking like a ferocious beast.

"It's just our food, little man." Carter went to the door.

Sydney grabbed hold of Dudley so he couldn't follow him. "Calm down."

He might need protection. Dudley kept barking until Carter reappeared with a delivery bag in hand, and his nose went straight in the air. *I'm not smelling anything good.*

"We're having salads."

So not my cup of tea. Dudley trotted over to the rug in the hallway and lay down for a short nap.

Carter took note of Dudley's disinterest. "I take it he doesn't care for salad."

"Not in the least."

"I can't get over how much he understands." Carter unpacked the bag, then got them drinks and utensils before sitting down. "You really think I could learn to do what you do?"

She nodded. "I can teach you what I know."

"I'd like that." He took a sip of water and glanced at Dudley. "But one thing doesn't add up. If he can understand and speak a thousand languages, and telepathically speak to you, how is it that he can't hear your thoughts?"

"I wish I knew. He doesn't know the reason, either." She drizzled dressing over her chicken Caesar, then stirred it in. "Makes me wonder how many animals I tried but failed to get a connection to and couldn't because they weren't telepathic like Dudley."

"You bring up a good point. Are there more dogs like Dudley, or is he one of a kind?"

Sydney looked over at her dachshund lying on the floor, eyes closed, and she had no idea if he was asleep or just faking it. "I asked him once, and he said that no one was smarter or a better conversationalist than he was."

Carter chuckled. "How many animals have you tried communicating with?"

"I'd say maybe forty or fifty, but none of them came close to his advanced level."

Carter took a bite of his Cobb salad. "How old is he?"

"Another question he refused to answer, but I'm guessing around five or six."

"I thought he was younger."

She leaned over and whispered, "He's getting a few gray hairs under his chin."

Carter studied him, then nodded. "If what you're saying is true, you two are exceptional. I thought how you found Zachary and Norma Jean was amazing, but this? You and Dudley have shattered everything the world knows about communication between man and canine."

Woman and canine, Dudley corrected as he sat up, fully awake.

Sydney smiled, taking a drink of water.

"He said something, didn't he?"

She nodded. "He corrected you by saying, 'woman and canine.'"

"You're absolutely right, Dudley. My apologies, Sydney. But seriously, have you thought about what this means? The world should know about you two."

And become a guinea pig for mad scientists? That's a hard pass.

"He's afraid someone will do research on him, and I happen to agree. Dogs, cats, monkeys. Their stories don't end well when they're brought to a lab," she said. "But I do want us to make a difference. In addition to helping the people and pets here in Pinecrest, I think our unique set of skills could help where others have failed. We might be able to train the untrainable. We could help troubled dogs get adopted and also help those already in homes with pet parents who might be a bit clueless."

"Or parents who might overindulge their dog who then becomes a brat." Carter took a drink.

"Are you by chance talking about Penelope?"

"Maybe."

"Dudley and I definitely need to meet her. What kind of dog is she?"

"A Cavalier King Charles spaniel."

Dudley snapped to attention. *They are the most gorgeous creatures in existence. Yes, we must meet with Miss Penelope immediately.*

Sydney laughed. "Apparently, Dudley is attracted to the breed and would be happy to speak with Penelope."

"Is that so?" Carter met Dudley's gaze. "I'm not surprised to hear you have an eye for the ladies, though she's a bit haughty I'm afraid."

No creature is immune to my charm.

"He says that no creature is immune to his charm."

Carter chuckled. "While you're winning her over, can you throw in a good word for me?"

You keep doling out hot dogs, and I'll have her loving you by the time we leave.

"He said he'd be happy to."

CHAPTER FIFTEEN

As much as they could have talked all night, Sydney seemed anxious to get her place set up. Carter had offered to help, but she declined, saying he'd done way too much already.

"Call me if you need anything at all." He opened the kitchen door for her and Dudley.

"I will," she said. "Thanks again for all of your help."

"No problem. Sleep tight, little man."

Dudley barked, then trotted to the guesthouse.

He watched Sydney carry on a conversation with Dudley as they went home. If it had been anyone else, he would have immediately dismissed her claims, but he'd seen them in action. Her explanation, as fantastic as it sounded, was the only one that answered his lingering questions. Still, it was difficult for him to wholeheartedly believe that she could communicate telepathically, and that a dog could understand a thousand languages.

Carter closed the back door and sat in front of his computer. The more he thought about it, the more absurd it sounded. But if her method for finding lost animals worked, who was he to judge what she believed? *He* didn't have to believe it.

Or did he? If he refused to accept her explanation, he'd be left with even more unanswered questions. How did Dudley know to turn around three times and bark, or run to the stack of firewood and back? The little dachshund definitely understood a lot more than the average dog, but to what degree?

Was a canine capable of understanding English fluently? If that was possible, and Sydney was being straight with him, was she telling him everything Dudley was saying? It felt weird to listen to her react to something he couldn't hear himself. It reminded him of listening to a child speak to an imaginary friend.

It was ironic how he had fought Russell on covering animal-related stories, because now, if true, he had the most remarkable story unfolding inside his guesthouse. How had Dudley learned to communicate so well? Were there others like him? What was his background? The big question was—were there geniuses in the animal world? If so, then humans had done them a tremendous disservice.

He searched online and began reading about animal communication. Sydney said anyone with an open mind could learn to do it. If he could become as skilled as Sydney, then he wouldn't have to wonder. He could talk directly to Dudley and find out for himself just how much the dog knew and understood.

He watched a few pet psychic videos that seemed completely bogus. The so-called psychics were telling pet owners all about their beloved pets, and who was going to dispute them? Their pets couldn't talk back.

Trying to keep an open mind, he continued to read about how it worked, but much of it seemed like a bunch of new age mumbo jumbo. Could he truly learn how to connect with an animal like Sydney had? He highly doubted it. The articles talked about getting in the right headspace to do this type of work, and he didn't think he could go there. He didn't meditate, he couldn't empty his mind and think of nothing, he wasn't susceptible to the power of suggestion.

But he could find a clue in a story that others overlooked. He could pull out the one disingenuous statement that would unravel an otherwise solid story. And he may have found a flaw in Sydney's. Through the dozens of articles he'd just read on how animal communication worked, there was one point pet psychics agreed upon—all life forms had the innate ability to speak telepathically.

As a journalist, that absolute was up for debate, but it didn't make sense for Dudley. If he was so smart and so good at communicating with Sydney, then he should be able to read her thoughts. Why was Sydney saying he couldn't? Was it so she could put on a show while she attempted to locate the missing person or pet? If she was telling the truth, and their abilities were real, then was Dudley telling *her* the truth? Was he pretending, or was he truly unable to read her thoughts? What if he had been telepathic at one time, but something had happened to sever that ability?

From now on, Carter would be looking at everything they did in a different light. He couldn't wait to document another session with them. Russell's idea of a fun, light, Friday column was anything but. It was now a serious business. Either Sydney had figured out a clever way to market herself, or she was part of a remarkable evolution in interspecies communication, and Carter was going to be there to document all of it.

I need a lift, please. Dudley set his front paws on the side of Sydney's couch, waiting for her to help him.

Sydney scooped him up and set him next to the armrest. "No jumping," she reminded him before she continued to unpack boxes.

When are we seeing Penelope?

"As soon as Carter talks to his mom, but I wouldn't get too excited. She might already have a boyfriend."

I highly doubt that. You humans constantly interfere with our love lives.

"Oh?"

How many dogs lunge on walks because they want to say hi to someone they're attracted to?

She hadn't thought of that. "A lot?"

A disgraceful amount.

"Sorry, but owners don't know if another dog will be friendly to theirs, and they aren't in tune with their fur babies like we are with each other. Besides, dogs have plenty of time to meet one another with dog parks, birthday parties, and playdates."

When's my playdate with Penelope?

Sydney groaned. He was like a dog with a bone. "I'll ask Carter about it tomorrow."

He watched as she put fresh sheets on her bed. *You fancy him, don't you?*

"What's not to like? He's a very nice guy." She unpacked her toiletries so she could take a shower.

Would you date him?

Her eyes widened. "I am not having relationship talks with you."

We just were—about Penelope and me.

"All males, no matter the species, have a one-track mind."

I'm just weighing my options.

"Regarding what?"

You and Carter. Three's a crowd.

"That's ridiculous."

Need I remind you why I'm living with you instead of Dana?

"You said you were figuring out a way to leave her."

Before she *left* me. Dudley quickly turned away, but not fast enough. For the first time, she saw vulnerability in his eyes. *None of that matters now. Her loss is clearly your gain.*

He was trying to be funny, but she wasn't going to let him dismiss his comment so easily.

"Hey." She went to him and set him on her lap. "I wouldn't dream of ever abandoning you. You should know that by now. I barely knew you, and I moved out of my apartment so that I could keep you. And as for Carter, anyone can see that he already loves you, so you're not going anywhere. Okay?"

People say that a lot.

"Like who? Were you abandoned by a couple or a family who promised the same thing?"

I don't recall, and I'm absolutely knackered. He wiggled to get down, so she lowered him to the floor. *Good night, Sydney.*

She'd definitely touched a nerve, and wondered what he'd gone through. She needed to find out so she could help him feel safe and secure. But it wouldn't be tonight. He had already shut her out with lightning speed.

CHAPTER SIXTEEN

Sydney awoke to the sound of birds chirping, and it was glorious. No loud banging from an apartment above her, no doors slamming, just wonderful sounds of nature. She took a deep breath in, then rolled over and yelped. Dudley was on her bed, inches from her face, staring at her. "How did you get up here?"

The two boxes at the end of the bed are just the right height for steps.

She leaned over, saw the boxes, and made a mental note to unpack them sooner than later. "Why are you in my bed?"

I couldn't sleep with all the racket.

"What racket?"

The birds.

"You don't like chirping birds?"

Perhaps I would, if I didn't know what was being said. Two males are fighting over territory. A female bird is yelling at her mate to go out and get breakfast for their babies. Another is complaining about the lack of room in their nest.

"Oh wow. I had no idea. I'm glad I don't understand bird. But speaking of breakfast, let's get you fed, and then we'll go for a walk."

I'm afraid I need to go out now.

"Okay, but go in the corner like we talked about, so you don't kill Carter's grass." She cracked open the door. "No barking. Carter might still be asleep."

Dudley grumbled something that she couldn't quite make out. She quickly got dressed in case she needed to run out after him, but he trotted back before she could put on her shoes.

How about serving me the other half of my hot dog?

"You need a balanced diet." She measured out kibble into his bowl and set it in front of him.

This is a pathetic breakfast. How about eggs and bacon?

"That would be nice, but even *I'm* not getting eggs and bacon. I still need to get to the grocery store." She held up a protein bar. "Here's *my* breakfast."

He stared at the bowl in disgust.

"I'd love for you to be able to eat people food, but you're stuck in a canine body, and canines have different nutritional needs than people. I'm sorry, but Dana bought you one of the highest quality kibbles on the market. If you really hate it, we can talk about switching you to something else later."

Later, as in this afternoon, when you buy me a steak at the store?

"Dream on. But do you know what I *could* buy if you don't eat what's in front of you? Cheap, terrible tasting kibble."

Dudley grumbled, stared at the kibble in his bowl, then slowly ate it.

She fought back a laugh before she went into the bathroom to fix her hair and throw on some makeup. "Ready for a long walk?" she asked as she came back out.

How am I to exercise on a full stomach? It's Sunday, which means it's time to lounge around all day.

"C'mon, King Durlindemore, you don't want your people to see you out of shape, do you?"

They won't if I stay in here.

She sighed, realizing how lucky she was that Dudley wasn't a Saint Bernard. He refused to get up, so she picked him up and set him on his feet in order to slip on his harness. When she opened the door, she saw Carter coming out of his kitchen door.

"Morning, Sydney, Dudley."

He was clean shaven and his hair looked slightly damp from a shower. "Got a minute?"

"Sure." She walked over with Dudley, and she could smell a fresh, woody scent of cedarwood on Carter, which made her want to get closer to him.

"A friend of mine just called me in a panic. She's lost her engagement ring, and asked if I knew how to get in touch with you. She's been reading about you in the paper and wondered if you two could find inanimate objects."

"I don't know. Can we?" She looked to Dudley.

If an animal or insect happened to be in the vicinity when the woman managed to lose it, then yes.

"Seriously? You can communicate with an insect?"

Naturally. They have a very small vocabulary.

"Okay, great." She looked at Carter. "Does your friend know where she lost it or could it be anywhere?"

"She was in the backyard."

Backyards are my specialty. Dudley rubbed his face in the grass, then rolled over on his back, basking in the morning sun.

"Dudley's confident we can find it, but I need to take him for a quick walk first."

Why? I can certainly take myself for a walk. But not right now. I'm busy sunbathing.

"You need to exercise every day," she said.

Carter stood over Dudley. "I take it he's not seeing eye to eye on your idea of a walk."

"Maybe you can talk some sense into him."

"Hey, buddy." Carter bent down and gave him a tummy rub. "Sydney's right. You need to exercise to stay healthy."

Would you tell him to move? He's blocking my sun.

"What's he saying?"

"He's not convinced."

"Okay, well, I was thinking of watching a movie tonight on my comfy couch with a snuggly blanket, but only those who exercise are invited."

Dudley's eyes popped open. *Are hot dogs on the snack menu?*

"No," she told him, then glanced at Carter. "He attempted to negotiate for another hot dog, but as we discussed, Dudley, hot dogs are reserved for special treats."

Carter rubbed his chin. "You know, he still has the other half in the fridge from last night, so technically he's not eating another whole hot dog."

Dudley rolled over and got to his feet. *Good on you, Carter. He's quite right, you know. Besides, wasting perfectly delicious food is a terrible thing.*

"You two are unbelievable." She threw her hands on her hips. "Fine. But this is it with the hot dogs."

We'll negotiate that later. Dudley trotted to the gate, then looked back at them. *Are we going or what?*

Carter chuckled. "At least you're getting him to exercise."

"I won a tiny battle over how many more to come?" She gave him an exhausted look.

Carter laughed. "He's quite the little manipulator, isn't he?"

"Look who's talking."

After their short walk, Sydney helped Dudley into the back of Carter's car, then hopped in the passenger seat, and they were on their way.

"As much as I'd like to record this session for the column, my friend asked to keep this to ourselves. She doesn't want her fiancé to know about the lost—but hopefully only misplaced—ring."

"Not a problem for me or Dudley. We can do our job with or without cameras."

But not without treats.

"Noted."

"Did he say something?" Carter asked.

"He was reminding me that he won't work unless treats are involved."

Carter smiled. "Sure. No problem, Dudley. I gave Sydney a whole bunch of diet treats." He eyed him in the rearview mirror.

Do you eat diet hot dogs?

Carter quickly glanced at her for a translation.

"He wants to know if you eat diet hot dogs."

Carter laughed as he turned down his friend's street. "Fill me in on how this will work."

"If your friend has a pet, Dudley will talk to him or her about the engagement ring."

"And if she doesn't?"

"Dudley will talk to the wildlife."

"What if the wildlife can't help?"

"I don't know." Sydney turned and looked at Dudley. "Do you want to answer that?"

It means I'll have to do some real work and search for it on my own.

"He's confident he'll be able to find it on his own."

"This I've got to see." Carter pulled into a circular drive in front of a gorgeous mansion.

Quite lovely. When shall we move in?

"Yes, it's a very nice place," Sydney answered Dudley as they got out. "What does your friend do for a living, if you don't mind my asking?"

"Tessa created a line of clothing for young moms, and her fiancé is in commercial real estate."

The door opened and a pretty brunette greeted them. "Thank you so much for coming."

"Tessa, this is Sydney and Dudley."

"It's so nice to meet you. Amazing how you found Zachary and Scout, and helped Pepper out of that enormous pine tree." Tessa snapped her fingers at her own dog. "Kahlua, get back."

A shy brindle terrier mix cowered behind Tessa. "Hi, Kahlua." Sydney held out her hand for the dog to sniff. Kahlua hesitantly inched toward her, but then got a whiff of Dudley and started barking. "It's okay, Kahlua. It's just Dudley."

"Let me put her in the other room." Tessa led Kahlua away before Sydney could ask her to stay.

Sydney eyed Dudley anxiously.

Perhaps we won't require Kahlua.

"Sorry about that," Tessa said, returning. "Now, what can I do to help?"

"You said you sort of know where the ring is?" Sydney asked.

"Yes, follow me." She led them out to a massive backyard that extended into a heavily wooded area. "It's out here, somewhere."

Not what Sydney had expected. How were they ever going to find it? "Do you remember what you were doing before you noticed it was missing?"

"I threw a toy for Kahlua, and it flung off my finger." Tessa teared up. "We just got engaged last night. The ring is too big, and my fiancé is coming home at lunchtime, specifically to take me to the jeweler to have it resized. I knew I shouldn't have worn it, and now I've lost it." Her voice broke with emotion.

"It's okay, Tessa. We're going to help you find it," she said confidently.

"I've got a metal detector in the trunk of my car," Carter said. "I'll be right back."

"Do you remember where you were standing when you threw the toy?" Sydney asked.

"Let's see." Tessa walked away from her, then looked back. "It could be in this area." She walked another twenty feet. "Or over here. I panicked, and now I don't remember exactly."

The human is of no help. I must now speak with Kahlua.

"Did Carter tell you how Dudley and I work?"

"No, but I read all the articles about you. Seems like you two not only work well together but have a great sense of the situation."

"That's a good way of putting it. I'm an animal communicator, and so is Dudley. We can actually communicate with other animals. Can you bring Kahlua back out?"

"Oh, she doesn't like other dogs."

"Dudley will calm her down, I promise. He's a very good communicator, and he'll be able to talk to her."

"What do you mean? How is Dudley going to talk to her?"

"It's easier to show you than to explain it."

Tessa looked more anxious than she already was. "I took Kahlua out of a shelter six months ago, and she didn't even know how to walk on a leash. She's afraid of everything and has a lot of issues. As you saw, she doesn't like strangers or other dogs. I really don't think she'll be calm enough for you to be able to talk to her."

"I understand your concern, but how about we try it for a couple of minutes?"

She sighed. "I'll go get her."

As soon as Tessa went back inside, Sydney tried to telepathically reach Kahlua to let her know what was going on, but the dog was too wary of her and didn't respond.

"Are you sure about this?" she asked Dudley.

I'm King of the Dachshunds. I can certainly talk to a skittish terrier.

Tessa brought her terrier out, and the second Kahlua saw

Dudley, she began lunging and barking at him. Dudley held his ground and barked back.

"This is a bad idea!" Tessa yelled over the noise. As she attempted to pull her dog back into the house, the terrier abruptly stopped barking.

Dudley barked a few more times, then started making long whiny sounds along with a few sneezes. Kahlua cocked her head, sat, whined back, then lowered her head.

"What is happening?" Tessa asked with a stunned expression on her face.

"Dudley is literally talking to Kahlua right now."

"Yes, I know dogs have quite a bit to say to one another, but I've never seen this kind of behavior."

Kahlua slowly walked over to Dudley, and they sniffed each other.

"This is amazing." Tessa couldn't take her eyes off the dogs. "I haven't been able to get Kahlua next to any animal. I've taken her to classes, which she failed. I've even had three dog trainers in here, but nothing has helped."

She was attacked by two dogs when she was on the street. One big dog and one little one.

"Oh, no. Is that why she's so scared?"

Yes.

"No, she was scared before the training," Tessa said, thinking Sydney had been talking to her, as Carter came back with his metal detector.

"Dudley is telling me that Kahlua was attacked by two dogs when she was a stray, which is why she's so afraid of other dogs."

"Dudley just told you that?" Tessa looked at her skeptically.

"She's a pet psychic," Carter said.

"Oh, I thought an animal communicator was someone who studied their behaviors, but, hey, whatever works," Tessa said. "And you might be right, Sydney. Kahlua was skin and bones by the time animal control picked her up. I've no doubt she had an altercation or two with other street dogs over food."

"If she ever starts feeling anxious, just reassure her that she's safe now, and this is her forever home."

Tessa bent down, next to her terrier. "Did you hear that, Kahlua

Lua? You're safe now. And Dudley is a sweet dog who is just here for a visit."

You humans are so slow. Kahlua's already over it, and I'm now asking her questions about the ring. She saw something shiny fly off her human servant's hand when she went for the toy.

"Thanks, Dudley." Sydney kneeled next to Kahlua. "Do you remember where you were playing with your toy?"

Dudley made a bunch of noises she hadn't heard before. He sounded like he was eating something while whining at the same time. Kahlua answered with the same sound.

"What?" Tessa laughed. "Is that like dog language?"

Before Sydney could say anything, Dudley and Kahlua took off toward the woods but stopped at the edge of the mowed lawn, where a three-foot section of tall wild grass took over before the woods began. Kahlua walked into the tall grass and sat down.

"What is it, Dudley?"

Kahlua said the ring landed somewhere in this vicinity.

Tessa pulled up a picture on her phone. "This is what my ring looks like."

The diamond was a two-carat round, brilliant cut with a platinum setting.

"Gorgeous," Sydney said.

"We'll be on the lookout for anything that sparkles," Carter assured her.

"Dudley, do you need to see it?" Tessa asked.

Hardly. You took a bath in perfume, so I'll be able to smell it before I see it.

"No, he'll be able to pick up your scent on the ring," Sydney said.

"But I only wore it for a few hours."

"That's long enough. Since Dudley and Kahlua narrowed it down to this area, can you show me how you threw the toy?"

"Sure." Tessa positioned herself in the grass, facing the woods. I think this is about where I was standing. I'm left-handed, so I threw the toy like this."

"Across your body, which means it might have flung off to the right side."

"That's correct."

Dudley barked at Kahlua, and they began zigzagging across the long grass.

"Let me see if I can get this to pick up anything." Carter ran the metal detector over the ground, moving much slower over the search area than the dogs, but he wasn't finding anything.

Dudley began sniffing wildly in another section, and then he started barking. *I smell perfume!*

"Dudley's got something." Sydney hurried over and Tessa joined her. They got down on their knees and ran their fingers through the tall grass. As Sydney gingerly moved along, something sparkly caught her eye. "I found it!"

Tessa saw what she was holding and let out an excited scream. "I can't believe it. You did it! You actually found it!" She slid the ring back on her finger, then threw her arms around Sydney. "Thank you so much."

Tessa got up and hugged Carter too. "Thank you!"

Kahlua barked, tail wagging, thinking it was a game.

"And thank you, Kahlua and Dudley." Tessa received a bunch of doggie kisses and laughed. "What a relief." She admired the ring on her finger before they walked back to the house. "I don't know what I would have done if it hadn't been for all of you. I searched for an hour before I called you, Carter. I would have never found it without you."

"We're happy to help," he said.

Tessa took out her wallet. "What do I owe you?"

Carter glanced at Sydney. "Nothing," she replied.

"I'm not taking no for an answer. What you just did today is an invaluable service, and you need to be paid for it. You're a legit pet psychic, Sydney. How's two hundred for you and Carter's metal detector?" Tessa pulled out twenties and offered them to her.

"That's way too much." She wouldn't take the money. "Plus, you're Carter's friend."

"Carter has a lot of friends, and it's not too much at all. I've been engaged for less than twenty-four hours. I would have never forgiven myself if I'd lost a two-carat diamond ring. Please, accept this. I want you to have it."

Sydney reluctantly took the money. "Thank you, Tessa."

"Dudley is amazing." She gave him a pat on the head. "If you ever want to arrange a playdate between Dudley and Kahlua, just let me know. Kahlua could use a friend."

"What do you think about that, Dudley?"

I'll be happy to help as long as I receive delicious treats, like chicken or steak. Training Kahlua to act like a normal canine is going to be a lot of work.

"He says he'd love that."

"Fantastic. I guess I'll see you soon, Dudley." Tessa gave Sydney her business card. "Maybe we can set up a time next week. I'd love to know why Kahlua gets all crazy in the car when we stop at a red light."

Dudley said something to Kahlua, then Sydney heard, *She thinks the car is a wind machine and hates it when her human servant turns it off.*

Sydney smiled. "Kahlua loves the wind on her face, and she hates it when you stop at the light because the wind stops. She's barking at you to turn on the wind again."

Tessa laughed. "Turn on the wind. That's funny, and it makes total sense. Kahlua would hang her entire body out of the car if I let her."

See what I mean? The terrier is nowhere near normal.

"Hold on to that ring, Tessa, and congratulations," Carter said.

"I will. Thanks again."

CHAPTER SEVENTEEN

Sydney let out a relieved breath as they walked back to Carter's car. "That went incredibly well."

"It exceeded *my* expectations. And this thing didn't help at all." He held up the metal detector before shoving it in the back of his trunk.

Once again, I did all the work. Dudley caught her eye as they got in the car. *Tessa should have paid us with steak.*

She shook her head, smiling. "I'm sure you'd love to be paid with a bunch of steaks."

Carter chuckled, glancing at Dudley in the rearview mirror. "You really are the smartest dog I've ever known."

Sentient being.

"Sentient being."

"Apologies, Durlindemore. I will never call you a dog again."

This guy is growing on me. I shall keep him as my manservant.

"I really wish I could do what you do, Sydney. I wish I could hear what Dudley is saying."

"Maybe you can. You just don't know it, yet."

"I read about animal communication last night. I even tried some of the exercises, like attempting to say hello to a neighborhood cat this morning. But I don't think he heard me."

That's a feline for you. Their best talent is ignoring people.

Sydney laughed. "Dudley said cats tend to ignore us, so I wouldn't assess your ability based on them. Besides, it takes time. I studied under one of the best, and like I said, my connections with animals don't always work."

"Have you had a chance to set up any more sessions from the list I sent over?"

"I have one Monday afternoon with a stubborn boxer, and then your colleague, Jamie, and her Rottweiler are scheduled for next Saturday."

"That's great." A text came in from Carter's mom. "Look at that. You're not even advertising, and you have another session. Want to meet Penelope?" Dudley barked excitedly. "No translation needed."

How's my breath? Dudley panted in her face.

"Terrible. You have dog breath."

That means it's perfect! Unlike humans, we don't care for the smell of mint. Dudley stared out the window, ready and alert.

"Hopefully, Penelope likes him more than me," Carter said.

"If Kahlua's change in behavior is any indication, I think the two of you will be getting along great by the end of the session."

Carter pulled in front of his parents' house, and Sydney had never seen Dudley so excited.

"Calm down," she said, holding on to him tightly. "I don't want to drop you."

Carter rang the doorbell, and Penelope immediately began barking.

The voice of an angel. Dudley remained perfectly still, listening intently beyond the door.

Sydney smiled, and leaned toward Carter. "He's already smitten, and hasn't even met her yet."

Carter chuckled as his mom opened the door. "Hi, Mom. This is Sydney and Dudley—here to help Penelope and me."

"Hi, Sydney. Please, come in."

"Thank you, but I'd first like to see her interaction with Carter." She moved aside for Carter.

"Hi, Penelope." He slowly walked in. She growled, then suddenly stopped. She threw her nose in the air and remained completely silent. "This is new. Why isn't she barking at me?"

"She might already smell Dudley." Sydney stepped through the door with Dudley in her arms, and Penelope immediately began barking. Dudley looked a little dazed. "Aren't you going to say something?"

Jeripdeezigmorfe.

Gibberish. Dudley sounded like a drugged dog who couldn't formulate a sentence. Penelope grew more agitated and barked louder, while Carter's mom looked very skeptical.

Sydney turned Dudley away from Penelope, breaking eye contact. "Can you focus, please?"

Dudley blinked, then looked at Sydney. *My apologies. I was temporarily blinded by her beauty.* He set his attention back on Penelope and began whining and sounding like he was chewing, followed by a few seconds of howling.

Instantly silenced, Penelope took a step back, sniffed the air, then cocked her head.

You can put me down now, Sydney. She lowered Dudley to the ground as he continued to speak. Penelope barked back, along with a few sneezes, before she sat in front of him, listening and watching him intently.

"What's he saying?" Carter asked.

"Unknown. Dudley?"

I'm telling her a little bit about myself, most importantly that I'm single.

"Seriously?"

"What?" Carter stared at her anxiously.

"He's...uh...breaking the ice." She looked a little embarrassed, then focused on Dudley. "Can you please ask her what the issue is with Carter?"

I'm getting to that. Dudley continued to talk, and strutted around a bit, appearing as if he was a comedian on stage, telling a story. Penelope came closer to him, and even closer. They touched noses, stared at one another, then ran off together.

"Is this normal?" his mom asked.

"Nothing is normal with Dudley," he said.

They finally returned, and Penelope had a small toy in her mouth. She ran up to Carter and dropped it at his feet.

His mom gasped. "Would you look at that?"

"Go ahead and throw it for her," Sydney said.

"You sure she won't bite me?"

"Positive."

He slowly bent down toward the toy as Penelope backed up, anticipating his throw. He threw it, and she ran to get it, but she didn't bring it back. She took it to Dudley instead.

"What just happened?" he asked.

"I think Dudley had a talk with her. Dudley, can you fill us in?"

Dudley had the toy but gave it to Penelope, then trotted over. *Penelope despises felines. Carter always smells like one, except for today. I told her he's not a cat and doesn't live with one. Though I'm unclear as to why she thinks he smells like one.*

"Penelope doesn't care for cats and thinks you smell like one, except for today."

Carter closed his eyes and dropped his head. "Chester. The office cat. Why didn't I think of that before? He likes to sit on my lap when I'm typing."

"That makes perfect sense." His mom's eyes widened in surprise. "I've only had Penelope for a few weeks," she explained to Sydney. "And Carter has been coming over here after work."

She nodded. "Dudley, can you please explain the situation to Penelope?"

Dudley made a bunch of noises with rolling barks, which Penelope answered back. She then came over to Carter so he could pet her.

"Amazing." His mom was absolutely delighted.

"Is she apologizing?" Carter asked, rubbing her ears, and Sydney looked to Dudley for an answer.

No, she's accepting his invitation. I told her Carter loves her so much that he's invited her over tonight for hot dogs.

"You didn't."

You're welcome. Dudley barked, and Penelope ran back to him.

Carter eyed the two. "What?"

Sydney let out a sigh. "Apparently, Penelope just accepted an invitation to your house tonight for hot dogs with Dudley."

Carter's mom laughed. "Your dog just asked my dog on a date?"

"This is new territory for me," Sydney explained. "But it *would* be a good chance for her to bond with Carter."

His mom watched the dogs play-fight over the toy. "I think Carter will have some stiff competition, but I'll drop her off after she has her supper, although she can't have a hot dog."

"Did you hear that, Dudley? Even Mrs. Hansen knows that dogs don't eat hot dogs."

Mrs. Hansen doesn't know that Penelope chewed up a four-hundred-dollar pair of shoes, either, so I wouldn't be getting any late-breaking news from her.

Sydney's eyes widened in shock. Carter noticed and gave his mom a hug before she could ask any questions. "Thanks, Mom. We'll see you tonight. Let's go, Dudley," he called out, but was completely ignored.

"Come on, Durlindemore. You'll see her soon." Sydney held up his leash. Dudley touched his nose to Penelope's, then reluctantly obeyed.

"Durlindemore?" His mom squinted in confusion.

"He's complicated," Carter said.

"It was nice meeting you, Mrs. Hansen."

"Lovely meeting you as well, Sydney." She watched Dudley trot past her. "And thanks for stopping by, Mr. D."

Dudley gave her a woof, then strode out the door.

"What did he say in there?" Carter asked as soon as the front door closed.

"Penelope chewed up a pair of your mom's very expensive shoes."

"Guess she'll know soon enough."

Penelope said they tasted terrible and were not worth keeping.

"Mrs. Hansen didn't buy them to eat."

Fair enough.

As soon as Carter started driving them back home, he noticed that Dudley had already fallen asleep in Sydney's arms.

"Looks like we tuckered out the little guy," Carter whispered.

She held back a laugh as Dudley started snoring softly. "Yeah, he probably hasn't had this much activity in a long time."

"I just realized something," Carter said, giving her a sideways glance. "This morning, I invited Dudley over for a movie if he would go on a walk, and now I've apparently invited Penelope by proxy, but I neglected to invite you. Would you like to come over tonight for a non-hot-dog dinner and a movie?"

"I'd love to, but since you went from a guy with no dogs to

having two in your house and on your couch, how about I make us dinner while you figure out the movie?"

"That sounds good to me."

CHAPTER EIGHTEEN

Carter had never been a messy guy, so his place wasn't ever that dirty. But he broke out the cleaning supplies and gave it a good scrubbing anyway. He wasn't sure what he was doing, allowing his new tenants into his life so quickly.

He already loved Dudley, but he had no idea where he stood with Sydney. They'd had that one moment where he had tried to kiss her, but her phone rang, and he hadn't attempted it again. At least they were becoming fast friends. Would they end up as more to one another? Or would it suddenly end like it had with Jade?

What if Sydney only thought of him as a landlord and a friend by default due to their proximity? If she was entertaining the idea of a closer relationship, like he was, what would happen if it ended? Too many couples with dogs broke up, and he already knew he'd be the one who was left heartbroken. He had no claim to Dudley.

He should have stopped his involvement with them before it started, but it was already too late for that. Dudley had weaseled his way into his heart the second Carter saw him scratching his back in the park grass. Then when Sydney upended her life for that dog, it made him care for her even more.

He was in the middle of mopping the kitchen floor when his sister called.

"Mom just told me what happened today," Lorelai said excitedly. "She said Penelope was acting like a totally different dog and that Dudley could understand English like she's never seen before."

His sister was expecting him, as the skeptic in the family, to shoot it down. Only he couldn't. "All true."

"I want to meet them," she said in a rush.

He let out a short laugh. "Get in line. The paper has been flooded with inquiries on the dynamic duo."

"Have her come to dinner on Tuesday." Lorelai's suggestion sounded almost like a plea.

"I'd like to get to know her first before my whole family weighs in."

"Fine." She huffed. "But don't take too long, otherwise, my dog might suddenly have a behavioral issue. Enjoy hanging out with Sydney and the dogs." She laughed. "I never thought I'd hear myself saying that."

In truth, he didn't, either. He hung up and stared out the kitchen window toward the guesthouse. For an entire year, it had pained him to look out there, but not now. He couldn't stop thinking about Sydney and Dudley. His feelings for them had already made him question his own beliefs. The telepathy between them seemed real. He'd witnessed too much in the past few days to believe otherwise. But as a journalist looking for undeniable proof, he needed to put telepathy to the test—or debunk it.

He wished he'd been able to record today's session with Tessa in order to scrutinize the footage later—just in case he had missed any subtle body language that perhaps Sydney wasn't consciously aware of displaying. His original theory that she had to be using training signals no longer held up. Kahlua's sudden change in behavior was too great, and so was Penelope's.

Maybe his focus should be on Dudley. Could the dachshund be giving signals to other animals that were far more complicated than what humans understood? Possibly, but that wouldn't explain how Dudley, Kahlua, and Sydney narrowed down the area of the missing ring so quickly—unless telepathy had been involved.

Then there was Penelope. How had she conveyed to Dudley that she hated cats when a cat wasn't present? How had Sydney known? He had never mentioned there was a cat at work until she relayed what Dudley had psychically said to her.

Maybe it was a wild guess on Sydney's part that had prompted Carter to tell her about Chester. That didn't feel right, either. Fake psychics might be able to pump information out of people without their knowledge, but not Sydney. She was too honest for cheap tricks.

As much as he wanted to find out everything he could about telepathy, he was going to push all of that aside tonight. He wanted to learn about Sydney the woman, not Sydney the pet psychic—though having Dudley around would most certainly make that difficult.

It had taken Sydney a lot longer to do the grocery shopping since she changed her mind a half dozen times on what she was going to make Carter for dinner. Though she wanted to impress him, she wasn't much of a cook and decided to keep it simple.

As she hauled the groceries in through the front door, Dudley barely moved.

What did you buy me?

"Nothing. I bought people food." She set the grocery bags down on the counter and began unpacking them. "As much as you think you belong in that category, you don't. You're a dog, which means you eat dog food."

How can you refer to slop out of a can as actual food?

"You have kibble."

How can you call dried-out pieces of God-knows-what actual food? He scrutinized every item that came out of the grocery bags. *Are those hot dogs?*

"Yes, and I'm giving them to Carter to pay him back."

For what? I ate half of one hot dog. Hardly worth repaying him with an entire package. And need I remind you, I never got my second half as promised, so I deserve a fresh one tonight.

"If you behave, maybe I'll cook you something better than a hot dog."

He licked his chops. *Do tell.*

"It's a surprise."

I'm not fond of human surprises.

"You'll like it, I promise."

I do hope you're right. What are you making for my manservant tonight?

"He's not your manservant. I'm keeping it simple—chicken fajitas."

Not a very romantic meal.

"We're still getting to know one another. Besides, with you and Penelope there, not much is going to happen."

Why not? She will have my full attention—except for when I'm begging for leftovers.

"Is it going to be like this every night? Because you can save your breath. You're not getting chicken fajitas."

New studies have indicated that it's best to change up Fido's food on a regular basis.

"Once in a while and with a gradual transition. That news story we heard on TV was talking about different brands of *dog* food."

I beg to differ, but I suppose I can be satisfied with your surprise.

"Good decision. And please don't comment on every little thing while I'm trying to carry on a conversation with Carter. I can't turn off the Dudley channel in my head."

Nor should you, for what I have to say is always of the utmost importance.

"Of course, it is. Why don't you take a little nap while I shower and get ready?"

Brilliant idea. This is why we make such a good team. Dudley ran over to her bed. *You took away my stacked boxes. I need a lift up.*

"What's wrong with the plush bed Dana bought you?"

It's marginally comfortable. Your bed suits me better.

"*My* bed, not yours."

He lowered his head and gave her big puppy eyes. *I was on the street for so long, sleeping on cold concrete, shivering in—*

"Oh, all right." She went over and picked him up. "But stay off my pillow."

Dudley tunneled under the blankets and settled.

She was very good at being the boss with every other dog she'd taken care of. How had she lost control with Dudley so quickly?

Carter hadn't realized how difficult it would be to choose a movie for them to watch. Should he go with a horror film so she would cuddle into him if she got scared? Maybe he should pick a rom-com. Every woman he knew loved rom-coms…which meant she'd probably seen them all. Maybe he should choose a dog movie—though most of them ended up with the dog dying at the end, so that might not be a good choice, either.

"Knock, knock," Sydney called out from Carter's open back door.

"Hey!" He hurried over to help carry in the groceries. She smelled of gardenias, and her smile brightened the room. Her hair was loosely pulled back, and she wore a short, casual dress. He felt like she belonged there.

He set the bags on the counter. "What's all this?"

"I thought it might be easier to cook over here than at my place, if that's okay."

"You're welcome anytime."

Dudley gave a woof, and Carter bent down to scratch his back. "How are you liking your new digs, little man?"

"He said, 'It's not an estate in the Hamptons, but it'll do.'"

Carter chuckled. "That's exactly what I thought when I bought the place."

Dudley pulled back his lips in an attempt at a grin.

Carter helped unpack the bags and found a toy for Dudley. "Can I give him this?"

"Sure, but don't be surprised if he doesn't go after it. He wanted me to bring it for Penelope."

Carter tossed it anyway, and Dudley just yawned.

Sydney set a sealed plastic bag of marinating chicken inside the refrigerator. "I hope you like chicken fajitas."

"Love 'em." He grabbed the last bag and pulled out hot dogs. "I take it these are for Dudley."

He barked in reply.

"Actually, they're for both of you, but not tonight." She retrieved a pot from a lower kitchen cabinet and filled it with water. "For Dudley's snack, I'm going to poach an unseasoned chicken tender, which will be a lot healthier for him."

"My mom makes that for Penelope as a food topper. Will there be enough for her if she's allowed to have a bite or two?"

"Of course." Sydney glanced at Dudley who appeared to be talking telepathically to her. "Well, it's not," she answered Dudley.

"What did he say?"

"That the poached chicken should be an appetizer before a three-course meal."

"Little man, if you continue to be so obsessed with food, I won't be able to call you little man anymore." Dudley gave him a snarky look, and Carter laughed.

"Shoot, I forgot his water bowl."

"I have something he can use." Carter retrieved a small glass bowl out of the cabinet. "Will this work?"

"Yes, thank you."

Carter filled it with cool water and placed it in the corner. "And what can I get you to drink? I have beer, freshly brewed iced tea, soda, and water."

"Iced tea sounds good."

Carter poured tea over a glass of ice and set it on the counter next to her.

Dudley stared at her and whined. "What's wrong?"

"He's wondering when Penelope is coming over."

"Anytime, little man. My mom should be here soon."

Dudley immediately wagged his tail. Just a coincidence, or had he understood?

"He's very happy to hear that." Sydney started slicing up an onion and bell peppers. "He's going to wait for her by the front door."

Dudley waltzed out.

"He talks an awful lot."

"Wouldn't you?" She seemed so unfazed by it all.

"Has anyone else been able to hear Dudley's thoughts?"

"Not that I know of."

"I wonder if other pet psychics could hear him."

She gasped as her gaze locked on him. "That's a great idea! I should take him to Isabelle, the animal communicator who taught me. Maybe no one else has heard him because they weren't trained to do so."

He'd thrown the idea out there as an off-the-cuff remark, but now that he thought about it, having her take him to another pet psychic would strengthen Sydney's assertion about telepathy. "Mind if I come along when you do?"

"Not at all. In fact, Isabelle might like the publicity. I'll give her a call tomorrow."

He studied her with renewed interest. Sydney wasn't making any of this up. If she was, she would have balked at the idea.

Dudley came running in with his wagging tail and excitement in his eyes. "Is she here, little man?" He barked in reply just as the doorbell rang. "Be right back."

With Dudley on his heels, Carter opened the door and Penelope blasted in without so much as a look his way. She came nose to nose with Dudley as she gazed into his eyes. Their tails were up, and they didn't move, seeming engaged in an unspoken conversation.

"I see Penelope's already fixated on Dudley," Carter said, watching the two.

"At least she's not barking at you." His mom shrugged. "I still can't get over how fast Sydney figured out the problem."

"She's very talented."

"Yes, well, I might need to hire Sydney for another session. That little vixen ruined a pair of very expensive shoes." His mom threw her hands on her hips and glared at Penelope.

"Oh, no." Carter tried to look surprised.

"It's a good thing I love her so much."

Dudley made a funny noise and the four-legged lovebirds were off, galloping toward the kitchen.

"Those two have become instant friends," his mom said. "Kind of like you and Sydney."

"Yeah." He smiled. "She's in the kitchen making us chicken fajitas. Come on in."

"I don't want to intrude." She waved him off. "But say hi for me." She headed for her car. "And no hot dogs for Penelope."

"What about a little poached chicken?" he called after her. "Sydney's making that instead."

"Penelope would love it." She blew him a kiss. "Have a great evening."

He stayed to watch his mom drive off before he went back inside. As he rounded the corner to the kitchen, he saw Dudley and Penelope patiently sitting next to Sydney, watching her every move.

"I just put the chicken in," she said to them. "It will be a while, so go chill."

"I see Dudley has derailed our fajitas." Carter got himself a beer.

"He wouldn't stop bugging me, but a little chicken will get them to settle."

"You have a good mom, Dudley."

The dachshund glanced at him, then at Sydney, who rolled her eyes, and Carter knew he'd said something.

"Another comment?"

"He said, 'I'm certainly no child, and Sydney enjoys doting over me,'" she repeated in her best version of a British accent.

"Has anyone ever called you cheeky, Dudley?"

"'Hardly,'" she repeated as Dudley. "'No one has the ability to hear my exceptional conversation except for lucky Sydney.'"

Carter broke into a big grin. "Yes, lucky you."

She laughed.

Once Sydney gave Dudley and Penelope their chicken, they took a nap, allowing her and Carter to finally have dinner.

Carter loaded up his fajitas with sour cream, cheese, and lettuce, then took a bite. "These are really good. I'll be your official taste tester anytime," he said with his mouth full.

"Hate to disappoint, but I don't spend a lot of time cooking."

"I don't spend *any* time cooking, so you already have me beat." He hadn't realized, until that moment, how much he hated eating alone.

"Have you had a chance to write up the Norma Jean session?" she asked, taking a drink.

He nodded. "I hope you won't be too upset, but I featured Dudley more than you in this one."

Dudley raised his head, now intently listening.

"That's fine with me," she said. "As for Dudley, and I quote, 'As it should be. After all, I'm the real star, and you, my dear Sydney, are my sidekick.'"

Dudley looked like a star at that moment with Penelope cozying up to him like a groupie.

"You're great at imitating how he sounds," Carter said. "What does Penelope sound like?"

Sydney pushed her brows together, then frowned. "I don't know. When I telepathically listen to other animals, I hear their words in my head, but I don't really hear their voice like I do with Dudley. However, Dudley knows what she sounds like." She glanced at Dudley who grunted. "Penelope is apparently well-spoken and has the voice of an angel."

"He's not at all taken with her, is he?"

She laughed. "Not one bit."

He studied them lying together. They looked like typical, normal dogs, but Dudley was far from it. "Now I'm curious to know how all animals sound. Do they have accents like we do? How varied are their personalities? Can some animals be slimy, deceptive characters and others be altruistic heroes? Do they have as big of a personality as Dudley's, or is he one of a kind?"

Sydney stared at Dudley, then quoted him. "'Naturally everyone in the animal kingdom sounds different, as do humans. As for personalities, canines are charismatic standouts on our planet, whereas humans rate slightly above average.'"

Carter leaned closer, lowering his voice. "You must be laughing all the time at his comments."

"He says he can hear you, so whispering is futile."

"Right." He sat back and cleared his throat, wishing he could have the same experience as Sydney. "Does Isabelle still teach classes?"

"As far as I know, but I'll find out when I call her." She studied him. "I really think if you allowed yourself to be open to the possibility, you could be good at it."

"Did everyone in your class successfully learn to communicate telepathically?"

"Almost. There was one woman who wasn't confident enough in her ability, so she often second-guessed the impressions she was receiving. I can teach you the basics before you take a class. Whenever you're ready."

"Thanks." He held her gaze until she was distracted, no doubt by Dudley, who was probably ready for the movie.

"Did you get enough to eat?" she asked. "There's still enough for one or two more."

"That was plenty and delicious. Thank you."

"No, Dudley, you don't get leftovers."

"Yeah, little man. It's too spicy for you."

"He says he has an iron stomach. But it doesn't matter, Dudley. I'm leaving the leftovers with Carter."

"Works for me." Carter gathered up their dirty dishes and took them over to the sink.

"No. You just had chicken," Sydney said to Dudley.

"Was he asking about movie snacks?"

"As a matter of fact, he was. See, you're already picking up on his thoughts."

He wanted to believe that to be true, but dogs were creatures of habit, and Carter was already learning Dudley's.

Penelope held eye contact with Dudley for a good minute, as if they were conversing. Then Dudley retrieved his toy and gave it to her, which made Carter wonder how deeply animals loved one another.

Dudley had asked Sydney to bring his toy tonight so that he could give it to Penelope, which meant Dudley had thought ahead. He'd used his cognitive skills to prepare for a date. Just how intelligent was he and other dogs, or other animals?

There was so much he wanted to ask the dachshund, and though he could through Sydney, he wanted to talk to him directly. Would he be able to hear him telepathically one day? That would be amazing, and he certainly wouldn't mind if that ability extended to him figuring out women. He'd love to know what Sydney was thinking—particularly about him.

CHAPTER NINETEEN

After Carter got Sydney some more tea, they went into the living room and sat down to watch a movie. Dudley had been talking to her more than she wished. She didn't want Carter to think she was avoiding getting to know him, because that's all she wanted to do.

"What are you in the mood for? A horror film, a rom-com, a movie about dogs?"

Dudley's ears perked up. *Does he even need to ask?*

She almost answered him and caught herself at the last minute. If she wanted Dudley to stop talking to her, she needed to ignore him. "A rom-com is good. I also like action movies if they're not too violent."

"I think Ryan Reynolds is in a new action film." He scrolled through the most recent movies. "Here it is."

"I saw the trailer," she said. "It looks good."

"Done." He ordered the movie. "Does anyone need anything before we start the show?"

"I'm good," she said, then looked to Dudley.

I believe Carter said something about a comfy couch and a snuggly blanket.

"That was before you invited Penelope."

"Is there a problem?" Carter asked.

She let out an irritated sigh. "He remembers how you promised him a movie on the couch with a snuggly blanket."

"He's right. I did." Carter went into another room, and returned with a plush throw.

"That's way too nice."

Looks perfect to me.

"I never use it."

"Okay, Dudley, but this is it, or I'm sending you back to the guesthouse."

I know what I'm doing, and you'll thank me later.

She didn't know what Dudley was talking about as she spread out the blanket.

Not between you two. Put us on the end of the couch.

And then she got it, but she didn't want to seem too obvious. "Okay, you can have the armrest, too," she said to Dudley, as if he'd asked for it.

She moved the throw to one side of the couch, then lifted Dudley onto it as Penelope jumped up herself. Dudley stretched out, making himself even longer than he already was, and once Penelope settled in next to him, they took up half the couch. Now, the only place for her to sit was right next to Carter.

You're welcome.

She sat down, as if it was no big deal, but she was practically in his lap. "Do you have enough room? I can put them on the floor."

"No, I'm good." He threw his arm over the back of the couch. "How about you?"

She nodded. "I'm sorry about all of this."

"What are you talking about? I had an amazing dinner with great company. And Penelope hasn't barked at me once."

"That's because she sees Dudley and only Dudley."

He laughed. "Yeah, she seems just as enamored with him as he is with her."

And Sydney was enamored with Carter. Their thighs were touching, and with his arm draped across the back of the couch behind her, it seemed so natural for her to cuddle into him, to put her head on his shoulder, to wrap her arm around his waist. Being so close to him stirred up feelings that she had buried. She wanted to know how it would feel to kiss him or to be in his arms. How was she going to get through a two-hour movie?

She glanced at Dudley and Penelope who were curled up together, peacefully sleeping. She wanted to look at Carter or say something, but she couldn't think of anything to say, so she forced herself to pay attention to the movie. Ryan Reynolds was on screen, in a tux, and was as gorgeous as ever. In fact, his profile reminded her of Carter's. His nose looked very similar, as well as his chin. Even Ryan's thin but perfect lips looked very similar to Carter's, though Carter had a sexier mouth. She often caught herself watching the way his lips moved when he was talking. They were sexy even when he wasn't talking.

Carter must have sensed that she was staring at him. "What?"

"The bottom half of your face is very similar to Ryan Reynolds's."

Carter ran his hand over his jawline. "But I'm way younger and cuter, right?"

She laughed. "Obviously."

"Good." He put his arm around her, and she fell into him. She fit so nicely next to him.

He glanced past her at the dogs. "I don't think I've ever seen Dudley or Penelope this quiet."

She sat up a little. "They're definitely good for one another."

Carter traced her arm with his fingertips, not paying attention to the movie either. "Is Dudley asleep or is he talking to you?"

"I don't know if he's asleep, but he's definitely not talking."

"Good." He held her hand, and suddenly Penelope got up to change positions causing Carter to let go. He kept looking over at the dogs.

"They seem settled now," she said, but Carter was already distracted.

"I read a lot of articles last night about telepathy and our sixth sense," he said. "One article said that as civilization evolved, we as humans stopped relying on our sixth sense. Children who are born with a strong sixth sense are often told to ignore it—that it's just their imagination."

"That's right." She looked at him with admiration, impressed that he'd taken the time to learn about it. "With what you do, as a journalist, I think your sixth sense, your intuition, is much stronger than you realize."

He snorted. "If it is, I don't see any evidence of it."

"Do you know who's calling before you answer the phone?"

"Sometimes, but I think everyone has that."

"Not everyone." She sat up and faced him. "I'm thinking of a color in my head. What is it?"

"Steel blue."

"Yes!" Her mouth dropped open. "You do have ability. I would have simply said blue, but you saw the exact shade of blue I was thinking about."

"I hate to disappoint you, but it was an educated guess. While I helped you unpack, I noticed that you had a lot of steel blue. Steel-blue pillows on your couch. Steel-blue plates, steel-blue towels."

"I never realized that, but I guess I do." She felt a little embarrassed, not knowing this about herself. "It's my favorite color."

"You can see what mine is."

She glanced around his family room. "Sage green?"

He nodded.

"I'm suddenly feeling a bit inferior about my own psychic abilities."

"You telepathically communicate *with a dog*."

"Maybe it's all him, and I have nothing to do with it."

"I doubt that, but why don't we test your psychic acuity?" He stared into her eyes. "Do you know what I'm thinking?"

She laughed and broke eye contact, but he remained locked on her, so she expelled a quick breath, then looked at him again. There was an intensity behind his eyes. It was as if he was looking right into her, reading her every thought, discovering her every desire. Her breathing became shallow as heat rushed to her cheeks.

A serious look came over his face, and she knew he was cheating. Whatever he'd been thinking, he was now thinking something else, something that aligned with what she was feeling.

His eyes drifted onto her mouth, lingering on her lips. She felt her pulse quicken and his lips parted as he slowly leaned toward her. His kiss was like no other—gentle, yet demanding. The sensation of his soft mouth, his breath on her cheeks, his strong arms sliding around her waist made her crave his touch. When he deepened the kiss, it awakened such a longing in her that she wasn't sure if she'd be able to control it.

She wrapped her arms around him, pulling him closer, and leaned right into Dudley.

Get a room.

She jerked up, breaking the moment. "Sorry."

"What's wrong?"

"I leaned into Dudley."

He eyed the dachshund. "Does he understand human relationships?"

She hesitated. How was she going to tell him that Dudley knew far too much?

Carter pulled away. "Did he say something to you?"

She cringed.

His eyes widened. "While we were kissing?"

Should she tell him or sugarcoat it?

"It's written all over your face now, so don't try to deny it." Carter let out an irritated breath. "What did he say?"

"Doesn't matter." She shrugged.

"Then tell me."

Her mind tried to think of something totally unrelated to his comment but couldn't think fast enough. "'Get a room.'"

Carter's shocked expression said it all.

"I know. I'm sorry."

"This is worse than if he had simply been staring at us."

"I know." She bit her lip. "Something I hadn't thought about until now."

Carter scrubbed his face with his hand. "I don't know if I can do this."

"Don't say that." Her heart beat faster, worried that he meant it. "This is new to me too," she reminded him, hoping he'd see that they were navigating this together. "We just need to schedule a dogless date night."

Or I can go to Penelope's.

Carter narrowed his eyes on Dudley. "Has he been eavesdropping this whole time?"

The beginning of a relationship was always so magical, but not for those who had to worry about constant interruptions by a third party.

"Dogs are always passively listening," she said. "Goes back to when they had to fend for themselves in the wild. But he can certainly remain in the guesthouse from now on. Or we could take him to your parents to visit Penelope."

Carter relaxed a little and leaned back. "Penelope would like that, and my mom loves dogs, so yeah, we could make that happen."

Well done, Sydney, though I'd much prefer the latter of the two choices. Dudley turned away and went back to cuddling with Penelope, which signaled to Carter that he'd heard everything they'd said.

"He *was* eavesdropping." Carter shook his head.

She couldn't disagree because she didn't want to lie. Would Carter decide that dating her was more complicated than he wanted to deal with? "I can make him go to the guesthouse right now, if it will make you feel more comfortable."

Carter glanced at Dudley, who had his eyes closed. "No, they're settled. Besides, Penelope would never forgive me."

She laughed, and he smiled before he puffed out a breath. He backed up the movie, and they watched it all the way through. Carter seemed to finally relax but not enough to kiss her again. This was going to be a problem. She definitely needed to set more ground rules with Dudley.

By the end of the movie, they were at least holding hands. When they got off the couch to say good night, Dudley went over to Carter, looked up at him, and poured on the puppy eyes, as if to say he was sorry for ruining their evening. Carter bent down to give him a tummy rub, and Dudley gladly took it.

Does he still love me? When she didn't answer, he started whining, staring at her, then at Carter. *Ask him.*

"What's going on?" Carter eyed Sydney.

"He's wondering if you still love him."

"What? Of course." He picked up Dudley. "Why would you think I wouldn't?"

Three's a crowd.

"'Three's a crowd.'"

"On a date? Yes. But we'll figure it out."

Dudley wagged his tail and gave him a lick on his nose before he wiggled to get down. He then ran over to Penelope to say good night to her.

Sydney was very glad to know that Carter considered it a date.

He took hold of her hand and brought her closer. "Thank you for dinner and hanging out with me."

"Thanks for having me. Us. And I meant what I said. We need to do a few dogless dates. If your mom isn't available, Dudley will understand that he needs to stay in the guesthouse."

Carter nodded, gently kissed her, then pulled away. Even his small kiss sent her flying. "I better take Penelope home before it gets too late."

"Okay," she said. "I've got another session tomorrow afternoon. I'll confirm it with the client and text you the address in the morning."

"Sounds good." He kissed her again, this time a little longer. When he finally pulled away, Dudley trotted to the back door. "Sleep tight, little man."

Sydney snores, so that's debatable.

"He said good night, and thanks for the tummy rubs."

You really need to get your hearing checked. Dudley headed toward the guesthouse.

"I selectively hear as well as you do," she said quietly as Carter watched them go.

I fear I might have taught you some bad habits.

She opened the guesthouse door. "You won't be on my next date, so you won't have to worry about it."

She looked back and saw that Penelope was right by Carter's side. At least one dog problem had been resolved.

CHAPTER TWENTY

"Come on, Penelope. Let's get you home." He headed toward the garage door and noticed that she wasn't following him. Instead, she was looking longingly at the door Dudley had gone through moments ago. "You've got it bad." She whined. "You'll see him soon. I promise."

As Carter got out her leash, he tried to connect with her telepathically. One of the articles he'd read said that he needed to picture what he wanted her to do in his mind, and simultaneously *tell* her what to do. Easy enough. He pictured her sitting right in front of him.

"Sit," he commanded.

Penelope ignored him. He tried again, but she refused to obey. He shouted her name in his head to see if she would react. She didn't. He was horrible at telepathy.

"Do you want to go home to your *mom?*" he asked. Penelope cocked her head and sat. "Good, girl." He slowly approached her with the leash. She waited for him to get a foot from her, and then she raced to the other side of the room, acting like it was a game.

"Come on now." His shoulders slumped. "I've got to get you home. Penelope, sit!"

She took off, racing around the house. The dog was now doing laps up and down his hallway without any sign of slowing down.

With a defeated sigh, he dialed Sydney. "I can't even put a leash on a dog."

She laughed. "I'll be right over."

Carter hung up and stared at Penelope. "I'm beginning to think that you and Dudley are in cahoots with one another."

Sydney knocked and came in. She was about to close the door when she saw Dudley racing toward her. "I told you I was only going to be gone a minute. You were supposed to stay in the guesthouse."

"What's his excuse?" Carter had to ask.

"He felt that if I got to see you one more time, he should be able to see Penelope."

Carter smiled. "Smart dog."

Dudley touched Penelope's nose, and they fell into their usual greeting of gazing at one another.

"Since Dudley has Penelope's attention, try putting on her leash," Sydney suggested.

He leaned over and hooked the leash onto her harness without a problem. "Thank you."

"Anytime."

He wanted to kiss Sydney again, but Dudley and Penelope began playing near their feet, and Penelope's leash quickly wrapped around their legs.

"Settle down," Sydney said, unwinding herself. "Say good night, Dudley, so Carter can take her home."

He touched noses with Penelope, then reluctantly sauntered out with Sydney.

As Carter drove Penelope back to his parents' house, he reviewed the night in his head. He had wanted to go slow after what happened with Jade, but how could he now? Sydney's dog was asking him if he still loved him. Dudley really *did* understand way more than he should. And though Carter first thought it was cool to have an extremely intelligent dog living in his guesthouse with a beautiful girl he happened to be attracted to, it was very awkward to have him around when they were getting to know one another.

"Do you comprehend as much as Dudley?" he asked Penelope when they stopped for a red light. Much to his relief, she didn't look at him or show any kind of reaction. Her head remained out the window, sniffing the night air, as a normal dog would.

He really enjoyed being with Sydney, having dinner with her, watching a movie with her, kissing her—not to mention that he couldn't stop thinking about her whenever he wasn't with her. But would he get used to having such an intelligent dog around, watching and possibly judging his every move? He wished he could talk to his friends about it, but they'd think he had finally lost it.

Carter pulled into his parents' driveway and took Penelope to the door.

"There's my angel!" He already knew his mom was talking about Penelope. She scooped the dog up in her arms and gave her a bunch of kisses, as if she'd been gone for a week.

"You know, Mom, when I accidentally broke your crystal vase, you never forgave me this quickly."

"That's because you were fourteen and knew not to throw a ball in the house. My sweet Penelope doesn't understand the difference between her toy and my shoe."

Penelope stared Carter down, as if she was daring him to disagree with his own mother.

"I'll make sure Sydney and Dudley have a nice long chat with her," he said, and Penelope's ears perked up when she heard Dudley's name.

"I'd appreciate that," his mom replied. "How did it go?"

"Penelope and I got along great—mainly because she forgot I was there. She and Dudley were inseparable."

"That's so funny. She doesn't have any interest in other dogs when I take her for a walk. In fact, she's very snooty to those who attempt to say hi. Sydney really knows what she's doing. How long has she been a dog trainer?"

"She's not. She's a dog walker, pet sitter, and animal communicator."

Her brows pulled together. "Is that like a behaviorist?"

His mom had already watched Sydney work, but she had no idea what an animal communicator was, and he wasn't going to be the one to explain it.

"Something like that."

"Well, I think Sydney's a sweetheart and quite pretty. Any woman who loves animals as much as she does proves to me that she's a selfless and compassionate person—one with good morals and ethics."

He wasn't sure if liking dogs said that much about anyone, but it seemed to match what he knew of Sydney. "She is."

"Why don't you invite her over for dinner on Tuesday, and have her bring Dudley? I'm sure Penelope would love to see her new friend."

He already knew his mom was going to make that suggestion because Lorelai had. They often pretended to come up with a shared idea spontaneously, but he knew they planned it.

"Great idea, Mom. I'll mention it to her tomorrow."

⁂

Sydney had never felt the need to step into the bathroom to change into her pajamas in the presence of a dog, but as Dudley constantly reminded her, he was no regular dog. It was like living with a male roommate. She also hadn't thought about how living with an exceptional canine would affect her human relationships, but she and Carter were certainly thinking about it now.

"Did you have fun tonight?" she asked him as she came out of the bathroom and saw that he'd not only found another way up on her bed, but he'd made himself comfortable on it.

He opened one eye. *Fun is an underwhelming description of how I'm feeling. I'm in total and complete love, and apparently you are too.*

"I'm in *like*. There's a difference."

You two are also in lust.

"That comes with falling in like with someone. What isn't normal is having a dog right there, who not only comprehends as much as a human adult, but also gives a running commentary."

I refuse to apologize for being a genius.

"I'm not asking you to, but Carter and I are going to need some space."

He has a bedroom.

"We only just had our first kiss. We're trying to get to know one another, which is very difficult to do with you so near."

Should things begin to heat up between you, I shall make myself scarce.

"Thank you." She let out a big sigh. "Now about your sleeping arrangements."

He's not here, and I don't take up much room.

She opened her mouth to give him a hard no, but he poured on the puppy eyes, instantly melting her heart. "Oh, all right, you can stay, but this is temporary. Do you understand?"

Of course I understand. I'm not an imbecile.

She got in bed and was about to turn out the light when she noticed him staring at her.

How temporary?

"If things progress with Carter, I can't have you sleeping in bed with us, which means you'll be sleeping in your own bed on the floor."

I told you I was different when we met.

"I know, but I hadn't exactly thought it through with regard to my love life."

This is what I was afraid of. First, I'll be kicked out of the plush bed, and then I'll be kicked out of the house.

"Don't be silly. I said I would never abandon you and I meant it."

What happens when Carter still feels uncomfortable around me?

"He won't. He's already too attached to you. I can see it in his eyes."

That could be temporary.

She turned toward him. "Is this what happened to you? Did someone else know how special you were, but it freaked them out too much?"

No. You're the first.

"Then what are you worried about? I moved for you, and we lucked out. We have a great place here with Carter. He loves you, I love you, and I'm pretty sure Penelope loves you."

She's a true angel. May my angel move in with us?

"I'm afraid not. It would break her mom's heart to give her up—but you can visit her every week."

I suppose that will have to do. Dudley released a dramatic sigh.

Sydney suppressed a smile. "Can Penelope comprehend as much as you?"

Hardly. Her understanding of the English language is infinitesimal compared to mine.

"Good to know." At least Carter could relax around Penelope. "I almost forgot to tell you. I'm going to take you to meet the woman who taught me animal communication to see if she can understand you."

Smashing. I look forward to conversing with another one of your species.

"Are you from outer space?"

Whatever gave you that idea?

"Just the way you talk sometimes. You've never told me exactly where you're from."

Rest assured, I'm not from another planet, though space visitors do walk among you.

She laughed.

I'm stunned by the fact that you all haven't figured out which ones they are. It's not as if they hide from you. How often have you noticed someone who appears completely out of place? Or how about those who are weirdly off pace with the rest of society?

"You're trying to tell me they're aliens?"

The movie Men in Black *is more accurate than you think.*

She shook her head, smiling. "It's enough for me to believe in a talking dog. I'm not ready to buy the aliens-live-among-us theory."

Suit yourself. Just offering up the intel.

"So where exactly are you from?"

Let's chat about that another day. Sleep tight, Sydney.

"You, too, Dudley."

CHAPTER TWENTY-ONE

Carter sat with Chester on his lap as he finished working on the article about their town's upcoming three-day art festival, which attracted artists and buyers from all over the country. From glass blowers to metal workers, artists working in any form could display their pieces.

Jade's work had always been extremely popular. He wondered how she was doing, and genuinely hoped she was happy in Paris. At last, thinking about her no longer brought on that familiar pain, and he had Sydney to thank for that.

"How did you do it?"

He glanced up to see Shep hovering, which prompted Chester to bolt.

"Do what?"

"Convince Russell to give you a weekly column."

"I didn't. There's local interest in Sydney and Dudley that has already contributed to more subscriptions."

"But you don't like covering animal-related stories."

"I do now." He eyed him suspiciously. "Why do you care anyway? You're always working on the top stories."

"I'm covering the Rotary Club luncheon this afternoon." His expression said it all.

"Sounds like it's time for you to move on to a mid-size paper."

"I'd love to," Shep said. "But if I left, this paper would go under, and I don't want to be the guy to put you or anyone else out of work."

Shep's comments were always a mixed bag of narcissism and

altruism. But what he'd never been was chummy with him. "Cut to the chase, Shep."

"Okay." He quickly pulled up a chair and fixed his gaze on Carter. "I thought we might be able to collaborate on something. I saw our mayor having dinner last night with a group of businessmen I've never seen in town before. I inquired at his office and was told I was mistaken, that Kessler had nothing on the books yesterday past five. I inconspicuously took a few pictures of the people he was dining with and managed to find out who they are. They're land developers who I believe are eyeing our town for a big project."

Carter leaned forward. "How big?"

"They were throwing around the word 'revitalization.'"

He stilled. "Revitalization isn't necessarily a good thing, especially for us. We're in the heart of Pinecrest. We must be sitting on some of the most valuable property in town. Did they say anything else?"

"A young guy in the group said that owners would sell or be *forced* to sell, though he didn't explain how that would be accomplished."

Carter rubbed the back of his neck, sensing Shep was on to something. "Kessler is slick. No doubt he has it all figured out." Carter searched for a folder on his laptop. "I just remembered something I came across recently." He found the folder and clicked it open. "I've been doing a little research on our mayor. Turns out his cousin is now a senior planner with Pinecrest's planning commission. Who better to help him cut through the red tape?"

"Which means he stands a good chance of getting approval for whatever he's up to before anyone can challenge him," Shep said.

"If you recall, Kessler came out of nowhere when he was running for mayor. His charming smile had a lot of locals forgetting that fact."

"This could be the investigation we've been waiting for, Carter. We could be the two who end up exposing him."

"I'd love nothing more, but Russell already warned me to back off. You know the mayor's brother-in-law is keeping the lights on with his advertising. We'd be out on the street if it weren't for him."

"Doesn't it all seem a little incestuous?" Shep asked. "Kessler fooled a lot of people to get elected, and now it's easy for him. He has his brother-in-law's influence to keep us in line while he puts his own people in place around him."

Carter sat back and heaved a deep sigh. "If you're right, this will have a huge impact on Pinecrest."

"Are you in?"

"Yeah, but we need to be smart about this. I don't think—"

"Can I have everyone's attention?" Russell came out on the floor, looking a little pale.

Shep turned around. "This doesn't sound good."

"I just got off the phone with our biggest advertiser, and he's pulling his support."

There was a huge gasp around the newsroom.

"Why?" Jamie asked. "We've added a record number of new subscriptions just in the last few days. Does he know that?"

Russell nodded. "I gave him the numbers, but he said his decision was final. Without him, I can't pay the bills. I have no choice but to shut it down."

"We're finished?" Jamie's mouth fell open, stunned by the news.

"I'm sorry." Russell looked around the newsroom at the few but faithful faces, and his eyes became glassy with tears. "Thank you all for your incredible dedication, hard work, and friendship. I will miss our family." He blinked away the moisture accumulating in his eyes. "Send me your receipts for any reimbursements, and I'll give everyone a call when your last check is ready for pickup."

As stunned silence fell over the room, Russell lumbered back into his office and quietly shut his door.

Shep swiveled back to Carter, and lowered his voice. "What do you think the odds are that the mayor had something to do with this?"

"One hundred percent." Carter set his elbows on his desk and leaned in. "Do you have any friends working in the mayor's office?"

"An ex-girlfriend."

"That might be worse." He blew out a sarcastic laugh. "I don't know anyone over there, either." He stared out the window, running options in his head. "If he can kill us this easily, we have to assume Kessler's got loyal spies everywhere, which means we'll need to quietly gather information on exactly what he's doing."

"I'll run over there today and sniff around."

"I'll start looking into the backgrounds of any city official who's been directly appointed by the mayor."

Shep grabbed his phone and stood up. "Text me if you find anything."

Carter nodded. "Be careful. With the snap of his fingers, he silenced the longest running newspaper in Pinecrest and put eight decent people out of work."

By early afternoon, Sydney was walking her second set of dogs—or rather, strolling. Dudley seemed in good spirits as two dapple dachshunds, Sugar and Spice, set the pace by sniffing everything in sight. Jammer, a French bulldog, was also along for the stroll, as well as Sarge, a senior pug, who enjoyed exercise as much as Dudley.

Knowing a snail could move faster than her current group, she pulled out her phone and dialed Carter. "Hey, so, change of plans. My new client called and has to postpone her session, but I managed to get a hold of Isabelle, the animal communicator I trained under, and she can meet Dudley at four."

"Uh. Okay. I can make that work." His voice sounded strange.

"What's wrong?"

"The newspaper was just shuttered."

"What?" She couldn't believe what she was hearing. "Why?"

"I don't know the full story yet, but the mayor's brother-in-law canceled all of his advertising, which was our biggest revenue source."

"Oh, Carter. That's terrible. I'm so sorry. Did it have to do with the article you wrote?"

"It didn't help, but Shep recently stumbled upon something else, and I think Kessler had *The Pinecrest News* shut down before any of us could report on it."

"That's a little chilling—to kill free speech like that."

"Yeah, everyone is in shock over here."

"Is there anything I can do?"

"No, but thanks."

"Well, forget I mentioned this afternoon. I can—"

"No, I want to be there," he said. "Especially since my column won't be running on Friday, which means you might not get any more clients than the ones you have currently. I'm really sorry."

"Don't even think about apologizing. You weren't working at the newspaper to get me clients. Besides, you already got the ball rolling, and it's picking up speed. Tessa recommended me to two of her friends, and Marjorie gave out my number to members of her book club."

"That's fantastic." He genuinely sounded happy for her, even though his journalistic future was in jeopardy.

"Yeah, I can hardly believe it myself. I really think we came together for a reason—all three of us, and just because *The Pinecrest News* folded, it doesn't mean your career goes with it. You're a great journalist, Carter. If you can't have your column in the paper, then you'll have it with another publication."

"Thank you. I love your optimism," he said. "Text me Isabelle's address, and I'll meet you there at four."

"I will. See you then." Sydney hung up. "I can't believe what just happened to Carter."

He might need a lot of TLC from you.

"Yeah. I just wish we could help him get his job back."

Perhaps he needs a better one with us.

"I'm not sure if we have enough work for him to join us full time."

I hereby bequeath any future earnings to you, dear Sydney, to give to him.

"A wonderful and generous idea. Thank you, Dudley."

I do hope this earns me a few more tummy rubs and visits with Penelope.

She smiled at her smart little doxie. "I think that can be arranged."

Carter felt a little shell-shocked as he said goodbye to the people he'd seen every week for the past two years. Russell seemed despondent and looked completely ashen.

"Are you going to be okay?" he asked his now-former boss.

"I always am."

"Don't believe that this is it, Russell. Think of it as a temporary but much-needed vacation. I'll figure out a way to get us back."

"That's exactly what Shep said." Russell picked up Chester, who was circling at his feet. "You two are more alike than you realize."

"We're definitely seeing eye to eye on where the corruption lies in this town."

"Don't do anything stupid."

"We won't." Carter gave Chester a long stroke down his back. "Be good, and mind your dad."

Carter put his things in the car, checked the time, and realized he needed to head to Isabelle's. He wasn't exactly sure how he was going to get the newspaper running again, and as much as he wanted to believe that he wasn't afraid of the mayor, he was. With lightning speed, the guy had decimated his place of employment and put everyone who had worked there in financial jeopardy.

He needed to find a new job, but doing what? He really liked working with Sydney and Dudley, and maybe she was right—that they'd been thrown together for a reason. But was that just on a personal level or a business one as well? He didn't have their telepathic talent, but he could put their website together and record all of their sessions. Then if Shep was able to determine that provable corruption was taking place at the mayor's office, he would dive into an investigation with him.

He and Shep would certainly have an easier time investigating now. Kessler wouldn't suspect two out-of-work journalists giving him any trouble. If Shep's hunch ended up being wrong, then no harm no foul. Carter would continue on with Sydney and Dudley, and somehow figure out a way to make a living in the process.

CHAPTER TWENTY-TWO

Sydney set Dudley in his car seat and put on the goggles Dana had bought him. "You are one spoiled pup."

Perhaps. However, I'm not one for accessories. Take these bloody things off me.

"They're to protect your eyes."

A bit much, don't you think?

"Yes, but you're so adorable in them. In fact, you look downright dashing." She took a picture and showed it to him.

You're quite right. I do look rather distinguished. I shall wear them with pride.

She couldn't stop smiling and only wished she'd been driving a convertible with the top down.

Dudley stuck his head out the window and filled his nostrils with all the neighborhood smells. *Tell me about Isabelle.*

"She's one of the top pet psychics in the country, which is why I decided to study under her."

She most certainly did well by you. I shall suggest she train all who choose to have a canine in their lives. Imagine how many misconceptions could be avoided if we were able to communicate easily.

"That would be amazing. With everyone using telepathy, maybe it would help lessen the burden on animal shelters. No more destructive behavior, pets getting lost, or doggies peeing on the rug."

About that last bit. My fellow canines are all very well aware of the rules. However, I've met a few chaps who merely prefer not to trudge all the way outside if the weather is disagreeable.

"Are you serious?" Her mouth dropped open. "That's disgusting."

So is the cone of shame humans force many of us to wear.

"Hardly in the same category. A pet collar is necessary for proper healing of a wound. I wouldn't dream of peeing in your house."

Perhaps you would if I made you wear a cone of shame.

"Never, and neither should any dog." She flicked him an irritated glance. "I assume you had to wear a recovery cone. What happened?"

An escape had gone horribly awry. I do wish I had longer legs.

She smiled. "I know how you feel."

As soon as they arrived at Isabelle's home, Sydney helped Dudley to the ground. A few minutes later, Carter pulled up behind her.

"Hey." She looked at him with empathy as he got out of the car. "Are you sure you're up for this?"

"No sense in going home and sulking," he said. "Besides, I'm very interested in what Isabelle has to say." Dudley came over to Carter for a scratch. "Hey, Mr. D."

Do you have a treat for me?

"Dudley said he's sorry to hear about your job."

Your translation skills are staggeringly poor.

"Aww, that's so sweet, and for that, you get a treat." Carter reached into his pocket and tossed him one.

Dudley snarfed it down, then eyed Sydney. *I take that back.*

Carter retrieved his digital camera from the back of his trunk. "After our conversation, I was thinking that since I now have free time, I can build your website. I can also accompany you to all of your sessions and shoot videos, which will work great on your website. You can even have an advice column titled *Dear Dudley*."

Sydney gasped. "Are you sure you can't hear Dudley? He suggested the same thing and came up with that exact title."

"What?" Carter laughed and glanced at Dudley.

Great minds and all that.

"He pretty much said great minds think alike."

"Well said, little man. I'll start working on it as soon we get home." They walked up to the front door. "Will Isabelle be okay if I film the session?"

"Yes, she's been on camera several times over the years and has no problem with it." Sydney rang the bell, and a few seconds later, Isabelle opened the door.

"So good to see you again, Sydney." The older woman gave her a hug.

"It's great to see you, too. Carter is behind the camera, and this is Dudley." She picked him up.

"Well, hello, Mr. Dudley. May I call you that? I feel like you're known by a more regal name."

She's good, he mentally said to Sydney. *Can you hear me, Isabelle?*

She laughed with excitement. "Loud and clear."

Sydney gasped and glanced at Carter. "She *can* hear him."

"Why don't we go sit down and have a nice chat?"

Are biscuits included?

"Oh, you are a funny one." Isabelle led them into a large solarium in the back of her house. Floor-to-ceiling windows ran the entire length of the outside wall. Several indoor plants decorated the room, some standing in huge ceramic planters, while others hung above their heads. A water fountain peacefully trickled in one of the corners, and very soft, new-age music played in the background.

Sydney loved this room. It was where Isabelle held her animal communication classes.

"Help yourself." Isabelle motioned to a pitcher of iced tea sitting on a table next to drinking glasses, a plate of cut lemons, and a bowl of sugar cubes.

"And for you, good sir." Isabelle motioned to a bowl of fresh water.

Thank you. He lapped up a little water, then focused on Isabelle.

"Now, Mr. Dudley, is there another name you prefer?"

I'm known as Durlindemore, King of the Dachshunds, but Dudley is growing on me.

"Both are wonderful names," Isabelle said. "Have you always been able to communicate so well?"

He glanced at Sydney. *Yes, although it takes two to have a conversation.*

"You are quite right." She chuckled. "Tell me, have you always had this gift?"

As long as I can remember.

"I take it from your accent that you traveled here from England."

"Dudley really has an accent?" Carter suddenly spoke up.

Isabelle nodded. "I'm sensing you flew over here with your family."

I was shoved in a cargo hold. Not to my liking in the least.

This was new. She'd asked him several times about his past, and he had always changed the subject, which led her to believe he didn't want to talk about it. Why was he now being so candid with a complete stranger?

"No, I don't suppose I'd much care for that, either," Isabelle said. "Who was the first person to hear you?"

Sydney.

"Had you tried to converse with others before her?"

Constantly. I've always been able to speak to other species, but Sydney was the first human to hear me.

"How did you know you could communicate with humans if Sydney was the first?"

Because, at one time, I could hear every human around me, and I tried countless times.

"That must have been overwhelming and somewhat depressing, to hear so many but none could hear you."

It was dreadful. However, I managed to switch them off. A necessity for me to stay sane. The things you humans think about are staggeringly trite. It's a wonder you've advanced as much as you have.

Sydney and Isabelle shared a smile, both hearing Dudley very clearly.

"Yes, I imagine so. We have creature comforts that your friends in the wild are lacking."

Precisely.

"I, too, must lower my psychic antenna to get a break from all the chatter," Isabelle said before she leaned in and intently stared him in the eye. "Since you can turn it off, I imagine you can easily turn it back on." She said it in a way that made Sydney think she knew a lot more about Dudley than he was willing to share with her.

Dudley's focus quickly darted to Sydney. *Enough about me. How did you learn telepathy?*

"I was born with it. My parents always thought I was making up dialogue for my cat, Sami, or a morning bird out my window, but I wasn't. I told them exactly what the animals around me were saying, only I never had as clear of a connection with any animal as I'm having with you. Why do you suppose that is?"

Dudley seemed to squirm under her scrutiny.

Sydney glanced at Carter to make sure he was filming them. She suspected something else was going on. She knew that look on Isabelle's face. Her teacher was receiving information from someone other than Dudley, most likely from her own spirit guides.

I'm suddenly very tired.

"Then I'll let you go. It was wonderful speaking with you, Durlindemore, King of the Dachshunds. I do hope you'll come back and see me."

Of course. I'd best be off now. He got to his feet, flapped his ears, and trotted out.

Carter lowered the camera and came over to them. "What just happened?"

Isabelle leaned in, keeping her voice down. "Carter, would you mind keeping an eye on Dudley for a few minutes while I speak with Sydney?"

He looked confused and a little anxious but did as she asked. "Uh, sure."

Sydney pulled out a bag of training treats from her jacket and handed them to Carter. "In case you've run out."

Carter nodded, then headed out just as Dudley returned to see why no one had followed him. "C'mon, little man. Let's get some fresh air and have a snack while your mom talks business."

Boring, she heard Dudley say as he sashayed out.

"What's going on?" she asked Isabelle, feeling slightly alarmed.

"He can hear your thoughts."

"What?" She squinted in confusion. "He told me he couldn't."

"He can hear everyone's thoughts, if he chooses."

She took a long breath, then let it out slowly. "I thought it was strange when he said I would always need to verbally speak to him. But why would he lie? I've looked crazy in front of people talking to him out loud when I could have easily talked to him telepathically."

"According to my guides, he was very hurt by his first family. I don't know all the details, but Dudley became very attached to a boy. Unfortunately, the boy's father didn't want Dudley around and decided to dump him at a shelter—only Dudley heard the man's thoughts and started barking at him. The man was so annoyed by his incessant barking that he stopped the car and left him on the side of the road instead."

Sydney put a hand to her mouth, as she felt her throat tighten. "Oh, Isabelle, that's horrible."

"Yes, I imagine it was." She took a sip of tea. "But he loves you very much, and Carter. I believe he pretends that he can't hear you so that you won't edit your thoughts. Right now, he knows exactly what you think of him."

All of her conversations with Dudley sped through her mind. He was more emotionally delicate than she realized. "This explains a lot—his need to move on, as he put it, from family to family."

"I don't think he understands that people can sometimes say or think things they really don't mean."

"Then I need to have a heart-to-heart with him as soon as possible." She shook her head, upset with herself for not figuring it out on her own. "Have you ever run across another animal who can communicate so well?"

"I wish I had. I've been doing this for forty years, and I've never met anyone like him. He's quite exceptional, Sydney."

"I know. Do you have any idea what would make him this way?"

"Nature, I suppose. Humans have geniuses and prodigies. I imagine animals have theirs, and Dudley is one of them. As you know, all creatures have the ability to speak telepathically with one another, but humans have allowed their own psychic abilities to wane. The reason you and Dudley have an exceptional relationship is because you two continue to strengthen that psychic muscle together."

"You're right," Sydney said. "I'm picking up more psychic information every day. You know, Carter wants to be able to do what we do."

"I sense that he's still conflicted about what to believe. He wants to believe in all of it, because of you, but at the same time, he just can't. Does that make sense?"

"Perfect sense."

"Give it time. The three of you seem right for each other in more ways than one."

Sydney smoothed down the back of her hair suddenly feeling awkward that her feelings toward Carter showed more than she thought. "You really think so?"

"I know so." Isabelle smiled. "He's taken with you just as much as you're taken with him."

She inhaled a quick breath. "Thank you, Isabelle, for that confirmation."

"Anytime, and keep me posted on Mr. Dudley. He's a very special canine."

"Oh, I know, and he never lets me forget it."

Isabelle laughed as they walked out together. "I'm going to check in with my guides again to see if they can give me any more information on his history. If so, I'll give you a ring."

She opened the door to see Carter and Dudley sitting on the stoop watching the neighborhood dogs walk by.

"Carter, if you ever want to learn how to communicate like Sydney, I'll be happy to work with you," Isabelle offered.

He stood. "I just might take you up on that. Thank you, Isabelle, for your time."

"My pleasure. Go easy on these two, Durlindemore."

I've stopped referring to them as my human servants. What more do you want?

"I think you know."

Sydney suddenly heard Isabelle telepathically say, *Trust opens many doors.*

Dudley took a good long look at her, then replied, *I'll keep that in mind.*

"What was that all about?" Carter asked as they walked back to their cars.

She wanted to share with Carter what Isabelle had revealed to her, but she thought it best to speak with Dudley first.

"Oh, she just told me that if Dudley ever wanted to hang out at her animal communication classes, he was more than welcome."

"That's it?"

"Yeah."

"She didn't have to send us away for that," he said. "I definitely want to learn this."

"Then I guess you better start being more open to the concept of psychic ability and the fact that it's very real."

"I will. I mean I *am*. Who said I wasn't?" Carter got a look of horror on his face. "Did Isabelle read my mind? Was she scanning me without my knowledge?"

Sydney laughed. "Her psychic ability is natural. She can't help it if she picks up on things others are hiding."

He looked even more horrified. "What's that supposed to mean?"

"It means you're blocking yourself from your own psychic ability."

"That's absurd."

"Is it? She told me that you want to believe in it, but you just can't."

Carter shifted and cast his gaze to the ground. "Okay. Maybe she's right, but does she know that I'm a journalist and being a skeptic comes with the territory?"

"If you truly want to learn animal communication then you need to be open to it without judgment."

"I'll feel ridiculous."

I suppose I can work with him, one-on-one.

"Dudley just said he can work with you."

"Really? You'd do that, little man?"

If it will make life easier, then yes, but humans are very hard to train. I expect delicious treats as payment.

"I think we can arrange that," she said to Dudley. "He'll do it for treats."

Carter laughed. "Okay, great. We'll start tonight. I've got to run a few errands, but why don't you come over for dinner around seven?"

"We'll be there."

As Sydney pulled up to a stoplight, she gave Dudley a sideways glance. He seemed engrossed in his surroundings, taking in the good sniffs and barking at any dog he saw on a leash, so she was fairly certain he wasn't trying to read her mind.

She couldn't believe it. Dudley could read her mind. This was a game changer—a good one in so many ways, but also an intrusive one. She wasn't someone who shared her most private thoughts with anyone, but now a dog could freely have access to them anytime he wanted. Who'd sign up for that? She'd have to watch what she said, worse, what she thought. How long could she keep that up before it became too exhausting?

And just how good was Dudley at reading a person's thoughts? Did he have to struggle hard to make a connection, or was it as easy as swallowing kibble? Was he hearing her thoughts right now?

She glanced at him. He was enjoying the fresh air and the sun on his face. He appeared to be in his own little world, but it didn't mean he was. Had he been eavesdropping on her without her knowledge? She had to know the extent of his expertise before she told Carter.

Sydney parked in front of Carter's house and helped Dudley get out of the car. She watched him as he trotted to the side gate. *Hello, Dudley. I know you can hear me.* He didn't respond to her at all. Was he pretending he hadn't heard her?

She opened the door for him, and they headed inside. She poured herself a glass of water, then sat down on the couch as Dudley slurped noisily from his bowl in the corner.

"We need to talk."

His head jerked up. *I thought you were rather quiet coming home. What did Isabelle say to you?*

I think you know, she said telepathically.

Dudley lowered his head and gave her puppy eyes.

"Why did you lie to me?"

Because I knew you would think the worst—that I've been privy to your every thought.

"Haven't you?"

Absolutely not. I'm a gentleman. I would never invade your thoughts without your permission. Besides, do you really think I want to hear, 'Does he like me? Does he think I'm pretty?'

"You *have* been invading my thoughts."

No, I merely assumed. I see how you look at him—similar to how I look at Penelope. When I met her, my thoughts were, does she fancy me? Does she find me exceptionally handsome? Because I am.

Sydney squelched a laugh, but she couldn't hide her smile. Even when the conversation was serious, he managed to lighten it. "Have you been reading Carter's mind?"

Perhaps a little.

She groaned.

Only because he isn't like us. I did it to protect you—to make sure his intentions toward you were honorable.

She should have scolded him for doing such a thing, but she couldn't. It was endearing.

They are honorable, in case you're wondering.

She nodded and wanted to know more but couldn't exactly do that without looking like a hypocrite. "Is it easy for you? To read our minds?"

It is when I ask the person's soul and am given permission. But if I want to know something on my own, without asking permission, then it's much more difficult and it drains the energy right out of me.

"Did you ask Isabelle if you could talk to her telepathically?"

She asked me. As you recall, she was hearing me as well as you were. She opened up her energy to me and invited me to speak with her telepathically. She's very psychic. I imagine she was conversing psychically before she could speak.

"Yes, she is very talented. I heard her telepathic voice for the first time today."

Your ability is getting stronger.

"That's what she told me. She also said something else—that you'd been abandoned."

He broke eye contact. *Happens to millions every year.*

"I know, but I'm sorry it happened to you. Will you tell me about it?"

I thought Isabelle already had.

"Not the details."

What does it matter? One cannot alter the past.

"It matters to me."

Dudley glanced out the window, then came over and curled up on her lap. *All right, then. I was a mere pup when a boy asked his mum if he could take me home. She said yes, and Oliver and I became inseparable. I walked to school with him, then waited by the front door all day for him to return. When he didn't have to go to school, we did everything together. We played in the woods. We ate lunch together, he read me stories, we took naps together. It was a perfect life. Then we moved over here.*

Soon his parents weren't getting along. There was always tension in the air, and Ollie began spending more time away. One day Ollie's mum said she was going back to England with Ollie but leaving me here. She said she'd send for me once they were settled in a new place. Ollie insisted I go with them, but his mum kept saying I'd be too much trouble.

They left without me, and Ollie's father went into a rage. When I attempted to comfort him, he picked me up and said we were going for a ride. He was so aggressive with me that I decided to read his mind. He was taking me to a shelter. I started barking at him, trying to make him hear me. But he couldn't. Worse, his thoughts told me that he never liked me. He believed his son loved me more than him. He became so impatient with my barking that he pulled over and tossed me out of the car. I never saw Ollie again.

Sydney wiped away the tears suddenly streaming down her cheeks. "Oh, Dudley. I'm so very sorry. That's just awful."

Dudley sounded so sad speaking of Ollie. Did this mean he'd prefer to live with the boy? She never dreamed of having to give him up. She'd loved him from the moment she realized he could be hers.

She felt a lump in her throat and pushed it down so she could speak. "If you know his last name and want to be reunited with him, I'll search for him and try to find him."

He looked up at her. *But then that would mean I'd need to leave you, and I've grown rather fond of you, dear Sydney.*

"I've grown fond of you too, Dudley," she said with a shaky voice. "But how can I keep you if you belong to another?"

I believe we come and go out of each other's lives for a reason. I was in Ollie's life when he needed a friend. But our separation marked the beginning of new adventures for him. And for me. Even though I loved Ollie tremendously, I sensed I was supposed to be with someone other than Ollie—someone who truly understood me. This is the reason I kept running away from every person who took me in—not because they were abusive or because I had trust issues. I was running to find you.

She blinked away the tears that kept coming. "But you didn't even know me."

I knew you were out there, but I didn't know where you were, until the night we met. The moment you started helping your friend over the phone, I realized it was you. You were the one I'd been waiting for and my search was over. It might have taken me years to find you, but I finally have, and I don't want to say goodbye.

"I don't, either." She hugged him tightly. "As long as you're happy here, I will never let you go."

He licked the tears off her cheek. *You were definitely worth the wait.*

CHAPTER TWENTY-THREE

Realizing the time, Carter hurriedly brought the bags of groceries inside. Shopping always took him longer than expected, because he spent half of the time running up and down the aisles, trying to find a particular item. Unlike his mom and sister, he didn't have the aisles memorized. He was a take-out and delivery guy, not a chef. Hot dog buns were on aisle twelve. What more did he need to know?

Except tonight—he wanted to impress Sydney by making her a great dinner, like she had for him. However, wanting and doing were two different things. After wandering up and down the aisles for what seemed like hours, he realized he needed to stick to what he knew. Grilling.

As soon as he got home, he took a quick shower, then fired up the grill out on his deck. It was such a clear night that he decided to set the table outside. Add in a few lit candles, and they were well on their way to a romantic dinner and a romantic night.

Or were they? Why did he agree to work on telepathy with Dudley? Maybe they could do a few exercises for a while, but then hopefully his lack of skill would deplete Dudley so much that the dog would return to the guesthouse and call it a night. Carter wouldn't mind that scenario. He'd finally be alone with Sydney.

"Are we too early?" she asked, walking over with Dudley.

"Not at all." He checked the temperature on the grill.

"It's so nice out here." She admired the lit candles. "Can I help?"

"I think I've got it covered. I'm not doing anything fancy, just burgers. And Dudley, I'm grilling you a beef hot dog."

Dudley barked, wagging his tail.

"No translation needed, but your mom will decide how much of it you'll get to eat." Dudley lowered his tail and whined, which made Carter laugh. He took a swig of his beer and eyed Sydney. "What can I get you to drink?"

"Did I see a bottle of root beer in your fridge the other night?"

"You did. Handcrafted, and it's pretty good."

"Sold."

He grabbed a root beer for her, then got to grilling. "I haven't had a chance to review today's session with Isabelle, but from where I stood, it was intriguing. I'd love to know what was being said. Maybe we can show it to Dudley and see if you two can remember the telepathic conversation."

Sydney took a sip of her root beer and sat down. "Sounds like you're becoming a true believer."

"It's difficult not to when I can't figure out another logical explanation for your extraordinary skills. Though I have to ask, did you tell Isabelle his real name?"

"Absolutely not. Even though I've studied under her, I wanted to see how much she could learn from Dudley psychically."

"Then I'm incredibly impressed. Durlindemore isn't exactly a name that rolls off the tongue."

"No, it isn't, and if you remember, she already sensed that his real name was more regal when I introduced him." She glanced at Dudley and smiled. "He just informed me that his regal stature is what gave him away, and that clearly anyone who lays eyes on him can see there is nothing common about him in the least."

Carter chuckled. "Yes, I see your point, Durlindemore. You know, hot dogs are a favorite among the common man, so maybe you shouldn't eat them."

Sydney listened to Dudley telepathically, then laughed. "He said, 'Even royalty must, at times, partake in food meant for the masses.'"

"True, but I'd never dream of forcing royalty to do anything," Carter said. "Why don't I eat it for you?"

Dudley began barking his head off, which made him laugh.

"I don't know what you said, but no need to fret, little man. It's all yours."

Dudley grumbled something that made Sydney's lips twitch in amusement, and Carter suddenly wanted to kiss that mouth of hers.

"I've got a new client tomorrow afternoon," she said. "A pit bull who's acting aggressive toward the owner's new boyfriend."

He suddenly pictured Sydney trying to get a hold of the pit bull and the dog biting her. Sydney hadn't yet had the session with Jamie and her Rottweiler, so this would be her and Dudley's first session with a big and possibly dangerous dog. "How aggressive?"

"Lulu is a sweet rescue. She's been that way for two years, but she doesn't like the new boyfriend. I've got to see if it's a protection issue, or if the guy is antagonizing her unknowingly."

That didn't make him feel any better. The boyfriend could be a hothead. "You know, I was thinking. If this is energy work, maybe you can start doing some sessions over a video call."

"That's a great idea. We'll be able to book sessions with clients in other states."

"Why don't you try it out with the aggressive pit bull?"

Sydney studied him. "Are you worried about me?"

"It's hard not to be. Pit bulls are responsible for most of the serious dog attacks."

"Most attacks are because the owner has no business being one. Pitties are one of the sweetest breeds I've ever known. I could do this session over a video call, but I really need to watch the boyfriend—the way he moves and how he interacts with Lulu."

He wasn't happy about her decision, but it wasn't his call. "I guess I'll have to trust the pet psychic on this one—though it doesn't make me any less anxious."

"I truly appreciate your concern, but Dudley and I discussed it at length before I accepted the booking. He said not to worry. He can charm the rattle off a snake."

"I'd like to see that." Carter took the hot dog off the grill and gave it to Sydney, who cut it into small pieces and let it cool down before setting half of it in front of Dudley.

The dog devoured it in seconds.

"You were supposed to eat that slowly." She gave him a reproachful look. "Oh no, I'm not falling for that."

"For what?"

"He's pretending he didn't get anything. He said, 'Eat what slowly?'"

Carter chuckled. "Sorry, little man, but I saw you chow that down."

Dudley groaned, then traipsed to the side and lay down.

Carter took the burgers off the grill and joined Sydney at the table. "I hope to get your website up this week." He squirted ketchup on his bun before adding lettuce and tomato.

"Thank you, but seriously, it can wait. You'll never find another job if you're constantly taking care of me." She cut her burger in half and took a bite.

"Maybe I like taking care of you."

She smiled, then looked at him in a way that made him think he had melted her heart. "Let me at least pay you for all of the work you're doing," she said.

"No chance. You're still paying rent on your apartment."

"Doesn't matter. Besides, Dudley gave up his cut of the session fee and asked me to give it to you, which is the right thing to do. You're filming the sessions, and now you'll be building my website and posting the videos. That's a lot of work and you deserve half."

"I couldn't."

"You can and will. No arguments. When you find another job, I'm going to have to hire someone else to record these sessions. That person will definitely expect to get paid, so you should, too."

He let out a resigned sigh. "Okay, but this is only temporary."

And he hoped it was. He didn't feel right taking part of Sydney's fee. He needed to find a job. His previous aspirations of moving to a bigger city and reporting on important breaking news suddenly didn't seem so appealing. Nowadays, criminals did a quick walk-through at the police department and were out on the streets reoffending within the hour. It was senseless and depressing.

The thought of leaving Sydney was also depressing. He was

perfectly content staying in his small town where very little happened. He couldn't think of anywhere else he'd rather be than sitting across from her, watching her eat potato chips. She was nibbling on the edges like a mouse, and it was absolutely adorable.

Good Lord.

Carter jerked back.

"What's wrong?" Sydney asked.

"Didn't you hear that?" Carter asked.

"Hear what?"

"I thought I heard a male voice say, 'Good Lord.'"

Dudley instantly sat up, now fully alert.

"That was Dudley," she said excitedly. "You heard Dudley?"

"Did I? How?"

"I don't know." She looked as perplexed as he felt. "You're relaxed and drinking. Dudley is relaxed and almost sleeping, which means neither of you is stressed out or guarding your emotions. Say something again, Dudley."

Dudley trotted over to Carter and sat in front of him.

"He's thinking of a number right now."

Carter suddenly felt the pressure to get it right. He stared intently into Dudley's eyes, but he heard nothing. He shook his head and flicked a glance at Sydney. "Can *you* hear his number?"

She nodded. "He's saying it over and over."

Carter still heard nothing so he closed his eyes, attempting to hear it or hoping it would pop in his head. "Twenty-four?"

Sydney slumped and Dudley went back to his sleeping spot. "It was thirty-seven."

"Not even close."

"But you heard him say, 'Good Lord,' when he did." She turned to look at Dudley. "Why did you say that anyway?" Sydney listened to him—a conversation Carter couldn't hear at all. "What do you mean, no reason?"

"Dudley, could you hear my thoughts?" Carter questioned.

Sydney's eyes widened, but she said nothing.

Dudley was staring at Sydney, and Carter really wished he could hear what was going on in that dog brain of his. "Mind filling me in?"

"He said he was dozing off and falling into a dream. He said he really has no idea why he said it." She shrugged.

Carter narrowed his eyes on Dudley. "Are you telling your mom the truth?"

Dudley broke eye contact and yawned.

"He said he doesn't have the capacity to lie like humans and that he's off to bed as it's been an exhausting day."

Dudley headed toward the guesthouse.

"Let me get him settled." She got up. "Don't stop eating. I'll be right back."

He watched Sydney take Dudley back to the guesthouse. It was a curious thing, what just happened. Had he actually connected to Dudley telepathically, or was his mind playing tricks on him? He was on his second beer, which might have something to do with it, but he could have sworn he heard a British accent.

Of course, this posed another question. Could animals lie? He could easily see how Dudley would comment on his observation of Sydney eating chips like a mouse. If Dudley hadn't heard him, then it was a very strange coincidence. Besides, Sydney had already said he couldn't hear her thoughts, so there was no way Dudley could hear his.

Unless the dog was lying.

Sydney let Dudley in and shut the door behind them. "I thought you weren't reading his mind anymore?"

I'm not. It just happened.

"You just happened to eavesdrop on his private thoughts?"

No. I honestly was dozing off and thinking about how delicious that hot dog was, and how much I cared about Carter. And then all of a sudden, it was as if our wavelengths were on the same channel. I wasn't focusing on him, or attempting to hear him. He was simply there—blathering on about how he was content to stay with you in his hometown and how adorable it was that you ate potato chips like a mouse.

She broke into a grin. "He said that?"

No. He thought that. I'm truly mystified. How could he have possibly heard me?

"This is very strange."
Perhaps it's the alcohol.
"He was drinking the other night and nothing happened."
But he's more relaxed tonight.
"And more of a believer."
There you have it. I was incredibly relaxed as well, so I must have left my psychic channel open.
"But why couldn't he hear the number you were thinking?"
Stress, I imagine. Or fear of what it would mean if he could actually hear me.
"What fear could he possibly have?"
Suddenly being able to telepathically speak with a canine would discredit what he's known to be true. I suspect his subconscious is grappling with that very thing.
"Makes sense."
Of course it does. I said it. He yawned again. *Perhaps you two can figure it out without my help. I shall be fast asleep in a matter of minutes.*
"All right. Sleep tight. Bark if you need me." She tucked him in and headed back to Carter.

Carter waited for her to come back and sit down before he finished his meal. "Did he say anything else about what just happened?"

She debated on whether to tell him the whole truth. She'd need to, eventually, and the longer she waited, the more it would feel like a betrayal. At the same time, she couldn't exactly reveal that she now knew what he thought of her eating potato chips. He had already freaked out about Dudley being so fully aware of what they were saying and doing the other night. She couldn't imagine how he'd react if he knew Dudley had just read his innermost thoughts.

"Dudley said he was thinking about how much he liked you, as he was dozing off, and how you'd made him such a delicious hot dog. In his extremely relaxed state, his energy was open to you, and he believes your brainwaves ended up on the same frequency for a second."

One side of his mouth raised. "He really said that?"

She nodded. "Quick psychic connections happen frequently."

"No, I mean, he was thinking about me?"

"Yes. He really likes you. In fact, I'd say he loves you. He shared a lot with me after today's session, and what he's been through. Like us humans, he guards his emotions because he's been hurt in the past. He's very happy living here. From some of the comments he made to me lately, I think he worries that it could suddenly change overnight."

"Why? Because I'm out of a job?"

"Because he was once separated from a boy he loved very much. I've assured him that I love him and will never abandon him, but he's a bit wary because he's been burned. It isn't much different than any of us. We fall in love with someone, and if we're lucky, that love is returned and there's a happily ever after. But sometimes it doesn't work out that way."

"I can understand what he's feeling. Poor little guy. What can I do?"

"Just be your wonderful self and know that if you could hear him briefly tonight, maybe he can hear both of us once in a while."

"Like right now? Do you think he can hear what we're saying?"

"No. He was practically snoring the moment he closed his eyes. All I'm saying is the more comfortable he feels around us, the more he might be able to pick up our thoughts, so maybe try to refrain from thinking things like, *I wish Dudley would go away.*"

Carter looked a little offended. "I'd never think that."

"Even when we were kissing the other night?"

"He heard me then, too?"

"No. That thought crossed my mind, so I was just using it as an example."

He nodded, but he still seemed a little distracted. Were there too many rules now, especially if he had to watch what he was thinking?

"Are you still okay with all of this?"

"Yeah," he said. "What bothers me is not being on the same playing field. I'm beginning to believe that psychic ability is real, and I want to be open to it, but I stress out every time I try something."

"That will go away the more you practice. We can still work on it tonight if you want."

"Okay."

They finished eating and moved into the living room to work. "Do you have a deck of cards?" she asked.

"Yeah." Carter disappeared down the hall, then came back with the cards in hand and sat facing her on the couch.

Sydney shuffled them. "First of all, psychic ability is about emotions and feelings. You're already better at this than you think."

"How do you figure?"

"As a journalist, I imagine you get a lot of hunches or gut feelings. Correct?"

"Yeah."

"Well, you're already using your psychic muscle. You know in your gut that something is off—even though your eyes might be telling you differently. Take a deep breath, close your eyes, and relax."

Carter had a serene look on his face, which made him very sexy in that moment, and she wondered if she'd be sleeping next to him someday soon. She fought the desire to reach over and kiss him. *Focus.* "You can open your eyes now."

He did, but he didn't move. His breathing was slower, his eyes looked clearer.

"Good. Now, I'm going to hold up a card, and you're going to tell me which suit it is. Hearts, diamonds, spades, or clubs. I will also telepathically tell you what it is. Clear your mind of everything except for this. You can either concentrate on the card itself, or try to hear me, or both."

She drew the first card. It was the ace of spades. She pictured the card in her mind, then psychically told him the card was black and the suit was spades. She then gently repeated spades over and over in her head.

Carter sat up straight, concentrating, then slumped and broke eye contact. "I feel ridiculous."

"Why?"

"I don't know." He shook his head and refocused. After a long moment, he said. "I want to say that it's black."

She smiled. "Correct. Take another breath and try to see the suit."

Carter did as she instructed and finally said, "Spades."

"Yes!" She reached over and gave him a quick kiss.

"Oh, this is a reward-type game. I didn't know. The pressure is on."

"Sorry. I didn't mean to do that. It was an impulse."

"I like your impulses."

She raised a brow. "Focus."

"I was, and then you distracted me."

"I know. I'm sorry." She waved the card in front of him. "Tell me the exact card."

"What do I get if I do?"

"Now you sound like Dudley. Name the card."

Carter let out a big sigh and tried to concentrate. "I don't know. The five of spades?"

"You threw that out as a guess. Try again. I'm telling you what it is." She stared at him, repeating the ace of spades over in her mind while also picturing it.

"I don't know." He shook his head. "The only thing coming to me is the ace of spades."

She smiled and gave him another quick kiss. Even though she pretended the first kiss was on impulse, it wasn't. Attributing positive reinforcement to something he didn't like doing wasn't a bad idea. It had worked with dogs for years.

"I was right?"

She nodded. "See how easy it is?"

"Especially if I keep getting kisses. Let me try another."

She held up a card—the seven of diamonds.

He crossed his arms, concentrating.

"Stay open."

"What do you mean?"

"Uncross your arms. You close off your energy doing that."

"So many rules." He uncrossed his arms and blew out a quick breath. "Okay, I can do this." He focused. "Is it a red suit?"

"Yes."

"Diamonds?"

"Yes! You're unbelievable." She gave him another quick kiss.

"Shouldn't the kisses be getting longer?"

"Focus."

"Three of diamonds."

"Wrong."

"The nine of diamonds."

"It was the seven of diamonds. Don't think. Feel. What's the suit on this next card?"

"Spades again."

She shook her head. "Take a deep breath, blow it out, and concentrate."

He did and put his attention back on the card. "Hearts. I think it's hearts."

"Yes!"

"Is it the queen of hearts?"

She laughed. "Yes! I can't believe how good you are at this." She leaned over and gave him another kiss, but this time, he wouldn't let her go.

He pulled her to him, ran his hand through her hair, and kissed her longer. And just like that, she couldn't think of anything but him. She slid her arms around his neck as each kiss intensified. He ran his hands down her back sending sensations all over her body. He pulled her closer just as his cell rang, which startled them both. He quickly reached for it to turn it off, then froze, as he stared at the caller ID.

His hesitation gave her enough time to see the name "Jade". He dismissed the call and went back to her, taking her in his arms. A few moments later his cell rang again.

She saw it was Jade again, and wondered who she was, since she'd never heard him mention a Jade before. "Do you need to get that?"

"No." He turned off the volume and flipped over the phone this time, but she stopped kissing him. He searched her eyes. "What's wrong?"

She wished she could read his mind because she didn't want to sound like she was suspicious of him. "I'm sorry. It's just, we haven't discussed our previous relationships with each other—not that I want to—but we also haven't discussed what we expect from each other. I prefer to date someone exclusively, and I'm really trying not to pry, but can I ask who Jade is?"

He sat back, took a deep breath, but wouldn't look at her.

"I understand if you don't want to talk about her. It's just that my last boyfriend got back with his ex-girlfriend while he was living with me, which is why I'm asking."

Shock registered on his face, and then anger. "I'm sorry that happened to you. You deserve better." He puffed out a breath. "Jade was my fiancée."

"Oh. Wow. Okay." Definitely not what she'd expected to hear. "How long ago?"

"It's been almost a year now. All of the sketches you saw in the guesthouse when you first came over were hers."

"I remember seeing one of a wedding."

He nodded but said nothing else.

Had the sketch been Jade's vision of their upcoming wedding? Did he still love her? How had they left it? Were they still in each other's lives? Carter wasn't offering up any information and that worried her.

"She's very talented," Sydney finally said. "Can I ask what happened?"

"She got accepted to a prestigious art school in Paris, so we broke off our engagement and ended our relationship."

"I'm sorry. That must have been very difficult for you."

"It was, but living in Paris had always been a dream of hers, and I wasn't going to ask her to give that up for me."

Her heart melted knowing he'd put Jade's happiness above his own. "At least you remained friends and still talk."

"I haven't spoken to her in months. That's why I was surprised to see her name pop up on my phone."

So why was she calling now? Did Jade want to get back together with him? If he had loved her enough to want to marry her, and no one had come between them, would he still have feelings for her?

"Hey." He took her hand, no doubt catching the look of concern on her face. "I'm with you now, so there's nothing to worry about. Okay?"

She forced a smile. "Okay."

He took her in his arms and she closed her eyes, cherishing the feeling, never wanting to give him up. They seemed so right for one another.

Maybe she was making too much of it. She shouldn't be surprised that he'd been engaged once. Who wouldn't want to date him, live with him, marry him?

Had Jade finally realized what a great guy she'd given up? If she'd only been a girlfriend to him and not a fiancée, Sydney wouldn't be giving her another thought. But he hadn't removed her from his life until very recently. Her sketches and art supplies had been as she'd left them, as if she'd run an errand and was coming right back. Had Carter been hoping that she'd return and they'd continue where they left off? Is that why he'd never boxed up her things?

Jade had tried to get ahold of Carter not once but twice. Had she left a voice message? Sydney really hoped she was worrying about nothing, and that his ex-fiancée had been calling just to say hi. But what if that wasn't the case? She'd never be able to compete with a talented artist from Paris who'd once held Carter's heart in the palm of her hand.

CHAPTER TWENTY-FOUR

As much as Carter wanted to continue where he and Sydney left off, Sydney seemed distracted after Jade had called. And he was too, but he was also pissed at Jade's poor timing. Why the hell was she calling now after she'd ghosted him for months?

He checked his phone after Sydney went home. Jade hadn't left a message, and he had no desire to call her back. He didn't want to think about her again, reopening old wounds. He meant what he said to Sydney—he was with her now.

But how could he prove it? She'd obviously been hurt from a past relationship as much as he had, and the last thing he wanted was for her to worry needlessly. He had tried to get the night back on track, but Sydney had left early, saying she was tired—but he knew her fast departure was because of the phone call.

If he wasn't able to spend the evening with Sydney, he could at least work on her website. He'd start by securing her domain name since she and Dudley had settled on *The Dachshund Whisperer*. He'd then work on the design layout and have a few options ready for her to take a look at tomorrow after the pit bull session. Hopefully, if Sydney had any doubts as to how he felt, she'd realize that he'd been thinking about her all night instead of his ex.

Sydney walked silently to the park with Dudley, Cocoa Puff, Pupperton, and Finn. It was a peaceful morning, but she couldn't enjoy it.

I knew I should have stayed with you at Carter's. Dudley cast a glance her way. *Did you two have a row last night?*

"No."

I can see you're horribly troubled about something, but I'm refraining from reading your mind. Should I go ahead and do that?

She couldn't help but smile. "Carter was engaged to be married less than a year ago, and his ex-fiancée called last night."

Oh dear. What did she want?

"I don't know. He didn't pick up."

That's encouraging. How was he acting?

"He was definitely surprised to see her name pop up on his phone."

And now you're worried he rang her back after you left and that things have changed between you two, especially since we didn't see him this morning.

She nodded.

I can do some intel gathering, and he won't suspect a thing.

"Thank you, but that's an invasion of privacy. As much as I want to know, I can't ask you to do that."

Then allow me to quell your fears. When I was tapping into his thoughts before, I never heard anything about an ex.

She let out the breath she'd apparently been holding. "Thank you for the reassurance." Her cell rang and she jumped for it, hoping it was Carter, but it wasn't. It was her new client. "Hi, Adriana. Is everything okay?"

"Not really. I broke up with my boyfriend last night."

"Oh, I'm so sorry."

"Thanks. Lulu never liked him, so that should have given me a clue. I hate to cancel on you so late, but now that we broke up, I no longer have the issue you were coming over to correct."

"No problem. Is there anything else Dudley and I can help Lulu with?"

"Not at the moment. I'll pay your cancellation fee."

"Don't worry about it. Hold on to my number, and give me a call if something else comes up. Take care, Adriana." She hung up and eyed Dudley. "Her boyfriend is no longer."

Smart woman. There must have been a good reason why Lulu didn't care for him.

"I was sensing the same thing. Of course, this means we just had our first cancellation."

Carter will be happy. He seemed terribly distressed about this one.

"He was. I think he's more psychic than he realizes."

I can confirm that.

She smiled at that fact. "I should probably call him to tell him."

You might want to wait on that. Pupperton is locked on to a squirrel.

Before she could respond, he pulled her into a run. "Heel!" She visualized Pupperton obeying, but he wasn't.

Dudley had a few choice barks to say to him, which not only made the big dog heel, but had him lowering his head to Dudley.

"What did you say?"

I told him that there would be no squirrel killing on my watch, and if he ever wanted to go on another walk, he needed to stop dragging us down the street.

"Wow. I only heard four barks."

Our language isn't complicated, and I got straight to the point. Most animals in the wild have easy languages, as seconds count when it comes to life and death.

"That makes total sense."

Of course it does. We don't unnecessarily complicate things like you humans.

"I suppose that's why I've preferred the company of canines over men."

Until Carter came along.

"He's an exception," she said. Pupperton started walking faster, but glanced back at Dudley to make sure it was okay for him to do so. "I think we need to get a good jog in for Pupperton. Are you up for it?"

Must we?

"If you want to keep eating hot dogs, we do."

Oh, all right. I suppose I can pick up the pace.

Sydney set her cell inside her jacket and zipped it up. "Let's go!"

Carter's cell rang, startling him awake. He was hunched over his computer and realized that he must have fallen asleep on the job. "Hey Shep," he said with a hoarse voice as he got up to stretch.

"You sound like crap."

"I was up all night, working on something."

"So was I," Shep said. "Can you meet me in a half hour at the coffee shop on Orchard?"

"Is this about the mayor?"

"Yeah."

"See you in a few."

Carter glanced at the time. Much later than he thought. Sydney must have wondered why he wasn't out on his deck this morning. He headed into the bathroom to splash water on his face and dialed her on the way. She wasn't answering, so he quickly changed his clothes and headed out, anxious to know what Shep had uncovered.

When he arrived, he found Shep sitting alone at the far end of the diner. Any other day, Shep would be chatting up a pretty woman, or regaling residents with tales of his heroic journalism. Instead, he was sipping coffee and poring over documents laid out on the table.

"Hey, Shep." Carter slid into the booth opposite him.

"Have you eaten?"

He shook his head. "I haven't even had my morning coffee."

"I can fix that." A waitress, who had been right behind him, turned over his coffee cup and poured him some fresh brew before topping off Shep's. "Do you need a minute or do you know what you want?"

Carter scanned the daily specials advertised on the table. "I'll take your veggie omelet with fruit," Carter said.

"Same." Shep threw a splash of milk into his coffee and stirred it in, then waited for the waitress to leave before he spoke. "I think you might be right as to why we were shuttered. Seems Kessler has his eye on any downtown business taking up prime real estate. From what I can gather, he's looking to transform our safe, sleepy, small town into a resort destination for the rich." Shep handed over an inch-thick folder of research he'd printed out. "Colton Enterprises is a land and real estate development company. Kessler was meeting with its CFO and his team the night I saw them. Our mayor happened to be an employee of that company three years ago. In fact, when he moved here, he was still working remotely for them for six months before he "quit" to run for mayor. I spoke with Russell late last night. He was approached to sell the building a few months ago but turned down the offer since it was his grandfather who had started the paper."

"And now that *The Pinecrest News* has been put out of business, there's no reason for Russell to hold on to the property." Carter thumbed through Shep's research. "I wonder if they're trying to get rid of the barber shop next door, and the arts and crafts store down the block."

"Wouldn't hurt to make some inquiries."

"I'll head over there after we eat." Carter set the research aside. "Makes sense as to why he'd target our block in particular. We're in the heart of downtown, we're in some of the oldest buildings, and the businesses don't bring in much revenue. Do you know when they're meeting next?"

"No, but I'm working on one of the assistants in his office to get her to spill any secrets."

From Shep's smile, Carter knew that meant he planned on dating her. "You know, Shep, I thought you'd be long gone, on your way to Chicago or New York for a bigger market. I'm really impressed with the amount of investigative work you've done on this, but I've got to ask—why are you so interested in taking him down?"

"Contrary to what everyone thinks, I happen to love it here. My family and friends are here. Everyone knows me and loves me. Is it a little too small for me at times? Sure, but life is much easier and friendlier here than it is in the Big Apple." Shep sat back. "What about you? More than once, I heard you ask Russell for bigger assignments. Are you planning on moving?"

"I was until I met Sydney. Now, I'm helping her get her own business started."

"Is that the only reason?"

"We're hitting it off, if that's what you're asking."

"That's great." Shep tried to hide his disappointment. "Do you believe what you wrote, that she can telepathically communicate with her dog?"

"At first I didn't, but I've been recording her communication sessions, and I can't explain how she gets some of the information that she does—unless she was having detailed conversations with Dudley."

"Maybe we should send the mutt in to gather intel on Kessler."

Carter laughed, but then his brain went into overdrive. Was there a way to get Dudley near the mayor to collect vital information? They needed a man on the inside. What about a dog on the inside? An extremely smart dog who could snoop around—maybe find some blueprints or a project proposal. He needed to talk to Sydney about it. After all, no one would ever suspect that a fat little dachshund was actually a Trojan horse.

Sydney was winded and Dudley was panting by the time they got to their usual bench in the park. She opened her collapsible water bowl for the dogs and poured cool water in it, then sat and took a sip of her energy drink. She retrieved her phone and saw that Carter had called but hadn't left a message.

"Here goes." She felt butterflies in her stomach as she called him back, and was relieved when she got his voicemail. "Hey, I saw that you called. My afternoon session has been canceled. Maybe we can have lunch and work on the website."

As she hung up, she noticed a carload of businessmen getting out of an SUV. "Do they look like hikers to you?"

Dudley eyed the men. *Not in the least. I wonder what these chaps are up to.*

One of the men carried what appeared to be architectural plans and laid them out on a picnic table as the others in his group huddled around it. That's when she noticed the mayor pulling up with his entourage.

"Something is definitely going on." She took out her phone and started snapping photos when Kessler walked over to the businessmen. "Maybe we can get closer," she said to Dudley.

She nonchalantly walked toward them with the dogs. She couldn't pick up what they were saying, so she moved even closer.

"...which extends all the way over there." One guy pointed to the far end of the park.

"Prime real estate," a younger guy said. "Once divided into large parcels and with exclusivity guaranteed, this development would attract wealthy clientele to the area."

"Is our option of high-density housing with the attraction of private hiking trails still on the table?" another asked before noticing Sydney. "Why don't we take this back to the office for further discussion?" They gathered their papers and left as fast as they came.

Sydney couldn't move, shell-shocked from what she just heard. "Was he talking about selling off part of our beloved park for housing?"

I fear you might be correct.

"Carter's going to want to know about this." She texted him to call her as soon as possible. He was going to freak out when he learned what Kessler had planned on doing to Pinecrest's largest park.

CHAPTER TWENTY-FIVE

Carter had spent close to three hours with Shep examining documents and strategizing. He'd been so immersed in his meeting that he'd missed Sydney's call. He was listening to her message about the pit bull session being canceled when he saw Russell's car parked outside *The Pinecrest News* building.

It was eerie—walking into the newsroom and not seeing everyone at their desks. Only Russell was there, in his office, packing up his things.

"Need any help?"

He turned around, looking a little startled. "Thanks for the offer, but I'm not in any rush. I'm having a hard time packing up thirty-five years of my life." Chester jumped on his desk and waited for Carter to come over and pet him. "I'm surprised to see you here," Russel said. "I thought you got everything yesterday."

"I did. I saw your car outside."

Russell pulled two journalism awards from his bookshelf and set them in an open box. "I still can't believe it's over. We were finally increasing our readership. Things were looking up."

Carter hated seeing him like this, which made him want to fight even more. "Don't you find it strange that the mayor's brother-in-law abruptly pulled his ads?"

"Yeah. He didn't give me any warning. In fact, when my wife and I ran into him just a few weeks ago, he said he planned on placing more ads with us this week. I just don't understand it."

"It was Kessler. He shut us down, and Shep and I are going to expose him."

"You two need to stop. You saw how fast he destroyed us. You're playing with fire."

"Comes with the territory when trying to expose corruption."

"Carter, your tax investigation was excellent, but sadly not enough people care."

"They will when they hear that he's planning on destroying our small town."

"How?"

"By clearing out our mom-and-pop businesses for a so-called *revitalization* project. His project is actually about turning our town into a resort destination for the rich."

"Who told you that?"

"Shep saw him meeting with commercial property developers. I don't think our paper was shut down because of its small readership. I think they want this entire block because we're in the heart of downtown. Shep told me they asked you to sell the building, and I'm willing to bet they've approached all of the business owners around here to do the same."

Russell slowly crumpled into his chair. "How did I not see it? I refused to sell, so Kessler pressured his brother-in-law to pull his advertising. He knew that our revenue would be so dramatically reduced, it would force me to fold." Russell dragged a hand over his weary face. He looked fragile, beaten down. "I never liked that guy from the start. He came out of nowhere and was suddenly running for office."

"I remember." Carter leaned against the doorframe. "Kessler knows nothing about running a small town. His background is in real estate. My guess is he put his sights on Pinecrest because of our perfect location to the Twin Cities."

"Of course he has." Russell shook his head in disgust. "If he turns our town into a resort destination, the locals will get pushed out when the price of everything skyrockets."

"We need to talk to the business owners," Carter said. "We need to know how many have already sold their storefronts. Hopefully, we can get to those who haven't."

"Steve next door leases, but I'll find out who owns it." Russell jumped on his computer.

"What about the little bookstore on the corner, or the dry cleaners?"

"I'm not sure, but I'll find out about those, too."

"Let me know. I'll start across the street." He headed for the door.

"Carter?"

"Yeah?"

"Thanks."

He nodded. "Just doing my job."

Carter spent the next hour going up and down the block, talking to managers and owners. Though a lot of the managers didn't know, the few owners he spoke with had indeed been approached with an offer, and some were even considering it. As much as he'd been an advocate for change and progress, he never wanted to live in a tourist town, especially one that catered only to the wealthy.

He glanced at the time. It was much later than he realized. He tried calling Sydney, but got her voicemail, so he headed back to the house for a late lunch and to hopefully see her there. He wanted her take on the mayor situation. Was there a way she and Dudley could help? He had to get his hands on incriminating documents in order to expose the mayor's plans.

He walked in his front door, threw down his keys, and sensed someone was in the house with him. "Sydney?" He poked his head into the kitchen to find it empty, then turned and let out a startled cry.

"Hey, handsome." Jade was standing in front of him, wrapped in a bath towel, combing out her wet hair as if it was an ordinary occurrence.

For a moment he couldn't speak. He just stood there, staring at her. "What are you doing here?" he finally asked. "How did you get in?"

"The key in the rock. I can't believe you still have it in the same hiding place." She laughed and gave him a kiss. He jerked back, and she seemed surprised by his reaction. "Aren't you happy to see me?"

"What are you doing, Jade? We're no longer together."

"We took a break."

"No, we broke up. You can't just come into my house, make yourself at home, and expect me to act like you never left."

"I know. I'm sorry. I thought our situation was a little different because we used to be engaged. I mean, it's not like I'm someone you only dated a few times. I seriously thought you'd be happy to see me. I tried calling you, but when you didn't answer I thought I'd surprise you."

"Mission accomplished."

The kitchen door opened, and Dudley came running in followed by Sydney. "Carter? I brought you some—"

Dudley was growling as Sydney rounded the corner and saw Jade in nothing but a towel. Her eyes met Carter's—shock, confusion, then betrayal registered on her face before she turned and ran out.

"Sydney, wait! It's not what you think."

She flew out the side gate without looking back. He wanted to go after her, but Dudley was aggressively barking at Jade. He hurried back inside. "Dudley, enough. I've got this."

Dudley immediately backed off, but he was grumbling, and Carter couldn't help but wonder what he was saying.

Jade watched the dachshund with amusement. "Things have really changed since I've been gone. Who just left?"

"My girlfriend."

She gave him a confused look. "I heard you haven't dated in months."

"You heard wrong."

She tightened the towel around herself. "So you haven't been pining away for me?"

He glared at her. "Who have you been talking to?"

"Doesn't matter." She shook her head. "Clearly that's not the case." She expelled a big breath. "Now that I've thoroughly embarrassed myself, I'll get my things and go."

As Jade went to change, he texted Sydney, asking her to come back so he could explain. Right after he sent off the text, he heard a ding in the kitchen. Sydney had left her phone and keys next to a bakery box, which he assumed she'd brought for him.

He let out a relieved sigh. "She couldn't have gone very far." He held up her phone to show Dudley, who was right by his side.

The dog had an odd look on his face, and Carter wished he knew what was going through the dachshund's mind. He suddenly remembered what Sydney had said about how he'd been abandoned early on in his life.

"Not sure what you're thinking, little man, but don't worry. Your mom is coming back." He bent down and gave him a rub. "I want you to know—"

Jade walked in fully dressed. "I never pegged you for a dog lover. What's his name?" She reached out to pet him, and he bared his teeth.

"Easy, boy." Carter held Dudley back.

Jade quickly pulled her hand away. "A little devil, isn't he?"

"He's very protective over the ones he loves."

"I can see that." She eyed Dudley with trepidation before turning her attention back to Carter. "I'm sorry for coming in unannounced." She handed over the house key, then headed to the door and stepped outside. "I'm glad you're doing well, Carter, and that you're happy."

He let out a breath, along with his anger, since her words seemed sincere. "Thanks."

"Please apologize to your girlfriend for me."

"I will."

"I'm only here for a week, but maybe I'll see you around."

He waited for her to get in her car, realizing that if she was only in town for a week, she'd probably just come over for something casual, and that wasn't him. It had never been him. When she pulled away from his house, he felt a sense of relief. If that didn't prove his heart was finally free from her, then nothing did.

He turned to go back inside when he noticed that Dudley was right under his feet. No doubt he had listened to their conversation. "Can you telepathically send Sydney a message and ask her to come home? Please tell her that my ex let herself in with a hidden key, and that I was equally surprised to see her here."

Dudley barked at him, but Carter had no idea what he was trying to say.

"I really wish I could understand you. I need to find Sydney. Can you lead me to her?"

Dudley barked again.

"Great." He closed the front door. "Okay, Dudley, pick up her scent."

Dudley looked back at the garage.

"What's wrong? Don't we need to follow her?"

Dudley pranced over to the garage door and sat right in front of it.

"Oh, right. You don't need to use your nose when you're probably talking to her right this minute. I'm guessing the car will be faster?"

Dudley barked excitedly and wagged his tail.

"Got it. C'mon."

After Carter grabbed his keys, he helped Dudley into the passenger seat, then pulled out of the driveway. "Which way?"

Dudley whined, staring out the window.

"I don't know what that means." Carter headed east. "Maybe she's walking into town." He drove slowly, searching both sides of the street. When he didn't see her, he turned around and went in the other direction. "Where is she?"

Dudley barked, but he couldn't understand what he was trying to tell him.

He drove slowly around a four-block radius, not understanding why he wasn't finding her. "Maybe she walked around the block and went back home." As Carter made a U-turn, Dudley began barking his head off. "What is it?"

Dudley's bark was nothing he'd heard before. He sounded alarmed.

"Is it about Sydney?"

He sat, whined, and sneezed.

"Okay. Do you know where she is?"

He nodded and barked once.

"Great. Is she in the guesthouse?"

Dudley barked twice and shook his head.

"Is she on foot in the neighborhood?"

Dudley barked once and nodded.

"Got it. One bark for yes. Two barks for no."

Carter headed toward town again. Dudley jumped on his lap

so he could see better out the window. "Am I going in the right direction?"

Dudley barked once.

He kept going straight until he came to the next cross street. "One bark for left, two barks for right, three for straight ahead."

Dudley barked twice.

Carter turned right and kept driving. He got to the next cross street and said the same thing, but Dudley didn't bark at all. "I don't understand. Am I going in the wrong direction?"

He barked once.

"Is she on this block?"

Dudley nodded, and barked once.

Carter turned around and slowly drove back up the street, searching for her, but he didn't see her. He was almost at the cross street again when Dudley barked.

He pulled over. "I don't see her, and I don't understand what you're trying to tell me." He let his shoulders fall, feeling defeated. "I'd give anything to be able to hear you right now. What else can I do?" He cast him a long glance before he set his gaze out the window.

Behind the white truck.

He gawked at Dudley. "Was that you or did I just make that up?"

At last! I've been telepathically yelling at you this entire time. Good on you for finally hearing me. Sydney's nearby. She's in that empty lot, behind the white truck on the right.

Carter's mind was reeling. He was hearing a British voice inside his head as clear as anyone speaking to him.

"I heard you, Dudley. I just heard all of that!" He reached over and gave him a big kiss on top of his head.

Dudley thumped his tail and Carter heard him say something incomprehensible before he helped his short-legged friend out of the car. The second Dudley's paws touched pavement, he took off running.

"Hold on!" Carter quickly shut the car door and hurried after him.

Dudley ran into a large empty lot with weeds so overgrown that he almost disappeared.

"Sydney?" Carter called out.

"Here!"

He heard her, but still couldn't see her, however, Dudley could. She was sitting on a tree stump with a blood-soaked sock tied around her foot.

He hurried over to her. "What happened?"

She held up a weathered piece of wood with a very long rusted nail sticking out of it. "I drove this right through my foot."

He winced, looking at the three-inch nail. "You're obviously tougher than me. If I had stepped on that thing, people would have heard my screams for miles."

She laughed. "It hurt so much that it knocked the wind right out of me so I couldn't scream."

"You're going to need a tetanus shot and a doctor to look at that. Stay here. I'm going to move the car closer."

Dudley remained right by her side as they waited for Carter to return.

"I got your messages," she said to Dudley. "Thank you for telling me what happened and what Carter said to his ex."

My pleasure. You'll also be happy to know that he now believes without a doubt.

"Really. What changed?"

He heard me.

She gasped. "When?"

Moments ago.

"How?"

As we began looking for you, we worked out a way to communicate by my number of barks. While we were in the midst of our search, I saw concern creep into his eyes. He was terribly worried about you and was becoming frustrated with himself for not being able to talk to me like you can. He was driving up and down this very block, but I couldn't figure out a way to tell him that you couldn't be seen from the car. I believe he was so desperate to understand me that he became vulnerable in that moment and opened his mind to hearing me.

"He finally let go and believed."

Dudley nodded. *Precisely.*

"That's incredible, Dudley. At least something good has come out of this."

I do believe this is just the beginning.

Misty-eyed, she picked him up and held him tight. "So do I."

A few minutes later, Carter came back, a little out of breath. "Can you stand?" he asked.

"I think so." She set Dudley down, then stood on her good foot. She slid her arm around Carter's shoulders, ready to hobble to his car, when he swept her off her feet. She let out a surprised squeal and threw her arms around his neck.

"I got you," he said, confidently.

She smiled broadly. "Yes, I'd say you do." She gazed into his eyes and saw his concern for her turn to relief.

He walked to the car with her in his arms while Dudley trailed behind carrying her shoe. Carter gently set her in the passenger seat, then lifted Dudley and set him on her lap. Before he shut the door, he kissed her.

Is this what your reunions are going to be like?

Carter's eyes widened. "I heard that! I heard you again, Dudley. You're amazing. I'm amazing. I can hear you!" He was so excited that he gave Dudley another kiss on top of his head.

Great. Human slobber.

Sydney laughed. "Miracles happen when you believe."

Carter looked deeply into her eyes. Because of her, he not only believed in telepathy but he also believed in love again. "Yes, they really do."

CHAPTER TWENTY-SIX

A few hours later, Carter carried Sydney into the house. He set her down on the couch, then brought her a cold glass of iced tea.

"Thank you, Carter, for everything." She took a sip. "But you're doing way too much for me."

"You heard the doctor. You need to stay off your foot for twenty-four hours." He moved the coffee table closer, got a pillow, and had her put her foot on it to keep it elevated.

"I think you missed your calling," she said, watching him fuss over her. "I haven't been this pampered since I was a kid sick with strep throat."

"This situation is actually better. With strep throat, you wouldn't be able to have pizza for dinner, which I'm about to order." He took a decorative pillow off one of his chairs and put it behind her back. "After that, I want to show you what I've done with your website."

She reached over, pulled him close to her, and kissed him. "What did I do to deserve you?"

Oh good. More snogging. Dudley settled on the floor by the couch.

Carter laughed, still stunned that he could hear Dudley. "What kind of pizza would you like?"

"I'm good with anything you choose."

And I'm good with anything that fits in my mouth.

Carter glanced at him. "You have not been forgotten, little man. I'll be the one feeding you tonight."

Then let's not bother Sydney. I'll tell you what I get for dinner.

"He gets a third of a cup of kibble," she said to Carter.

And a hot dog.

"No hot dog."

But I helped rescue you.

"He has a point." Carter shrugged.

"Dudley believes he deserves a hot dog every hour of every day." She raised a brow to her chowhound, then set her gaze back on Carter. "I have a little chicken breast left over from lunch. He can have a small, and I mean small, portion, which you can mix in with his kibble."

"What do you think of that?" Carter turned to Dudley.

I can work with it. He got up. *Allow me to show you where everything is and help you determine what a small portion is.*

He trotted to the back door as Sydney shook her head. "That dog is incorrigible. Thank you for doing this. I think I left my keys on your kitchen counter, but the guesthouse should be open."

"Found them." He brought over her phone in case she needed to call him. "I've seen how fast Dudley eats, so we won't be long."

Carter let Dudley out the back door and walked with him to the guesthouse. "I'm sorry I had a hard time believing that Sydney could hear your thoughts."

No apology necessary. You're wired to be skeptical.

"You're not only smart but incredibly wise."

Yes, I might have mentioned that a time or two.

Carter laughed. "Are others as bright as you?"

Many species are incredibly intelligent, but can other canines carry on conversations like me? Perhaps, though I've never run across any.

Carter opened the guesthouse door for him. "It must have been frustrating for you to have discovered this great gift of yours, and then find out that you couldn't use it."

Frustrating, debilitating, agonizing, yes, it's been all of those things and more.

"Now that you've found Sydney, do you know what you want to do with your special ability?"

Like Sydney, I want to make a difference. Call me selfish, but I'd prefer to help my canine community first—to be a voice for those who don't have one.

"Who better to speak for the canine community than the King of the Dachshunds—though Sydney and I think you should be the King of all Canines."

Smashing idea.

"I think your plans are very noble. Sydney's a huge advocate for animals, so I already know she'll be on board."

I do believe that's why we found one another.

Carter was so grateful he could finally hear Dudley because he had been missing out on the deeper side of him—the considerate, selfless, and compassionate side. "Let's get you fed." Carter found his kibble and doled out a third of a cup into his dish.

This is one area where Sydney and I don't see eye to eye. How can she feed me kibble?

"It's not that she wants to. It's more like she has to in order to keep you healthy, and this brand is one of the best out there. You might think like a human, but you reside in a canine's body, which has different nutritional needs."

You sound exactly like her. Did she tell you to say that?

"No—although it is the truth." He found the container with chicken and popped open the lid. "But there's no harm in a little chicken topper." He cut off a big piece, shredded it into smaller pieces, then showed Dudley. "How does that look?"

His eyes widened. *I do like your definition of a small piece.*

"Yes, well, don't get me in trouble."

I wouldn't dream of it.

After Carter and Sydney shared a pizza together, he showed Sydney and Dudley their new website.

"I didn't get as far as I'd wanted, but this is what I worked on last night."

She gasped with delight. "Oh, Carter, it's gorgeous."

The background was a beautiful picture of Mulberry Park with vibrant green grass, colorful shrubs, and flowering trees in full bloom. *The Dachshund Whisperer* was written across the top of the website, and in the center was a close-up photo of Sydney holding Dudley. She was talking to him, and he was looking off in the distance with determination in his eyes.

"We don't look too bad, do we, Dudley?"

She set him on her lap so he could see it better. *We exude experience.*

She laughed. "I wouldn't go that far."

"He's right. That's why I chose it," Carter said. "So this area to the left can be a description of what you two do—basically explaining what animal communication is, and then over here on the top right, users can have access to some of your video sessions. Below the videos can be *Dear Dudley*—the advice column."

It does have a rather nice ring to it.

"Then on the tabs up here, we'll have your bios, client testimonials, services, prices, media interest, and how to get in touch the old-fashioned way—meaning not telepathically."

"Clever." She couldn't stop smiling. "I'm so touched, Carter."

"It's not done yet. If you think of anything I should add or change, just let me know."

There should be more pictures of me.

"Yes, I had a feeling you might say that." Carter ruffled his fur. "We need to make time for a photo shoot of you wearing glasses for the *Dear Dudley* column."

Brilliant. I'm quite handsome in spectacles. I'm told I look distinguished.

"This is absolutely perfect, Carter. Thank you." She leaned over and kissed him. It was meant to be a short kiss, but it turned into a longer one until Dudley whined, and they reluctantly broke apart.

She studied the web page. Carter had really done a great job. It looked so professional, but would it garner more clients? She only had one session booked for next week.

"Once I drive traffic to your website, you and Dudley will have more work than you can handle," Carter said.

"I hope you're right." She forced a smile.

It worried her that people's interest in her could suddenly fade, especially since the newspaper was out of business. Having Carter out of work equally worried her because he was spending all of his time helping her instead of looking for steady employment. What if the calls didn't come in like he assumed?

I've no doubt this website will generate loads of clients for Sydney and me. Thank you, Carter.

"You're very welcome, little man." Carter gave him a rub.

She eyed Dudley. *Were you listening to my thoughts?*

Dudley snuggled into her and gave her a kiss on the hand, which told her he had heard every word.

CHAPTER TWENTY-SEVEN

Carter's alarm blared at seven, and he debated whether or not to roll over and go back to sleep. Daylight was creeping into his room, so he forced himself out of bed and checked his phone. He had sent Shep a few texts last night and still hadn't heard from him, which was unusual for his competitive colleague. Something told Carter that he should check on him. He didn't want to wake Sydney, especially since she'd taken a painkiller last night for her foot, so he left a note attached to his back door saying he would return shortly.

He'd only been to Shep's house once, but Carter remembered where it was. He lived near the outskirts of town in a modest house on five acres, which Carter found odd, since Shep was an attention seeker. Wouldn't he want to live downtown where all the action was? The guy had always been a bit of an enigma.

Carter drove down the long drive and saw Shep's car parked in front of his house. He knocked on the front door, waited, then knocked again.

"Shep, it's Carter," he called out. He was peering through one of the windows when the door finally opened.

Shep was still wearing the clothes he had on the previous morning. His usually perfectly coiffed hair looked like it had gone through a tornado. His face was full of stubble, he had bloodshot eyes, and he smelled like he'd taken a bath in a bottle of whiskey.

"What the hell happened to you?" Carter asked, inviting himself in.

"I did everything you said I shouldn't do. I went to the mayor's office and demanded answers, which of course I didn't get. Even as I was being thrown out, I said that I wasn't going to stop until I found out the truth." Shep raised his chin and waved his finger in the air, acting out the scene for Carter before he slumped his shoulders in defeat and handed him a letter. "This was nailed to my door when I got home."

Carter quickly scanned the piece of paper. "The city is threatening to take your land through eminent domain?" He gave Shep a doubtful look. "They can't do that."

"They can and they will. An anonymous source sent me information late last night. They're planning on building a two-lane highway right through my property and my neighbors' properties to connect the freeways north and south of Pinecrest."

"Did this anonymous source send any documentation to prove these claims?"

"No. He or she does not have access. Everything is under lock and key in his office."

Carter took a long breath and rubbed his eyes. "If a whistleblower can't get to those documents, then I'm not sure how we can."

"My source also said that a big meeting was pushed up to this afternoon and is being held at the mayor's home."

"Which means they're trying to keep all of this quiet," he said. "We need eyes on him immediately. You go to the mayor's office, hang out in your car, and text me when he's on the move. I'll wait outside his residence and try to get photos of everyone who shows up for the meeting."

"We're going to need more than photos."

"I know. We need a little spy in there with them, and I might just have one."

Inside his car, Carter hooked up a hidden spy camera to record picture and sound on Dudley's harness, then he connected it to his phone.

"What's the plan?" Sydney asked, watching him.

"Shep's going to text me when the mayor leaves for home. When he arrives, we can send in Dudley to gather information."

"I still don't understand how this is going to work. Kessler's property is fully enclosed, with security cameras."

"Dudley will gain access when Kessler opens the gate."

"And then what?" she asked. "Dudley might be a small dog, but he's not invisible."

I'm very stealthy. You'd be surprised.

"Once he's inside, he's going to sneak around and try to stay out of sight. If he gets noticed, then I'll go to the front door and explain that I've lost my dog."

Perhaps I should have a snack for energy.

She shared a look with Carter, pretty sure Dudley didn't need a snack, but she'd also feel awful if he ran out of steam. She broke off a small piece of chicken jerky, and he gobbled it down. "I'm so disgusted by what Kessler plans to do with our town. What do you think they were discussing when I noticed them in the park?"

"I think they plan on bulldozing part of the park to sell it as prime real estate."

"That's just awful. It's such a beautiful area."

Since I won't be able to hear you two verbally, I'll make an attempt to hear you telepathically. Do I have permission to hear your thoughts?

"What's this?" Carter looked at Sydney.

Even though she had already alluded to the fact that Dudley might be able to hear their thoughts, she hadn't yet told Carter about what she'd learned from Isabelle. She opened her mouth to tell him the whole truth, then shut it, realizing it was not the time to discuss it.

Carter looked at them a little confused. "I thought he couldn't hear our thoughts."

Right, however, since you can now hear me as well, Carter, I thought I'd give it a go.

Not exactly the truth, but perhaps it was best to ease Carter into the idea that Dudley was privy to his every thought.

Carter's brows pushed together with suspicion.

"Asking one's permission allows a shared psychic channel to open," she explained. "If Dudley is able to connect with both of us psychically, this operation will go a lot smoother."

He thought about that, then nodded. "I see your point. Dudley, you have my permission."

Excellent.

A text came in on Carter's phone. "It's Shep. Kessler's on the move." He texted back. "I'm letting him know that we're in place." Carter watched his phone and read the texts as they came in. "Shep's following him to make sure he's not going to another location."

"Dudley, get ready," she said.

"Shep just lost him at a stoplight but said it looked like he was on the way home."

"Let me take Dudley for a walk to get him closer."

"What about your foot?"

"It's fine." She hooked Dudley to a leash, got out of the car, and walked him across the street to hang out by Kessler's driveway. A text came in from Carter, and she read it out loud. "He's seconds away."

Dudley started sniffing the grass and lifted his leg as the mayor pulled up to his security gate and waited for it to open.

Unleash me.

Sydney removed his leash. "Good luck."

Dudley ran into the open gate behind the mayor's car, and Sydney hurried back to Carter.

"Is the camera working?" she asked, climbing inside his car.

"Perfectly." Carter angled his phone toward her so she could see Dudley's progress. "Since we can only see Dudley's point of view, I'm assuming he's hiding behind a row of bushes."

The camera slowly panned across the bushes before the mayor's driveway came into view. A moment later, Kessler pulled his car into the garage.

And that was Dudley's cue. He took off toward the backyard, the camera's view bouncing along with him. Once the backyard came into view, he put on the breaks and scanned across the area, which revealed a massive deck attached to the back of the house.

He made his way up the steps to the deck and peered through a sliding glass door. Two seconds later, a yellow Labrador ran up to greet Dudley with his tail wagging. Dudley began speaking to him, and the Labrador cocked his head one way, and then another.

"What's he saying?" Carter asked Sydney.

She shrugged. "Ask Dudley telepathically."

"Shouldn't he have already heard me?"

"Maybe, but often when we speak, our thoughts are somewhere else. If you picture Dudley in your mind and telepathically speak to him, it works a lot better."

"Okay." Carter closed his eyes and concentrated on asking the question telepathically. *Dudley, what are you saying to the mayor's dog?*

Brilliant. I can hear you, Carter, Dudley transmitted telepathically. *I'm asking Fitzcollindorf to open the door.*

"Fitzcollindorf?" Carter asked Sydney.

"The canine's real name."

The Lab began whining, and moments later, a housekeeper let him out but immediately closed the door behind him. Fitzcollindorf greeted Dudley, then lunged at him, asking to play.

Not what I had intended.

"We've got cars coming up to the gate," Carter reported.

Received. I'm telling Fitzcollindorf to bark to get us inside.

The Labrador's backside suddenly filled the screen. "I'm assuming Dudley's plan is to hide behind Fitzcollindorf," Sydney said, trying not to laugh.

"In or out, Max." The housekeeper sounded irritated. "I'm not playing this game today." As Max AKA Fitzcollindorf walked inside, Dudley ran. The housekeeper gasped. "Get back here!"

The spy cam jerked around as Dudley dashed through the kitchen and into the foyer. Then it stopped as Dudley slowly walked behind a group of people heading into a dining room.

Dudley ran under the table as the mayor's guests sat down. The POV was of feet—three men wearing dress shoes along with two women in high heels. The mayor entered and stood at the head of the table. While the audio was a little muffled from being under the table, everyone could still be heard.

The mayor sat down. "My apologies for having to cancel our dinner, but—"

"I'm so sorry, sir." The housekeeper could be heard but not seen. "I have no idea where he came from."

"Who?"

There was silence.

"Oh. I thought, uh, Max came in here. I apologize for the interruption," the housekeeper said. "There are drinks and sandwiches over there on the hutch. Can I get you anything else?"

"No," the mayor said in a dismissive tone.

"She sounded like she was stalling to look for Dudley," Sydney said.

Dudley slowly made his way from under the table toward the far end of the room, where no one was sitting. He then scrambled behind a large potted plant in the corner, but all Sydney and Carter could see was the plant itself.

"Dudley, can you move to the right?" Carter asked.

Nothing happened.

"You have to think it as you're saying it," Sydney said.

"My thoughts are all over the place," he admitted. "Can you tell him?"

"Sure."

A moment later, Dudley moved. She and Carter could now see two men and one woman sitting on the left side of the table with the mayor on the end.

"You're so good at telepathy," he said. "Have him move to the left of the plant."

Dudley got Sydney's message and did as requested, but the plant obstructed everyone except for the woman at the end of the table.

"No good. Have him go back to the other position, so we can at least see three at the table with the mayor."

Dudley moved into his first position. He sat still as the spy cam filmed a young man removing proposed plans from cardboard tubes and spreading them across the table.

"Phase one will concentrate on the heart of Pinecrest," the young man said. "The newspaper is already gone, and the bookstore should be closed by the end of the week. The owner of the convenience store is interested in selling and so is the owner of the dry cleaners. It's a no-go with the coin and stamp collection dealer. It's family-owned, has been at that location for years, and they have no interest in leaving."

"Then we'll persuade them to sell," a shifty-looking man said.

"Why does the bookstore need to close?" the woman off-camera asked.

"No one has time to read anymore, and if they do, they'll do it on their phone," the shifty-looking man replied. "An outdoor corner café is better suited there. These three blocks will be earmarked for retail—jewelry stores, designer clothing shops, and upscale restaurants."

The same woman spoke up. "Mayor, as we move forward with this project, I must caution everyone about changing Pinecrest too dramatically or too quickly. We don't want to alienate our local residents who might not be able to afford shopping in their own town."

"We won't be alienating them," the mayor said. "Who do you think will be the employees?"

The other people around the table laughed.

"Whoever that woman is, she seems to be the only one who cares," Sydney said. "Is there a way to find out her identity?"

"We have her on video from when Dudley moved left, so I can find out."

The man in the middle pointed to the architectural drawings. "As of this morning, this area here is now zoned for a five-star hotel, which will put Pinecrest on the map as a tourist destination."

"Very good." The mayor smiled. "Once residents understand the potential and projected revenue our project will bring, I can't see anyone complaining. Now what about Mulberry Park? We get quite a few hikers and families who use it daily. Since we'll be removing access to half of the hiking trails, what can we offer to offset the pushback we'll inevitably receive from our residents?"

"We'll promise them more smaller parks around town," the young man replied.

"Or we can keep the park and build the luxury townhomes elsewhere," the unseen woman said.

"We can't if we want all the shops and eateries within walking distance," the man sitting across from her said.

"She's right," the other woman spoke up. "There are restrictions in place that will still need to be addressed. The family who donated the land specifically stated in the terms of agreement that their property would only be utilized as a park or a nature preserve."

The mayor sighed with displeasure. "Put it on the back burner. Phase one will be the revitalization of the town center as well as construction on our new two-lane highway."

"Sir, maybe we should also hold off on the highway," the man in the middle said. "It must be put in front of the voters, and getting the residents to approve it is going to be costly and time-consuming."

"I disagree," the shifty-looking man chimed in. "We're only impacting the property of five residents. We'll give them a good price to sell."

"No need," the mayor said. "That's what eminent domain is for."

The men laughed at the table. As the on-camera woman got up to get something to drink, she saw Dudley.

"Hi there, little guy. You must be Max."

The mayor stood up to see who she was talking to. "That's not Max."

Dudley barreled out the dining room and into the foyer as the mayor yelled for his housekeeper, who came running.

"Yes, Mr. Kessler?"

"There's a strange dog loose in my house. Did you bring your dog to work?"

"No, sir. He must have slipped in with your guests."

"Well, get rid of him!"

"Yes, sir."

The housekeeper turned and saw Dudley sitting right behind her. She reached for him, but he raced to the front door as Max appeared, barking. She grabbed hold of Max's collar, then quickly threw open the front door. Dudley gave a bark to Max and bolted out. He headed toward the security gate, which opened as he approached it, allowing him to escape.

Sydney hurried over, picked him up, and got him in the car. "Great job." She kissed him on top of his head.

"Yes, well done, Durlindemore." Carter gave him a scratch behind his ear.

I do hope you didn't need video of the design plans. They were simply too high.

"I assumed they would be, but luckily the audio sounded clear. As soon as I post this, the mayor is going to have a lot more headaches than just me and Shep."

Carter called Shep on the way home and told him to come over, while Sydney and Dudley went to give potty breaks to her afternoon clients. Once Shep arrived, Carter showed him the spy cam recording, and he was able to identify everyone in the meeting. The unseen woman who had objected to destroying the mom-and-pop retail stores was the assistant to the deputy mayor.

When Shep listened to her voice, he recognized it as the concerned citizen who had contacted him a few weeks earlier, wanting to speak with him off-the-record. But when Shep called her, she sounded scared and would no longer speak to him. Shep believed that she was the whistleblower.

Over the next few days, Carter's home became headquarters to *The Pinecrest Underground*. While he edited the spy cam footage, Shep wrote an article exposing the real reason why the longest-running newspaper in Pinecrest had been shut down.

Russell and Jamie also helped out by contacting all of the paper's subscribers, informing them of a breaking news story about Pinecrest's corrupt mayor, which could only be found on the new website.

The video and article from *The Pinecrest Underground* went viral and half the town was protesting in front of the mayor's office soon after. Sydney, Dudley, and Carter happily joined them.

Sydney held up a "Fire the Liar" sign while Carter carried one that read, "Protect Pinecrest." Even Dudley got in on the action. He wore a "Bark to Save the Park" vest.

Every dog who walked by Dudley came over to him, checked out his vest, and gave a bark in support before trotting away. It was such an unusual scene that people started commenting on it.

"Are you telling them to bark?" Sydney asked Dudley.

Naturally, as they cannot read English. But I gather we are achieving your intended goal.

Several residents shot short videos with their phones, no doubt posting them to their social media accounts.

"Well done, little man." Carter snapped off some shots for their own website just as a TV reporter from the Twin Cities showed up to cover the demonstration.

And Dudley held court like the king that he was.

"I'm beginning to think dogs can read English," a woman said to her friend behind Sydney as several demonstrators came to stop to watch the parade of canines greeting Dudley.

"They must really like Mulberry Park," the reporter said to no one in particular. He seemed a little lost, and Sydney could only surmise that it was his first day.

"Yes, it's a favorite among all of Pinecrest's residents," Sydney replied. "It would be a travesty to see it destroyed, as the mayor is intending to do."

"But we're not going to allow that to happen," an older woman spoke up, just as many demonstrators received alerts on their phones.

Sydney quickly opened her news feed and frowned. "No! The mayor is claiming our video of their secret meeting is a deep fake."

Carter's jaw tightened as he read the mayor's statement for himself. "I should have known he'd try something like this."

"He's not going to get away with it," she said defiantly, before she noticed the reactions of everyone around her. They'd stopped demonstrating, and were looking around at everyone else, as if they were wondering what they should do.

The TV reporter abruptly stopped an interview and went over to discuss this breaking news with his crew.

Dudley broke away from the crowd of dogs around him and hurried over to Sydney and Carter. *Do you see that French poodle over there and the woman with her?* he telepathically asked the both of them.

"Not now," she said to Dudley.

What I have to say is of the utmost importance. Meravasellion, the French poodle, just informed me that her human servant is the mayor's mistress.

Carter snapped a quick photo of an attractive woman who looked barely twenty. "Did you happen to get her name?"

Brooklyn Knutson, and that's not all. The mayor apparently wears boxers with hearts all over them and has a rather large mole on his back.

Carter broke into a big grin. "Dudley, you are amazing. It's time to fight fire with fire."

As Carter ran off to make a few calls, Sydney got Dudley some water.

How about a hot dog for my stunning detective work?

"You definitely earned it, however, I'm not sure where to get one." Sydney scanned the shops nearby. "I see a sandwich shop across the street. Will you settle on some turkey instead?

I suppose that will have to do.

Since it was barely eleven in the morning, Sydney only ordered for Dudley. "One turkey sandwich, but hold the bread and everything else. Just the turkey, please."

The employee gave her a strange look.

"It's for my dog."

He glanced over the counter, and when he saw who it was, his face lit up. "Dudley!"

Should I know this commoner?

"Looks like you have another fan." Sydney picked Dudley up so the employee could see him better.

"I can't believe you talked that cat down from the tree," the employee said. "You're a rock star, my man. Whatever you want. It's on the house."

My sincerest apologies. He's clearly a genius. I'll take everything.

"That's so kind of you," Sydney said to the employee. "A couple of slices of your fresh turkey would be wonderful."

You cannot be serious. Tell the man that you were mistaken. Have him drop the whole turkey in a bag, and we'll take it from there.

"Two slices, coming right up." He sliced off the turkey as

Dudley grumbled something incomprehensible, and Sydney didn't need any translation.

The second she took Dudley outside to eat, a woman recognized them and booked a session to help her parrot. A few minutes later, an older man booked one for his anxious dog.

"We're on our way, Dudley." She gave Dudley the last piece of turkey.

With all of these new bookings, I do hope you're blocking out time for my naps.

She chuckled. "No need to worry. You'll have plenty of time for that." Her cell chimed with an incoming text. "It's Carter. The mayor has been made aware of the sensitive information you shared with us today and is, at this moment, weighing his options."

I do hope he's smarter than he looks.

"So do I."

After Sydney took her regulars on their afternoon walk, she debated whether or not to take Dudley home. It was almost three in the afternoon, and she was getting worried about Carter. She hadn't heard anything more from him.

"Are you ready to go back home to take a nap?"

He yawned. *Smashing idea.*

She loaded him in the passenger seat when her phone rang. "Everything okay?" she asked Carter.

"The mayor just resigned."

"What?" She suddenly heard an explosion of cheering through the phone. "Where are you?"

"I'm back at the demonstration," he yelled louder. "Come over when you can."

"On my way." She hopped in the car and glanced at Dudley who was already fast asleep.

Sydney arrived at the mayor's office, and it looked like the entire town was there celebrating.

Dudley stirred and glanced outside when she parked and turned off the car. *This isn't home.*

"No, but there's a very good reason for it. Because of you, the mayor just resigned!"

Dudley looked pleased with himself. *I never doubted it for a moment.*

She got him out of the car and set him on the ground. "Let's go find Carter."

As Sydney and Dudley approached the area where they'd been demonstrating earlier, Carter came up from behind them.

"We did it!" He grabbed Sydney and planted a big kiss on her, then he picked up Dudley and did the same. "You are the most awesome sentient being in the entire world."

For the first time probably ever, Dudley was speechless. He pulled back his mouth into a smile and allowed himself to be smothered with kisses.

Shep came over and shook Carter's hand. "Thank you for saving my house and helping to save our town."

"It was my pleasure." Carter smiled. "We make a good team."

"A great team." Russell joined them. "With Kessler gone, we're back in business!"

"Congratulations," Sydney said to everyone.

"And, Carter, I promise I won't send you to cover any more animal-related stories."

"I don't mind them so much anymore, although I might have to cut back on my hours. Sydney and Dudley have been flooded with new clients."

"I can work with that," Russell replied, "but, Shep, that means you'll be our one and only star."

"A burden I'm more than happy to accept," Shep said, making everyone laugh, right as a microphone was shoved in his face.

"So you're the one who took down the mayor," a female TV reporter said. "How exactly did you do that?"

"I didn't do it alone. There was a lot of investigative teamwork involved," Shep surprisingly said, appearing to be extremely comfortable on camera. "And of course, you now know about the whistleblower in the mayor's office."

"Was she the one who obtained such damning evidence?" the reporter asked.

"No, that was another member of our team," Carter replied.

"I've seen the authenticated leaked video of their secret meeting," she said. "Was this team member hiding in the ex-mayor's residence, or had a camera been preset?"

Sydney shot Carter a quick glance, letting him know that she'd answer that one. "He'd been allowed access prior to the meeting."

"He should be hailed as a hero," the reporter said into the mic. "Will we get to know the identity of your team member?"

"I'm afraid not," Sydney replied. "He's asked to remain anonymous."

I did not. When did I say that? I love the spotlight.

The TV reporter turned and looked directly into the camera. "Well, whoever you are, the residents of Pinecrest are indebted to you for saving their beautiful town."

After the news crew moved on to interview other demonstrators, Russell eyed Carter. "You might want to keep up *The Pinecrest Underground* in case another city official decides to go rogue."

"Oh, I plan on it."

"Will we be seeing more adventures from *The Dachshund Whisperer* in our paper like we had planned?" Russell shifted his gaze between Carter and Sydney. "Or will readers only be able to find those on the official *Dachshund Whisperer* website?"

"I think we can stick with the original plan," Sydney said. "We'll save the best sessions with the most exciting photos for the paper."

"Thank you, Ms. Elder." Russell let out a relieved sigh. "In those last few days, before we were shuttered, your stories were the most popular with our readers."

Shep frowned at Russell. "You told me my stories were the most popular."

"Second most popular." Russell patted him on the back. "But I've no doubt you will be number one once again."

"I should hope so," Shep said, a little deflated, as they walked away.

"What exactly happened?" Sydney asked Carter.

"We informed the mayor that if he continued to push his lie about the video being fake, we'd release the information about his mistress."

"I bet he regrets taking on *The Pinecrest News* now."

"No doubt," Carter said. "Who would have thought that the real Dachshund Whisperer was actually an outspoken dachshund who came to the rescue more than once?"

I would. I would have thought that. I can't believe it took you so long to figure it out. I'm The Dachshund Whisperer, not Sydney.

Carter eyed Dudley. "Now what will Sydney's title be? The Dachshund Listener?"

As it is with all my subjects.

She rolled her eyes and Carter laughed. "I'm still trying to get used to the fact that I can hear you, Mr. D."

You're welcome.

Carter carried Dudley as they crossed the street and headed for the park.

Sydney studied Carter as they walked. "I imagine this is *still* a bit of an adjustment for you."

"It is—though it's not because I can finally hear him, but because he talks so much. He's like a child who won't stop babbling."

I heard that. I'm no more a child than you are a dachshund. I'm a sentient being, a visionary with a consciousness well ahead of my time.

She squelched a laugh. "You can't argue with that."

I should hope not. But back to me. When do I get my TV series?

Carter suppressed a smile. "I'm not sure if the world is ready for that, Durlindemore."

It would be a travesty for the world not *to know me. And though I cannot yet predict the future, my series will obviously be number one in the ratings.*

"No doubt," she said, turning toward Carter and petting Dudley's head. "But I'm not sure if *I'm* ready to share you with the world."

"I happen to agree with Sydney. The three of us are perfect together." Carter kissed her, squishing Dudley between them.

Yuck. I'm going to need to lay down some ground rules with you two.

She set Dudley on the ground, then gazed into Carter's eyes. "You're right. We are perfect. Perfect as a team helping others, and perfect together when we're not."

He gave her another kiss in agreement before he dug around in his pocket and produced a key. "I want you to have this. Being your landlord, I already have a key to your place, so I think it's fair that you have one to mine."

She stared at the key in her hand, and the last bit of insecurity seemed to dissolve into nothing. "Thank you." She beamed.

Dudley sat at their feet. *Why don't you two cut to the chase and move in together? That way I can have my own room.*

Carter remained focused on her. "Does he have an off switch?"

"You're the one who wanted to be an animal communicator."

"What was I thinking?"

She laughed as he cupped her face with his hand and slowly kissed her. His kiss was gentle, loving, heartfelt—

When you two become a permanent item, I'll require my own room with my own king-size bed. I am the king of my people, after all. I must be able to look out the window to survey my kingdom. I'll require the ability to get up and down on my own. A doggie ramp, perhaps, or a lift if you have the capability to build one. I prefer to sleep under things, so perhaps one of those canopy beds. Penelope adores them. Speaking of Penelope, when do I get to see my queen again? Hello? Are you listening? You've been kissing for an awfully long time, when I was the one who crushed the mayor and won the day once again. Shouldn't I be receiving a hot dog right now?

Sydney slid her arms around Carter's neck. "I'm free for a dogless date tonight if you are."

He chuckled, slipping his arms around her waist. "You just read my mind."

EXCERPT

Turn the page for a special look at…

Colorado Christmas Magic
by Caitlin McKenna

CHAPTER ONE

Hearing insistent meowing, Charley Dawson glanced up from her laptop to find her three-year-old cat perched on top of his treehouse, staring out the window of her one-bedroom apartment.

"What is it, Clarence?" She rose from the kitchen table to see what held his interest—the house directly across the street was lit up like a Christmas tree with big bright bulbs of red, blue, green, orange, and yellow. She ran her fingers through his short white fur and had him purring instantly. "I know you like the lights, bud, but we're not decorating this year. We're through with Christmas."

Clarence gave a short meow of disappointment before jumping down and running off, leaving Charley mesmerized by the lights. She used to love Christmas—how it ushered in that warm, comforting feeling of home where nothing seemed impossible. The Christmas season sprinkled happiness in the air, ordained love to reign supreme over everything, and made the world feel like it was a better place.

But for her, the magic of Christmas was gone. Over the past several years, the season only managed to bring her heartache. Last year's sorrow came from her then-fiancé, Hunter, who coldheartedly dumped her on Christmas Eve. After he left her, she'd cried on the couch with Clarence, staring at her Christmas tree, believing no Christmas would ever be joyful again.

With a sigh, she turned away from the window, gathering her long blond hair into a ponytail, then slid into the chair in front of her computer. She took one last bite of the sweet and sour pork before pushing it aside. The cold Chinese takeout reminded her of her love life—every relationship started sweet but ended sour.

She couldn't believe she was twenty-nine and still single—not that being single was a bad thing—but she had envisioned herself as a happily married career woman by twenty-five and a new mom by thirty. She was nowhere near meeting her goals, and she couldn't understand how true love kept eluding her—especially at Christmas.

She frowned at the blank page on her computer screen. For an hour's worth of work, she'd only come up with the title of her next blog post: "The Truth About Christmas." Did her readers sincerely want to know? Her popular blog, The Cold Hard Facts, was a real hit with Authentic Lifestyles readers. She debunked myths, urban legends, and uncovered the accurate but sometimes unpleasant truths behind long-held beliefs and traditions. She also exposed too-good-to-be-true business opportunities, shameful vacation getaways, and other consumer scams. Because of this, her boss suggested she break tradition and write something nice about the happiest time of year.

Bah, humbug. For Charley, Christmas was the most miserable time of year. Without having anyone to share things with, what was the point? Holiday parties became obligations; cooking ended up being a chore. She'd have to spend too much time baking for people who didn't appreciate it, and endure too much shopping chaos to buy gifts no one really wanted. "The truth about Christmas? Skip it!"

Abandoning her blog, she got up to pour herself a glass of wine and moved her pity party to the couch. Turning on the TV, she searched for anything that didn't involve love or hopeless romantics or jovial couples enjoying Christmas together. Even the commercials needled her with actors appearing so darn cheerful. No, she was definitely done with Christmas and love, once and for all.

But when channel surfing brought her to It's A Wonderful Life, her favorite Christmas movie of all time, she was immediately sucked in. "Clarence!" she called, putting her feet up on the coffee table. "Your show's on."

Clarence appeared from behind the couch and jumped into Charley's lap, as if he sensed she needed some affection. She snuggled in with her beautiful white angel and found herself weeping not twenty minutes into the movie. Then when George Bailey bitterly wished he'd never been born, puffy-eyed Charley found herself making a different kind of wish—a last attempt before she gave up for good. She wished—and out loud, mind you—for her soulmate to come find her since she wasn't getting the job done herself. The second this heartfelt wish passed her lips, the electricity in her apartment cut out.

"Just perfect. Exactly what I need. Oh, I get it. Are you trying to tell me that another one of my wishes will never see the light of day?" She cast her eyes upward into the darkness, assuming the power would snap on at any moment. But it didn't. "I figured as much."

With a loud meow, Clarence jumped off her lap. The tiny bell on his collar jingled as he ran down the hallway toward her bedroom.

Wiping off her tear-streaked face with the bottom of her sleeve, she rose and fumbled around in the dark, attempting to locate a flashlight. She finally managed to find one in the junk drawer right as the power popped back on and her favorite Christmas movie was playing once again.

As she started to close the drawer, she caught sight of an old photo strip buried under takeout menus. She and her high school sweetheart, Jack, had spent the day at the Santa Monica Pier, eating cotton candy, riding the Ferris wheel, and taking silly pictures of themselves in a photo booth.

With a bittersweet sigh, she caressed the strip of photos. How happy her sixteen-year-old self looked. Why hadn't she been able to find that kind of deep connection with anyone since Jack? *Because Love lost my address.* She shoved the photo strip back in the drawer and slammed it shut.

"Chocolate. I seriously need some chocolate." *Anything to get my mind off Jack.*

On the hunt, she scrounged around in the pantry, surprised she couldn't find one little morsel. She moved on to her handbag, her workbag, yes, even her gym bag. When she came up empty-handed, she checked the freezer for bits of chocolate in the form of ice cream, but to her dismay, she was cleaned out. She had no choice but to settle for the two complimentary fortune cookies she'd received with her takeout. She never cared for fortune cookies. The fortunes never applied to her and the cookies tasted dull and boring—much like her love life.

Charley snagged them off the kitchen table anyway, slumped on the couch, and popped opened the plastic wrapping on the first one. She snapped the cookie in half, crumbling it everywhere, then yanked out the fortune. YOU WILL REUNITE WITH THE ONE THAT GOT AWAY.

"Yeah, right." She crumpled it up, tossed it on the coffee table, then opened up the second cookie for a redo. YOU WILL REUNITE WITH THE ONE THAT GOT AWAY.

She sat up straight. It was a little weird to get the exact same fortune in two different cookies, and even more strange to get them right after she found pictures of Jack. "Ridiculous."

Jack had stolen her heart from the moment he'd spoken to her only to trample it to dust a little over a year later. She had tried to forget about him, she really had, but couldn't. She often wondered what had happened to him. She'd attempted to find him on Facebook but eventually gave up. Jack hadn't cared much for social media when it became popular, so she suspected he'd never changed his viewpoint on the subject. That made her even more curious as to where he lived and how he was doing. Did he ever think of her, or was he happily married? Maybe he had a gorgeous girlfriend and they were one of those couples she had recently passed by on the street, so happy and jolly that Christmastime had finally arrived.

Stupid fortune cookies.

Irritated at herself for thinking about him, she took to her blog and told the world exactly what she thought of Christmas. She was so certain her writing on the subject was sheer perfection that she posted it without waiting to reread it when she was in a better frame of mind.

The following morning, while shoving down smashed avocado

on toast before darting out the door for work, she wondered if her life would ever change. It felt like every time she moved forward, she ended up right back in the same place.

As she drove to work, she couldn't stop thinking about Jack. Even though they'd met in high school, their relationship ended up being more than just infatuation or young love. The spark between them had been incredibly honest and deep. They had shared so much with each other that she truly felt she'd found her soulmate. She hadn't been able to see herself with anyone other than Jack. Why did his parents have to move him so far away?

Charley pulled into an underground parking lot off Sunset Boulevard and discovered she'd forgotten to turn on her phone. As she headed into the lobby and straight into an elevator, her cell began blowing up. She smiled, feeling downright confident her readers were, at that very moment, agreeing wholeheartedly with her sentiments about Christmas.

Yet when she stepped off the elevator and opened the onslaught of messages, that wasn't the case at all. She remained glued to her cell screen, reading negative comment after negative comment. Heart pounding, she weaved her way through the hallways of Authentic Lifestyles Magazine without ever looking up.

"Miss Scrooge?" she uttered in shock, abruptly halting in place. She bristled as she kept reading, frozen to her phone.

Bright, peppy Olivia Lancaster came bounding up from behind Charley and glanced over her shoulder. "You bashed Christmas?" her best friend asked incredulously before she snatched the phone and scrolled through the barrage of insults left on the blog.

"I didn't bash Christmas, Liv. I merely suggested skipping it."

"You did more than that." Liv's eyes widened with every comment she devoured. "'Despicable,' says Devoted Fan, 'Unforgivable' comes from Fact Junky, and 'You've lost me forever,' cries Quirky Girl."

"That seems a little extreme." Charley plucked her phone out of Liv's tight grip. "I'm not going to apologize for telling it like it is."

"No, of course not," Liv said with a big snort of a laugh. "No one would ever accuse you of holding back."

"It's my job." Charley raised her chin. In truth, she actually enjoyed squashing people's over-joyous perceptions of long-held beliefs. (Wrong-held beliefs, according to her.)

"I'm just glad I get to write about fashion. Lunch later?" Liv asked, walking back down the corridor.

"Sure." Charley headed to her desk where she fired up her computer, anxious to defend her position to her readers. She took a determined breath, let it out, then pulled up her blog. The comments continued to pour in, an additional fifty-four in a matter of minutes. She skimmed through the newest ones, trying to find anyone who would agree with her. Finally, her eyes fell on:

I despised Christmas—

At last, a like-minded reader.

Until I fell in love.

"Bah, humbug." She slammed back in her chair.

"Here ya go!" An overly enthusiastic guy held out her morning mail, and she could only assume he was a new intern.

"Thanks." She rifled through a half dozen letters and stopped on a silver envelope embossed with gold script. She took note of the return address. 1 Kringle Lane, St. Nicholas, Colorado.

Intrigued, she opened it.

Dear Charlotte Dawson,

You're invited to spend a complimentary week at The Carroll Inn, a five-star bed-and-breakfast in St. Nicholas, Colorado: Home of the famous Scrooge Legend.

Scrunching up her face, she flipped over the letter, expecting to see additional information, but the back of it was blank. Pretty expensive solicitation for a gimmick. Without another thought, she crumpled up the paper and pitched it in the trash.

Now, where was I? She returned to her keyboard and began typing:

Dear Devoted Fan,

While I understand—

"Charley?" the familiar voice of her boss rang out. Paul was standing in the doorway of his office, twirling his glasses in his hand. "Can I see you for a moment?"

She rose and followed him. Paul was a cool boss. Being

called into his office was usually a good thing. He advanced his employees faster than any editor in chief around. She'd already reaped the benefits from working for him. When she'd come to him as an intern, he noticed her hard work and promoted her to fact-checker only one month later. Then, when he learned how successful she was as a blogger, he allowed her to become a permanent guest blogger with the magazine. Hopefully, Paul's request to see her meant another promotion.

He waved her in. "Great initiative, Charley. Yes, you can go and investigate the legend. I'm sure you'll want to debunk it."

She gave him a puzzled look. "What exactly are we talking about?"

"The invitation you received to St. Nicholas, Colorado." Paul held up the crumpled letter she'd thrown away minutes earlier.

She widened her eyes in astonishment. "How did you get that?"

"Didn't you leave it on my desk?"

"No. I just threw it away. As in minutes ago."

"Doesn't matter." He rocked back in his chair. "The important thing is you're going."

"To Colorado?" Charley asked with more disdain in her voice than she'd intended. "In the dead of winter? People can actually die in the dead of winter. That's a cold hard fact."

"Here's another cold hard fact—you leave first thing tomorrow."

She refused to budge. Her level-headed boss obviously wasn't thinking clearly. "But, Paul, it's freezing there."

She had lived in Los Angeles her entire life, and rarely had she ever ventured into the land of snow and freezing temperatures.

He pushed out a loud sigh, crossing his arms on top of his desk. "Charley, your blog is a great moneymaker for our magazine. Separating fact from fiction has driven your readership and our subscriptions to an all-time high. But you might have crossed the line this time."

"My blog is titled The Cold Hard Facts for a reason."

Paul reached over piles of paper on his desk and snagged a printed version of her latest post. He cleared his throat before reading it aloud. "'Face it. The holidays are a chore—the decorating, the shopping, the never-ending line at the post office, not to mention the hours of cooking, baking, and cleaning. Why torture yourself? No time to make Christmas cookies? That's what store-bought is for. Tired of spending hours wrapping presents? Send an eGift card instead. No time to trim a tree? Do yourself a favor and just skip Christmas altogether. It's not worth the hassle.'" He tossed the printout back on his desk and eyed Charley over the rims of his reading glasses. "You keep writing like this and you can rename your blog The Cold Heartless Facts."

She ran her hands over the arms of the chair, trying to feel justified for her comments even though, deep down, she knew she'd been off the mark. "I'm doing everyone a favor. I'm only voicing what everyone's thinking."

"Is that so? Then why does this one post of yours have more negative comments than all of your previous posts combined? Care to explain, Miss Scrooge?"

Shoot. He had seen the comment, the very comment that still gnawed at her. "Fine." She let out a defeated sigh. "I'll go." If she could debunk a legend and put the screws to Christmas, then subjecting herself to miserably cold temperatures would be well worth it.

"That's the spirit." Paul had a playful smirk on his face, so she knew the pun was intended.

"You know, the legend has to be a hoax because I've never heard of it."

He took off his reading glasses and leveled his gaze on her. "I thought that's why you put the letter on my desk."

"I didn't put—" She stopped herself. How the letter got to his desk was truly a mystery, but one she'd have to tackle later. "Have you ever heard anything about this famous Scrooge Legend?"

Paul put his glasses back on and pulled up the town's website. "It's right here. 'Welcome to St. Nicholas, Colorado, home of the famous Scrooge Legend, where any Scrooge who enters the town will end up loving Christmas as much as Santa.'"

Charley exploded with a laugh. "Ridiculous."

Paul arched a brow. "Prove it."

ACKNOWLEDGMENTS

I am deeply grateful to my good friend Valerie Repnau who worked tirelessly on editing my story. You are a true saint.

A heartfelt thank-you to my dear friend Lucy Lin, AKA Eagle Eyes, who dropped everything to help get me to the finish line.

I am forever thankful to both my wonderful sister, Lynn, who has always been my creative sounding board and my amazing husband, Jay, who keeps reading everything I write. I'm very blessed to be surrounded by a loving, supportive family, including my dachshunds, who sit by my side as I create stories. I love you all.

A big shout-out to my support team: Steve Apostolina, Joan Crossman, Wendy Cutler, Lori Gordon, Jennifer Jakes, Kim Killion, Luisa Leschin, Carole Rycki, Nik Shriner, Maura Swanson, Pepper Sweeney, DeEtte Tikotzinski, Lynnanne Zager, and all my readers who make the long hours working in front of my computer worth it. You all rock!

ABOUT THE AUTHOR

Caitlin McKenna enjoys writing witty and whimsical love stories. She is an author and screenwriter of several romantic comedies and a few thrillers. In addition to her writing, she is a seasoned voice-over actress and voice-casting director and has worked on hundreds of films and television shows. Caitlin lives with her husband and two spoiled dachshunds in southern California.

Connect with Caitlin:
Website:
https://www.caitlinmckenna.com

Email:
AuthorCaitlinMcKenna@gmail.com

Twitter:
https://twitter.com/caitmckenna

Instagram:
https://www.instagram.com/authorcaitlinmckenna/

Facebook:
https://www.facebook.com/authorcaitlinmckenna/

Made in the USA
Columbia, SC
14 March 2025